"This sweet series launch from... ... ...mance between a socially awkward Amish woman and the Amish man who once humiliated her . . . Fuller's fluid prose and the chemistry between the leads are sure to entertain. This winsome romance charms."

—*PUBLISHERS WEEKLY* ON *THE COURTSHIP PLAN*

"Sparks fly between a forthright heroine and a practical joker with a protective streak . . . but they're not the kind of sparks Charity Raber longs for after embarking on a courtship plan. The two can't agree on anything except that they definitely don't belong together. Does God have a different plan? Kathleen Fuller will keep you guessing with her endearing characters, compelling writing, and unexpected plot twists. A heartwarming and humorous read."

—RACHEL J. GOOD, *USA TODAY* BESTSELLING AUTHOR OF THE SURPRISED BY LOVE SERIES, ON *THE COURTSHIP PLAN*

"Kathleen Fuller is a gifted storyteller! Her latest, *The Courtship Plan*, made me laugh through the hilarity of Charity Raber—but also cry as Charity deals with trauma in a believable way. Endearing characters and precious life lessons make this novel another heartfelt winner!"

—LESLIE GOULD, BESTSELLING AUTHOR OF *PIECING IT ALL TOGETHER*

"Return to Birch Creek for another delightful Amish Mail-Order Bride novel by Kathleen Fuller. *Love in Plain Sight* combines Fuller's engaging style with a strong plot and compelling characters who will steal your heart. Don't miss this 'must read' story that's sure to remain a lifetime favorite."

—DEBBY GIUSTI, *USA TODAY* AND *PUBLISHERS WEEKLY* BESTSELLING AUTHOR OF *SMUGGLERS IN AMISH COUNTRY*

"Kathleen Fuller's emotional and evocative writing draws readers into her complex stories and keeps them cheering for her endearing characters even after the final page."

—PATRICIA DAVIDS, *USA TODAY* BESTSELLING AUTHOR

"Katharine Miller has everything she ever wanted, until she realizes what she's gotten. *Love in Plain Sight* is Kathleen Fuller at her best. She shines the spotlight on an unlikely heroine who runs away to find herself . . . and discovers what true love looks like."

—SUZANNE WOODS FISHER, BESTSELLING AUTHOR OF *MENDING FENCES*

"Fuller continues her Amish Mail-Order Brides of Birch Creek series (following *A Double Dose of Love*) with the pleasing story of Margaret, the youngest of four sisters who visits Birch Creek, Ohio, to stay with her aunt and uncle to avoid the temptations of *Englischer* life . . . This charming outing, filled as it is with forgiveness, redemption, and new beginnings, will delight Fuller's fans."

—*PUBLISHERS WEEKLY* ON *MATCHED AND MARRIED*

"This is a cute story of two sets of twins learning to grow up and be adults on their own terms and finding love along the way. It is another start of a great series."

—*PARKERSBURG NEWS AND SENTINEL* ON *A DOUBLE DOSE OF LOVE*

"Fuller (*The Innkeeper's Bride*) launches her Amish Mail-Order Brides series with the sweet story of love blooming between two pairs of twins . . . Faith and forgiveness form the backbone of this story, and the vulnerable sibling relationships are sure to tug at readers' heartstrings. This innocent romance is a treat."

—*PUBLISHERS WEEKLY* ON *A DOUBLE DOSE OF LOVE*

"Fuller cements her reputation [as] a top practitioner of Amish fiction with this moving, perceptive collection."

—*PUBLISHERS WEEKLY* ON *AMISH GENERATIONS*

"Fuller brings us compelling characters who stay in our hearts long after we've read the book. It's always a treat to dive into one of her novels."

—BETH WISEMAN, BESTSELLING AUTHOR OF *HEARTS IN HARMONY*, ON *THE INNKEEPER'S BRIDE*

"A beautiful Amish romance with plenty of twists and turns and a completely satisfying, happy ending. Kathleen Fuller is a gifted storyteller."

—JENNIFER BECKSTRAND, AUTHOR OF *HOME ON HUCKLEBERRY HILL*, ON *THE INNKEEPER'S BRIDE*

"I always enjoy a Kathleen Fuller book, especially her Amish stories. *The Innkeeper's Bride* did not disappoint! From the moment Selah and Levi meet each other to the last scene in the book, this was a story that tugged at my emotions. The story deals with several heavy issues such as mental illness and family conflicts, while still maintaining humor and couples falling in love, both old and new. When Selah finds work at the inn Levi is starting up with his family, they clash on everything but realize they have feelings for each other. My heart hurt for Selah as she held her secrets close and pushed everyone away. But in the end, God's grace and love, along with some misguided Birch Creek matchmakers stirring up mischief, brings them together. Weddings at a beautiful country inn? What's not to love? Readers of Amish fiction will enjoy this winter-time story of redemption and hope set against the backdrop of a beautiful inn that brings people together."

—LENORA WORTH, AUTHOR OF *THEIR AMISH REUNION*

"A warm romance that will tug at the hearts of readers, this is a new favorite."

—*THE PARKERSBURG NEWS AND SENTINEL* ON *THE TEACHER'S BRIDE*

"Fuller's appealing Amish romance deals with some serious issues, including depression, yet it also offers funny and endearing moments."

—*BOOKLIST* ON *THE TEACHER'S BRIDE*

"Kathleen Fuller's *The Teacher's Bride* is a heartwarming story of unexpected romance woven with fun and engaging characters who come to life on every page. Once you open the book, you won't put it down until you've reached the end."

"Kathleen Fuller's characters leap off the page with subtle power as she uses both wit and wisdom to entertain! Refreshingly honest and charming, Kathy's writing reflects a master's touch when it comes to intricate plotting and a satisfying and inspirational ending full of good cheer!"

"Kathleen Fuller is a master storyteller, and fans will absolutely fall in love with Ruby and Christian in *The Teacher's Bride*."

"*The Teacher's Bride* features characters who know what it's like to be different, to not fit in. What they don't know is that's what makes them so lovable. Kathleen Fuller has written a sweet, oftentimes humorous, romance that reminds readers that the perfect match might be right in front of their noses. She handles the difficult topic of depression with a deft touch. Readers of Amish fiction won't want to miss this delightful story."

"Kathleen Fuller is a talented and gifted author, and she doesn't disappoint in *The Teacher's Bride*. The story will captivate you from the first page to the last with Ruby, Christian, and other engaging characters. You'll laugh, gasp, and wonder what will happen next. You won't want to miss reading this heartwarming Amish story of mishaps, faith, love, forgiveness, and friendship."

"Enthusiasts of Fuller's sweet Amish romances will savor this new anthology."

"These four sweet stories are full of hope and promise along with mis-understandings and reconciliation. True love does prevail, but not without prayer, introspection, and humility. A must-read for fans of Amish romance."

—*RT Book Reviews*, 4 stars, on *An Amish Family*

"The incredibly engaging Amish Letters series continues with a third story of perseverance and devotion, making it difficult to put down . . . Fuller skillfully knits together the lives within a changing, faithful community that has suffered its share of challenges."

—*RT Book Reviews*, 4¹/₂ stars, on *Words from the Heart*

"Fuller's inspirational tale portrays complex characters facing real-world problems and finding love where they least expected or wanted it to be."

—*Booklist*, starred review, on *A Reluctant Bride*

"Fuller has an amazing capacity for creating damaged characters and giving in-sights into their brokenness. One of the better voices in the Amish fiction genre."

—*CBA Retailers + Resources* on *A Reluctant Bride*

"This promising series debut from Fuller is edgier than most Amish novels, dealing with difficult and dark issues and featuring well-drawn characters who are tougher than the usual gentle souls found in this genre. Recommended for Amish fiction fans who might like a different flavor."

—*Library Journal* on *A Reluctant Bride*

"Sadie and Aden's love is both sweet and hard-won, and Aden's patience is touch-ing as he wrestles not only with Sadie's dilemma, but his own abusive past. Birch Creek is weighed down by the Troyer family's dark secrets, and readers will be interested to see how secondary characters' lives unfold as the series continues."

—*RT Book Reviews*, 4 stars, on *A Reluctant Bride*

"Kathleen Fuller's *A Reluctant Bride* tells the story of two Amish families whose lives have collided through tragedy. Sadie Schrock's stoic resolve will touch and inspire Fuller's fans, as will the story's concluding triumph of redemption."

—Suzanne Woods Fisher, bestselling author of *Mending Fences*

"Kathleen Fuller's *A Reluctant Bride* is a beautiful story of faith, hope, and second chances. Her characters and descriptions are captivating, bringing the story to life with the turn of every page."

—AMY CLIPSTON, BESTSELLING AUTHOR OF *A SEAT BY THE HEARTH*

"The latest offering in the Middlefield Family series is a sweet love story with perfectly crafted characters. Fuller's Amish novels are written with the utmost respect for their way of living. Readers are given a glimpse of what it is like to live the simple life."

—*RT BOOK REVIEWS*, 4 STARS, ON *LETTERS TO KATIE*

"Fuller's second Amish series entry is a sweet romance with a strong sense of place that will attract readers of Wanda Brunstetter and Cindy Woodsmall."

—*LIBRARY JOURNAL* ON *FAITHFUL TO LAURA*

"Well-drawn characters and a homespun feel will make this Amish romance a sure bet for fans of Beverly Lewis and Jerry S. Eicher."

—*LIBRARY JOURNAL* ON *TREASURING EMMA*

"*Treasuring Emma* is a heartwarming story filled with real-life situations and well-developed characters. I rooted for Emma and Adam until the very last page. Fans of Amish fiction and those seeking an endearing romance will enjoy this love story. Highly recommended."

—BETH WISEMAN, BESTSELLING AUTHOR OF *HEARTS IN HARMONY*

"*Treasuring Emma* is a charming, emotionally layered story of the value of friendship in love and discovering the truth of the heart. A true treasure of a read!"

—KELLY LONG, NATIONAL BESTSELLING AUTHOR

THE MARRIAGE PACT

Also by Kathleen Fuller

The
MARRIAGE
PACT

An Amish of Marigold Novel

KATHLEEN FULLER

ZONDERVAN

The Marriage Pact

Copyright © 2025 by Kathleen Fuller

This title is also available as a Zondervan e-book.

Published in Grand Rapids, Michigan, by Zondervan. Zondervan is a registered trademark of The Zondervan Corporation, L.L.C., a wholly owned subsidiary of HarperCollins Christian Publishing, Inc.

Requests for information should be addressed to customercare@harpercollins.com.

Names: Fuller, Kathleen, author.
Title: The marriage pact / Kathleen Fuller.
Description: Grand Rapids, Michigan : Zondervan, 2025. | Series: Amish of Marigold ; 3 | Summary: "Perry and Daisy's fake relationship is fooling everyone . . . but they're the ones who might be getting fooled"--
Provided by publisher.
Identifiers: LCCN 2024048244 (print) | LCCN 2024048245 (ebook) | ISBN 9780840713384 (paperback) | ISBN 9780840713414 (epub) | ISBN 9780840713612
Subjects: BISAC: FICTION / Amish & Mennonite | FICTION / Small Town & Rural | LCGFT: Christian fiction. | Romance fiction. | Novels.
Classification: LCC PS3606.U553 M37 2025 (print) | LCC PS3606.U553 (ebook) | DDC 813/.6--dc23/eng/20241021
LC record available at https://lccn.loc.gov/2024048244
LC ebook record available at https://lccn.loc.gov/2024048245

Printed in the United States of America

25 26 27 28 29 LBC 5 4 3 2 1

To James. I love you.

Bontrager Family Tree

THOMAS BONTRAGER (68) M. MIRIAM BONTRAGER (68)
Children: *Phoebe (47), Devon (39), Owen (38), Zeb (37), Zeke (37), Ezra (35),
Nelson (33), Perry (31), Jesse (30), Mahlon (28), Mose (28), Elam (25)*

PHOEBE M. JALON CHUPP
Malachi (30), Hannah (22)

MALACHI M. JUNIA
Joseph, Thomas, Emma Mae, Katie, Rebecca

DEVON M. NETTIE
twins Samson and Susan, Clara, Noah

OWEN M. MARGARET
Vernon, Karl, Levi, Titus, Uriah

ZEB M. AMANDA
Mary Rose, Dorothy, Eli, Marietta, Alice

ZEKE M. DARLA
twins Thomas and David, Charlene, Aaron, Will

EZRA M. KATHARINE
Paul, William, Kristina, LeAnna

NELSON M. ELLA
John, Neva, Rachel, Perry

JESSE M. CHARITY
Cevilla, Shirley, Ranae, Kaylene, Lisbet, Malinda, Joy

MAHLON M. MATTIE
Gertie, Gideon

MOSE M. VONDA
Jolisa, Aaron

ELAM M. ADAH
Christopher

And then there was one . . .

Ten of the eleven Bontrager brothers gathered inside the family's expansive horse barn on this chilly, early spring day to discuss the latest family quandary. Perry, their only single brother, was about to be in a peck of trouble.

He was back home in Marigold nursing a serious cold while Devon, their oldest brother who lived in Fredericktown, was in Birch Creek on a quick visit. Phoebe, the eldest Bontrager sibling and their one and only sister, wasn't invited to this particular meeting. She had already tried to help him, to no avail.

Devon leaned against one of the huge vertical beams, his expression dubious. Identical twins, Zeb and Zeke, were seated on a hay bale near one of three dusty windows, their arms identically crossed. The rest of the brothers—Owen, Ezra, Nelson, Jesse, the second pair of identical twins, Mose and Mahlon, and the youngest, Elam—were alternately sitting and standing throughout the barn entryway, their faces a mix of amusement and annoyance. They all had blue eyes and varied tones of dark brown hair, some straight, some wavy, and one corkscrew curly.

They were also all married.

Horses stirred in their stables, as if they were curious about the unusual conference. It was a rare sight to see the brothers gathered in the barn all at once. When they were younger, before having wives and families of their own, they worked the family farm with their father, Thomas, while their patient mother, Miriam, kept them fed, clothed, and content. The Bontragers weren't without their hard times or their family squabbles. But they were a close-knit, caring, and incredibly *huge* Amish family.

"So what if he's not married yet?" Devon finally said. "He's only thirty-one. There are and have been plenty of older single people in our districts."

"Cevilla, for instance." Mahlon scratched his bearded chin. "But I doubt Perry will be in his eighties when he gets married for the first time."

"Not if *Mamm* has anything to do with it." Owen regarded his brothers. "She's been trying to fix him up. With *everyone*."

"*Trying* being the operative word." Ezra, the tallest, stretched out his long legs. "I think she's run out of single women to beg and plead with."

"I could put another bachelorette ad in the paper."

Every Bontrager turned to Jesse in horror.

"*Nee*," Zeb and Zeke exclaimed at the same time.

"Are you *ab im kopp*?" Nelson smacked him on the side of the head, flipping Jesse's straw hat to the ground.

"Ow." Jesse grabbed his hat off the barn floor, but he was grinning. "Hey, if it weren't for me, none of you would be married. Except Devon," he added when his oldest brother scoffed. "But the rest of you owe me."

The men's collective groan brought the horses to life. They pawed in their stalls, and one mare neighed, as if agreeing with the disgruntled men.

Jesse snickered. "I'm kidding."

"*Gut*," Nelson said. "Or you'd be walking home tonight."

"We all agree. No ad." Zeb, who, other than Perry, was the most stoic of the brothers, moved to the center of the barn. "Maybe Jesse and Nelson can marry him off."

Jesse's good nature disappeared, while Nelson looked at Zeb in serious panic. "What?" they said in unison.

"He lives closer to you guys," Owen said. He managed Bontrager Farms and lived on the property with his wife, Margaret, and their five sons. "Besides, *Mamm* is getting desperate."

Mose held up his hands. "She's even making *Daed* a little nuts."

Elam looked at Jesse and Nelson. "You and Devon don't have to constantly hear about Perry's 'woeful bachelor' status."

All three brothers who didn't live in Birch Creek shook their heads. "*Mamm*'s been talking to Charity," Jesse said.

"And Ella," Nelson added.

"Even Nettie." Devon sighed.

"She's obsessed," Ezra said. "Since her and Phoebe's attempts at matchmaking didn't work, she told Katharine she's starting a circle letter with the sole intent to find Perry a *frau*."

"She wrote twelve letters just this morning." Owen grimaced. "It's only a matter of time before Marigold is inundated with single women."

The men held a moment of silence for Perry.

Zeke spun a stalk of hay between his fingers. "I know I resisted getting married at first—"

"We all did," Devon said.

"Not me." Ezra leaned back and smirked.

"—but Perry has taken avoiding women to the next level." Zeke shook his head. "I'm starting to wonder—"

"If there's something wrong with him," Zeb finished.

"He's fine," Nelson said. "He just hasn't met—"

"The right woman." The twins spoke in precise unison.

"Someone should at least warn him," Devon pointed out.

"I nominate Jesse." Elam grinned.

Jesse balked. "Hey—"

"All in favor, say aye," Zeb said.

"Aye." Nine voices rang out in the cavernous barn.

"Now wait just a minute," Jesse said, scowling. "Don't I get a vote?"

"*Nee*," they all said together.

He rolled his eyes. "Fine. I'll give him a heads-up."

"Glad that's settled." Devon opened the barn door. A cool spring breeze blew inside, stirring the hay on the dirt floor. "We're starting to sound like a hen party." All but Jesse and Nelson followed him out the door.

"Do you really think we should get involved in this?" Jesse asked.

Nelson glanced at him. "What do you mean, 'we'? You're the one who's going to talk to him."

"*Ya*, but things are never that simple. Not when it comes to our *familye*."

Nelson sighed. "True. Well, all you have to do is tell him about *Mamm*'s letters. Then let him handle the rest."

They headed out of the barn. "You're right," Jesse said. "Perry can take care of himself."

Nelson nodded. "For his sake, I sure hope so."

Chapter 1

"Did you enjoy the pot roast, Maynard?" Daisy Hershberger perched on the edge of the couch, waiting for him to lower the newspaper in front of his face and answer her.

"Uh-huh." Seated in a comfortable chair across from her, he crossed his legs and turned the page.

A cozy fire crackled in the wood fireplace, and the scents of the supper Daisy had spent the afternoon making lingered in the air. Everything had been done from scratch, down to the yeasty rolls and flaky pie pastry. She loved cooking, and she'd heard one time that the way to a man's heart was through his stomach, or something like that. Maynard ate every crumb, but he was so quiet and reserved, she still wasn't sure if he enjoyed the meal.

She glanced at the wicker basket on the floor near the sofa where she kept her cross-stitch supplies—aida cloth, a case of colorful embroidery floss, several wooden hoops in various sizes, a packet of needles, and tiny scissors. Her current project was a scripture verse for her older sister's birthday, and she was almost finished. In fact, she could wrap it up tonight if she went back to work on it while Maynard read the paper.

While she liked the coziness of them being together, basking in the warmth of the living room fireplace inside the house she lived in with her parents, her mind wasn't on cross-stitch, and she didn't want Maynard to read the paper. She wanted him to sit next to her on the couch—the closer the better. Even though her parents were in the kitchen playing checkers and could walk in at any time, she yearned for him to put his arm around her and kiss her on the temple or— *gasp!*—on the cheek. If her parents saw, so be it. It wasn't exactly a secret that she liked, nay loved, Maynard Miller.

Except, apparently, to him.

Daisy sighed and waited for him to notice her frustrated exhale.

He didn't move. Just kept reading, the paper blocking her view of his face.

She tried conversation again. "Were the mashed potatoes creamy enough?"

"*Ya.*"

"What about the peach pie? Was that *gut*?"

He flipped down one corner of the paper, his reddish eyebrows flat over pale blue eyes behind silver-framed glasses. "I already said it was, right after I ate it."

"Oh. That's right."

Maynard went back to reading, and Daisy returned to fretting. It had taken almost three weeks to sync up their schedules so he could come over for supper. He always had an excuse for refusing her invitations. He was too busy at work. He had to get up early in the morning for work. He needed to do more work. And she had no reason to doubt he was telling the truth. He was a carpenter for the number one furniture maker in Dover, Delaware, and they were busy year-round. Their hickory rockers alone had a two-year waiting list.

But every time she was about to give up on him, he would surprise her. Like tonight. When she made a final attempt to get him to come over, he'd easily agreed. It was because of those times that she still held hope that someday, one day, he would come to his senses and realize they were meant to be together. In the meantime, she had to do her part to stoke the flame he kept neglecting.

"Maynard?" she asked tentatively.

After a long pause he said, "What?"

Surely, he wasn't annoyed with her. She had cleaned the house until it shone, had cooked his favorite meal, had fixed warm apple cider and brought it to him, made sure the fire was the perfect temperature, and when he pointed at the newspaper on the coffee table, she'd handed it to him. Maybe that had been her mistake. If she had told him no, he would be forced to at least look at her.

Who was she kidding? She never told Maynard no. In the eighteen months she'd known him after he and his family had moved to Dover from upstate New York, she had always said yes. She wished that someday soon she could give him the ultimate yes after he asked her to marry him. Of course, they would have to hold hands first. And share a kiss or two, at the very least. There would be plenty of hand-holding, snuggling, kissing and . . . *other things* . . . after their wedding. *Sigh.*

He yanked the paper onto his lap. "Are you ill, Daisy?"

"What? *Nee*, I'm fine."

"You're not acting like it."

Then maybe you should take my temperature. Slowly. Her cheeks flamed. But the idea of Maynard gently touching her forehead with

7

the back of his hand, then lightly stroking her cheek as he gazed into her eyes—

"You're acting *seltsam*." He put his feet on the floor, the newspaper rustling as he moved. "Are you sure you're not sick?"

She nodded and folded her hands on her lap, disappointed he hadn't noticed her new emerald-green dress or how it brought out her hazel eyes. At least she thought it did. She couldn't exactly ask her parents that question without them thinking she was, um, *seltsam*. "Do you like my dress?"

He quickly glanced at her. "Looks like the rest of your dresses."

"Nice?"

Maynard lifted the paper again. "Suitable."

She muzzled her annoyance. For the umpteenth time, she reminded herself that he was the man God had set apart for her. She knew it the moment he and his parents had walked into church service that fateful Sunday morning. Her knees turned wobbly at the sight of him, and she couldn't concentrate on the singing or the sermon. At the age of twenty-five she had finally, *finally* experienced what her siblings, friends, and cousin Grace already had—the excitement of falling in love. In church, of all places! But it made sense, because Maynard was heaven-sent.

Sometimes it was hard to keep that fact in mind. Like when he was consumed with work, or how he always left with his parents immediately after church service was over, eliminating any possibility of him taking her home or just going for a buggy ride.

She had to be going about this all wrong, thinking that being subtle would get his attention. She'd never made any overt romantic overtures toward him, although she had few opportunities to do so. At her request, he'd taken her home a couple of times when their small singles group met once a month to do community service activities.

Those rides had been quiet. But nice too. She always enjoyed a good buggy ride.

She also assumed it was the man's place to get the romance ball rolling. That's what her sisters said when they met their husbands. Her cousin Grace had mentioned the same thing in the letters she wrote to Daisy after she met her fiancé, Kyle. She could ask her brother, Nathan, if that were true for all men. He was also married, but talking about romantic stuff with him seemed kind of icky. He was almost ten years older than her, and they weren't exactly close.

Maynard was a bit different from other men she knew. What if he was waiting on her to make the first move? His shyness had to be getting in the way of moving their relationship forward. *I should have realized that before now.*

Time to test the waters. Wiping her damp palms on her dress, she said, "Uh, Maynard—"

"Now this is interesting." He tapped the paper. "They're calling for an extra-hot summer this year. Probably a record breaker."

"Maynard—"

"Then again, they've always predicted record-breaking winters, and we've had normal ones for the past five years."

"Would you . . . um . . . ." She swallowed. Talking about love was harder than she thought. "Um . . . ."

He glanced at the clock on the wall, then frowned. "It's that late?"

She looked at the time. Barely seven o'clock.

He folded the paper and put it on the coffee table.

She jumped from the sofa. "You're leaving already?"

His brows furrowed, as if she were speaking a foreign language. "It's past seven, Daisy," he said as he stood up.

"But you just got here!"

Maynard adjusted his glasses. "You know I like to be in bed by eight."

She couldn't let him leave now, not when she was mustering the courage to tell him they needed to take their relationship to the next level. And pronto.

True love was worth the wait, but she was getting tired of waiting.

"How are things going?" *Mamm* came into the living room, a tight smile on her face. *Daed* appeared right behind her.

"I was just telling Daisy that I have an early morning tomorrow."

Daisy pinched her lips together. There was no point in trying to change his mind. He was resolute about his eight o'clock bedtime. Besides, her mother and father were looking at them strangely, making her suspect something might be amiss. In a last-ditch effort for some kind of connection, she purposely brushed her pinky finger against his.

"*Danki* for supper," he said to *Mamm* in his usual monotone voice. If he'd noticed Daisy had touched him, he didn't draw attention to it.

"Daisy made it all." *Mamm*'s stressed look gave way to a genuine smile. "She's quite the cook."

He didn't acknowledge *Mamm*'s compliment as he picked up his hat from the rack by the door and placed it on his mop of bright red hair.

"Drive home safe, Maynard." *Daed* tapped *Mamm* on the shoulder and they went back to the kitchen.

Disappointed, Daisy walked with Maynard to the front door as he put on his coat. Despite it being early spring, the evenings were still cold. She took his scarf off the rack and handed it to him, watching for any kind of reaction to her secret pinky touch as he wrapped the navy blue flannel around his neck. Nothing. Maybe she had brushed his finger too lightly. She hadn't felt anything either.

"Good night, Daisy."

Their eyes easily met since they were the same height, around five six. "When will I see you again?" Ugh, she sounded desperate, but she couldn't help it. *Soon. Please, make it soon.*

"Depends on my work schedule." He opened the door, letting in a rush of cold air that instantly cooled her cheeks. "I'll let you know."

"Okay."

But he was already halfway down the porch steps. As she always did when he left her house, she watched him drive down the driveway. Only when he was out of her sight did she close the door and press her forehead against it. *Why didn't anyone tell me love was so hard?*

Then the perfect solution hit her out of the blue. Yes, that was the answer to their problem. Loving Maynard was difficult, but that was going to change, and now she knew exactly how to make that happen.

"Daisy."

She spun around and saw her mother standing there, tugging on the handkerchief in her hand. "Is something wrong?" Daisy asked.

"*Nee, nee,*" Mamm said a little too quickly. "Nothing's wrong. With me, anyway. Why don't we sit down."

Daisy silently complied and sat next to her on the sofa. While she waited for her mother to speak, Mamm kept fiddling with her handkerchief, finally shoving the balled-up fabric into the pocket of her apron. "How did things *geh* with you and Maynard tonight?"

"*Gut.*" They could have gone better, though. And they would the next time she saw him.

"You didn't say that with much enthusiasm."

Oops. She gave *Mamm* a bright smile, and it wasn't too forced. "Sorry. I just have some things on my mind."

Her mother's expression turned wary. "What things?"

Daisy took a deep breath and blurted the truth, even though she was sure her mother already knew it. "I love Maynard."

"Oh dear," *Mamm* mumbled.

Or maybe her mother didn't know how she felt about him. First Maynard, now *Mamm*. Daisy hadn't realized she'd kept her feelings so locked up. She thought she was an open book.

Mamm's smile looked strained. "How do you know?"

"I've always known." Her smile widened. "And now I know something else."

"What's that?"

"I need to tell him how I feel."

Her mother reached for her pocket, then clenched her hands together on her lap. "What if he doesn't return your feelings?"

"I'm sure he will."

"Then you two have been dating all along?" *Mamm* looked confused. "I thought . . . hoped you were just friends."

"We are."

"Then it's possible he doesn't love you."

She wasn't going to let a small detail derail her. "How would he know if we've never talked about it?"

"Oh, Daisy, you're not thinking this through."

"I'll *geh* see him after work tomorrow and we'll have 'the talk.'"

"Tomorrow?" *Mamm* said weakly.

"Once I tell him how I feel, God will do the rest." She beamed.

"Don't you think you're being presumptuous?"

She thought she heard panic in her mother's tone, but she had to be imagining it. Her parents had always been supportive of her and Maynard. Well, maybe supportive wasn't the precise word, but they never said no when she told them he was coming over for supper or commented when he drove her home.

But Daisy was too excited to pay complete attention to her mother's words. All she could think about was surprising Maynard after work and having "the talk" with him. Then they would officially be a couple.

"What's the hurry?" *Mamm* held up her palms. "I'm sure your conversation can wait a little while. A few days . . . months. A year or two, even."

She let out a long-suffering sigh. "*Mamm*, I've been patient. I also think I've been too much of a friend to Maynard and not enough of a girlfriend."

"But—"

She popped up from the couch, excited that she would finally get what she'd yearned for—Maynard's love. *And kisses. Don't forget the kisses.*

"Daisy—"

"*Gute nacht, Mamm!*" She danced to the stairs and floated up to her room. Her whole life was about to change, and she couldn't wait.

Daisy woke up the next morning primed and ready to talk to Maynard. She decided last night that being straightforward was best, although she did briefly entertain being coy and flirtatious, only to nix the idea because she had no clue how to flirt or be coy. She couldn't risk making a mistake at this critical juncture in their relationship.

When she entered the kitchen, she was surprised to see her mother and father at the table, and they weren't eating breakfast. By now, *Mamm* would be frying up her father's favorites—scrambled eggs, a thick slice of ham, and three pieces of buttered toast.

"*Gute mariye.*" *Daed*'s smile was strained and *Mamm* was practically stretching her handkerchief to the breaking point. "Have a seat."

Alarmed, Daisy sat. "Is something wrong?"

Her parents exchanged a look before her father spoke. "We just need to talk to you, that's all."

"Before breakfast?" Now she was positive something was wrong. Her father was a stickler about his morning meal.

"We have some news," *Mamm* said, looking a little less stressed, although that might be because *Daed* was holding her hand now. "*Aenti* Rosella wants you to help her plan Grace's wedding."

Daisy grinned, no longer concerned. She loved planning weddings, and from all accounts, she was good at it. She excelled at organization, from her bedroom to her schoolwork to her cross-stitch supplies, and she had helped plan her four older sisters' nuptials. When she started her part-time job at the local scratch-and-dent store three years ago, she had taken charge of keeping the stockroom neat and orderly—not always the easiest task.

"That is wonderful," Daisy said. "I can't wait to help her and Grace this summer."

Mamm shook her head. "She wants to plan it now. In Marigold."

"Okay. When do I leave?"

"This morning."

Stunned, she looked at both her parents. "I can't *geh* today. I have to let Mr. Brickman know I need time off."

"Already done," *Mamm* blurted. "He said to take all the time you want."

Daisy frowned. "When did he say that?"

"I called him thirty minutes ago."

"But the store doesn't open until eight."

"I have his personal number, remember? In case of emergencies?"

This didn't seem like an emergency to Daisy. And she didn't understand why she had to leave today instead of tomorrow, or next week, or even in June or July, when it would make the most sense. "Isn't the wedding in November?"

"It's been over two years since you and Grace have seen each other," Mamm said, standing up with *Daed*. "It will take time to figure everything out. I'll fix breakfast while you pack. The taxi's coming to get you in two hours."

"Two hours?" Daisy shook her head. "I have to talk to Maynard—"

"Rosella and Grace need your help." *Daed* was stern as he gestured for Daisy to get up. As soon as she did, her parents herded her out of the kitchen toward the living room to the staircase.

"You know how picky Grace can be," *Mamm* said.

"Since when?" Her cousin was the most laid-back person Daisy knew.

As they reached the bottom of the stairs, she turned and faced them. Lowering her voice, she leaned close to *Mamm*. "I'm having 'the talk' today, remember?"

Something flickered in *Mamm*'s eyes. "I'll tell him you said goodbye."

"But—"

"I reserved a ticket for you," *Daed* said. "It will be at the bus station."

"You don't want to let your *aenti* and cousin down, do you?" *Mamm* said.

Ugh. There it was. Guilt. Besides, her parents were presenting a united front, one she couldn't seem to breach. Dazed, she made her way upstairs to her bedroom. *What just happened?*

A few minutes later, a knock sounded at the door. Her mother opened it. "Can I come in?"

Daisy nodded and *Mamm* walked inside and shut the door. "I'm sorry we're rushing you, Daisy. We found out last night that your Aunt Rosella was wanting your help so soon."

"Why didn't she just call me?"

"I . . . well, you know how busy wedding planning can get."

"She has seven months."

"And those will fly right by." *Mamm* took her hands. "I know you're concerned about not telling Maynard. I promise I'll talk to him. And you can call or write to him from Marigold anytime you want."

"Except when he's working." She tried to keep the bitterness out of her tone. Daisy had never been one for talking on the phone, and idle chatter was forbidden by the *Ordnung* anyway.

"Of course." *Mamm* squeezed her hands. "He is *such* a busy, busy *mann.*"

What did she mean by that? She inwardly sighed. She didn't have it in her to disobey her parents, and they had already booked the taxi and reserved the ticket. But as soon as she helped Grace and Rosella, she was coming right back to Dover and straight to see Maynard.

Mamm grabbed Daisy in a tight hug. "Trust me, this is for the best. I'll let you pack."

She waited for her mother to leave, then frowned. This seemed odd. Her placid cousin was in an awful hurry for Daisy to visit her in Marigold, Ohio, months before her wedding. Not that it wouldn't be nice to spend time with Grace. They were inseparable up until eight years ago when Grace's family had moved away. Daisy had been the first one to hear about Kyle, and of course she had told Grace about Maynard . . . with a little embellishment. *Okay, a lot.*

She sat down on the bed, her mind on him again. Her family's timing couldn't be worse. Now she'd have to wait to talk with him, just after finally coming up with a plan.

Then she regrouped. She would enjoy her visit with her cousin, aunt, and uncle, and write plenty of letters to Maynard. Maybe she would even call just to hear his voice. Surely that wouldn't violate the *Ordnung*. As soon as she returned home, they would discuss their future. Perhaps even set a wedding date for this year. *I've waited long enough.*

Chapter 2

A ren't you a perfect specimen." Perry Bontrager took a pair of
small tweezers and a clean white handkerchief from his leather
apron and plucked the injured butterfly off the seat of his buggy. The
Vanessa cardui, commonly known as the painted lady, was one of
the most prevalent butterfly species in Ohio, and this one was an
absolute beauty—the vibrant-orange center of the wings with perfectly
spaced rows of black dots at the base were outstanding. The rest of
the wings were black and white, with a striped top and a bottom
fringed with white peaks against the dark background. He looked at
the red eyespots. Definitely female. He wasn't sure why the creature
was wounded, but he'd examine her more closely when he got home.

He set the butterfly carefully in his handkerchief and placed it
on the empty seat next to him. He was covered in dirt and mud from
spending the day shoeing horses for an English family three miles
from his house. The horses were favorites among his regular customers,
both Amish and English. Calm, easy to deal with, and affectionate. It
had been a long but productive day. And finding a gorgeous butterfly
in his buggy put the cherry on the sundae.

He slipped off his apron and set it next to the mini anvil, iron rods, and blacksmith tools already in the back of the buggy. Then he removed the back brace he'd started wearing four years ago while he'd apprenticed with Andrew Beiler in Birch Creek. *"Better start protecting your back now,"* the stocky man said, a few gray hairs in his long beard punctuating his wise words. *"You'll be in a world of hurt later if you don't."*

Perry arched his back and heard the faint cracking noise the movement made. The work was physically demanding yet satisfying. He couldn't imagine working any other job.

Soon he was on his way home, glancing at the butterfly to make sure she was okay. If she decided to fly off, he'd be glad for her. If not, then hopefully he could nurse her back to health and set her free.

As he drove, the *clip-clop* of his horse's hooves faded in the background and he took in the gorgeous sunset in front of him. The fiery orange mimicked the color of the butterfly's wings, and he was filled with a sense of awe. He was always amazed at the endless beauty of nature, and how God's majesty and creativity were on display at all times, from a tiny insect on the ground to the vast sky above. He made it a habit to practice not only noticing these things but prayerfully reflecting on them. There were times when he was too busy, especially if he had a lot of work lined up, but he had a day off tomorrow, and he could relax during the drive.

His home came into view, and he was eager to put up his horse and inspect the butterfly. That plan changed when he saw Jesse's buggy parked near the house, his oldest three daughters playing in the front yard. Out of his eleven brothers, Jesse was the only one who had all girls, and they kept him hopping. Every single one of them had her daddy wrapped around her finger.

As he pulled into the driveway and parked next to Jesse's buggy, eight-year-old Cevilla, seven-year-old Shirley, and six-year-old Ranae hurried toward him. "*Onkel* Perry!" Shirley said, her quick stride putting her a few feet ahead of her sisters. Jesse ambled behind them, looking a little weary. Perry heard that Wagler's Buggy Shop, where Jesse worked with the owner, Micah Wagler, had increased their business this year to the point that it was almost nonstop, so he wasn't surprised his brother looked so tired. Then again, his rambunctious girls were probably partly to blame too.

He set the buggy brake, glanced at the butterfly again, and was getting out when Shirley started to climb inside. "Whoa!" He scooped up the handkerchief before disaster struck. At Shirley's surprised and slightly hurt expression, he took her hand and hauled her inside for a big hug. Crisis averted. "I didn't mean to scare you," he said, tucking the handkerchief behind his seat so the butterfly wouldn't get crushed. He thought for a second that his nieces would like to see the insect, but he didn't want to risk further injuring her.

All was quickly forgiven, and Shirley scooted over as Cevilla scrambled inside. "Can we *geh* for a ride, *Onkel* Perry?" Shirley asked. Her navy blue kerchief was slightly askew, and a few red corkscrew curls poked out from underneath the hem, the combination of her mother's red locks and her father's unruly hair.

"Please?" Cevilla asked, looking up at him with round, blue eyes.

"Not today." Jesse scooped up Ranae before she could join her sisters and set her down on the gravel driveway. "Your *onkel* and I have some business to discuss."

That was news to him. Perry's eyebrow lifted as Jesse motioned for his other two daughters to go play in the front yard with Ranae. "What kind of business?" he asked, following his nieces out of the buggy.

Jesse pushed his straw hat back from his forehead. "I've been tasked with giving you a warning," he said, his expression grave.

"About what?" Perry braced himself for terrible news.

"*Mamm* is writing letters. Lots of them. About you."

"Huh?"

"More accurately about your bachelor status." Jesse gave him a sympathetic look.

Perry leaned against the buggy, struggling to hide his exasperation. "I better *geh* talk to her." *Again.* He couldn't get through to his mother that he was satisfied being single, and he had good reason to be. He wasn't sure his brothers understood it either. They'd all gotten married in their early twenties, and in Jesse's case, he had been only twenty. Ever since his youngest brother, Elam's, wedding two years ago, his mother and sister had been single-minded in finding him a spouse, with disastrous results. Phoebe had finally given up six months ago, and he thought *Mamm* had done the same.

"You can try, but it's probably pointless." Jesse grinned. "Guess you'd better get married so she'll finally leave you alone."

Perry tried to smile, but after so many years of being teased about still being a bachelor, and in his mother and sister's case, trying to manipulate him into finding a *frau*, he was tired of it. His brother was right about one thing—it was useless to try to convince his mother to stop. He knew she was only concerned for his future, and she had admitted her real fear two years ago after a horrendous attempt at a date with a young woman from Birch Creek, who not only had a fear of horses but also talked incessantly about absolutely nothing. Totally unsuitable for him.

"*I don't want you to be alone,*" *Mamm* had said, her voice breaking. "*Or lonely.*"

He'd tried to tell her he didn't mind being alone. In fact, he enjoyed *not* being surrounded by people all the time. He loved his family, but at times they were too much for him. For years he hadn't quite understood why he liked his solitude so much. All he knew was that he wasn't lonely when he was alone. He had his job, his house, his garden, his—

"Charity wants you to come over for supper soon," Jesse said.

"Sure," Perry answered quickly, relieved to get off the topic of *Mamm* and her pleading letters. How embarrassing.

"She's on a Greek food kick. Tonight she's making moussaka."

"Moo-what?"

"Eggplant, ground meat, bechamel, and a bunch of other stuff I don't remember."

"Sounds *gut*." He liked dining with Jesse and his wife, not just because they were family, but because he always knew Charity would make something interesting and delicious from one of the cookbooks she'd started collecting shortly after she and Jesse tied the knot.

Perry watched his nieces as they ran around the large oak tree in the center of his yard. When Shirley slapped Ranae on the back and told her she was "it," the little girl tumbled to the ground.

"Be careful," Jesse hollered.

But Ranae popped up from the ground and continued running. "I'm okay, I'm okay," she said, then squealed with laughter as she caught Cevilla and tagged her.

Jesse shook his head. "How did *Mamm* handle all twelve of us?"

"Only by the grace of God." Perry grinned.

"There's something I wanted to ask you." Jesse turned to him. "Ferman needs a job."

"I thought he was doing fine at the buggy shop."

"He was, but we're so busy and he's so . . ." A flash of guilt crossed his face. "He's seventy-five and has a bad hip, although he tries to hide that it's hurting him. But that's not the main problem. Believe it or not, he's too social."

Actually, Perry did believe it. He'd seen the man make the rounds at church. He was a nonstop talker.

"He's spending too much time jawing with the customers. That would be fine, except he's not getting things done around the shop in a timely manner."

"Because he's slow," Perry said.

"*Ya.* I know he's grateful for the work, and both Micah and I don't want to let him *go* without another job in the wings. I thought he might be able to help you."

Perry paused. He'd never had an assistant before. "Does he know anything about farrier work?"

Jesse shrugged. "Not sure."

Perry's horse whinnied behind him. "I don't know," he said. "I'm doing fine on my own."

"He's *gut* company, even though he can get a little cranky when his hip is bothering him. He seems to be able to set that aside when customers show up. But I understand if you don't want to hire him. This is more for his benefit than yours."

"I'm not completely against it," Perry said. Especially now that he knew he'd be helping Ferman out. He liked the man even though he didn't know him all that well, the age gap between them being the main reason. Perry's reluctance to stay for the customary after-service meal was another. He liked to spend Sunday afternoons at home. "I'll consider it and let you know."

"*Danki.* Micah will be relieved. I think Ferman will too." Jesse put two fingers at the corners of his mouth and whistled, getting the girls' attention. "Time to *geh* home, *maed.*"

They immediately ran toward their father and uncle, but with less energy than before. "Looks like they tuckered themselves out," Perry commented.

"I wish." Jesse lifted Ranae and balanced her on his slim hip and kissed her small, rosy cheek. "They usually get their second wind after supper. Tell *Onkel* Perry bye."

All three girls waved, and they got into Jesse's buggy. Perry climbed into his vehicle and waved back as they passed by. When they were behind him, he reached for the handkerchief and opened it. The butterfly was still there. He touched the tip of her left wing and it fluttered slightly. Quickly, he parked his buggy inside his barn, left his tools in the back, unhitched his horse, and put him up in his stall with plenty of feed and water. Then he went to the front porch to go inside.

He'd barely turned the knob when the door opened on its own. The lock had been broken for a week, but he hadn't worried about it since he and his neighbors, Howard and Rosella and their daughter, Grace, were the only ones who lived on their street for at least half a mile. The seclusion was part of the reason why he'd bought the place, and he never worried about anyone breaking in.

But it was one thing to have a broken lock, another for the door-knob to barely work. He'd work on fixing it tomorrow.

He entered the kitchen, got an empty glass jar from the cabinet and a paper towel. He set the handkerchief on the counter, leaving it open so the butterfly could be free. But she lay there, her wings still. He frowned, took the lid off the jar, and tore the paper towel in half, then in fourths, then folded one of the quarter pieces twice and set it inside the lid. Even though the lid had several small holes in it, they wouldn't interfere with his purpose. He grabbed a small amber bottle with a dropper in it from near the sink and put several drops of flower nectar on the paper towel. Carefully he lifted the butterfly and put her feet on the paper towel to taste the nectar.

Perry crouched down until he was eye level with the counter and watched to see if she would eat. After a few minutes, she finally lifted her proboscis and started to consume the nectar. What a relief. It was possible she was only hungry, and once she regained her strength, she would leave to find her normal source of food.

He stood and headed for the shower. The butterfly wasn't the only one hungry, but he had to clean up first before he made his supper. As was his habit, he stripped off his dirty clothes in the mudroom off the kitchen and deposited them in a basket next to the wringer washer. Three steps down the hall and he was in the bathroom. Living in such a small house on a basically deserted road gave him privacy he could only dream of when he was in Birch Creek, and he took advantage of it.

After showering and changing into pants and a long-sleeved collarless shirt, he slicked back his wet hair and returned to the kitchen, expecting the butterfly to be long gone.

Instead, she was sitting next to the paper towel. He smiled and went to her, giving her another once-over. Her wings seemed fine, her body didn't show signs of injury, and despite being calmer than any butterfly he'd ever encountered, she appeared normal. He let her stay on the counter as he heated up some potato soup on the stove, buttered a slice of bread, and filled a glass with water. Once he prayed over his supper, he ate, keeping his eye on his new little friend. If she didn't leave by bedtime, he'd put her in the jar with more nectar and let her go in the morning.

Perry took a bite of bread and chewed, his mother's quest back on his mind again. It wasn't only that he liked being alone and wasn't lonely that kept him from wanting to find a spouse. He was different, and the more years he spent on earth, the more he realized that.

Because, while he enjoyed his job as a farrier, his true passion was drawing, studying, and nurturing butterflies. Not exactly the most common of pastimes among Amish men. Not even in the top thirty. *Or on the list at all.* His family didn't even know about it.

For that reason and a few others, he knew he would never find a woman who truly understood him, never mind his unusual leisure activity. At one time he thought he had, but that ended up being a mistake. There were single Amish people and single English ones. Not everyone was meant to marry. He happened to be one of those people . . . and that was perfectly fine with him.

~·~

"We're here, young lady."

Daisy felt a sharp tap on her shoulder. Her eyes opened as the bus brakes squealed to a stop. At first she didn't know where she was or who was nudging her. But when she turned to her seatmate, an elderly English woman named Peg who had spent the trip from Dover knitting socks for her husband, she realized her location—Mount Eaton, Ohio.

Peg stuffed a half-knitted sock into her large pink tote bag that said "Knitting Keeps Me from Unraveling." "Is someone here to pick you up?" she asked, taking off a pair of bright red reading glasses and adding them to the bag.

"There's supposed to be a taxi waiting for me." She was in an aisle seat and couldn't get a good look out the window. "Dad said the driver will be in a silver sedan."

Peg clucked her tongue. "Lots of silver sedans in the world. Anything else to identify it?"

"Dad didn't say."

Daisy grabbed her small suitcase from underneath the seat in front of her and stood.

Despite her parents' insistence that Grace wanted her to remain in Marigold for a month, she planned to stay no longer than two weeks—plenty of time to help plan her cousin's wedding. The sooner she returned to Dover, the sooner she and Maynard would be a couple.

She stepped off the bus and searched the parking lot. Not a single silver sedan in sight.

"There's my George." Peg appeared next to her and waved to a short, balding man with a huge smile coming toward them. "It's good to be home." She turned to Daisy. "Is your ride here?"

"Not yet."

"Will you be okay? We can wait with you."

Daisy smiled. What a kind gesture, but she didn't want to inconvenience Peg. "I'm sure the taxi will be here soon."

Peg waved goodbye to Daisy as George met her on the curb. He kissed her cheek, then picked up her suitcase and the pink knitting bag and they headed to their car.

During the trip, Peg mentioned she'd been married almost fifty years, was in Dover to visit her younger sister, and that she not only knitted but crocheted, tatted, weaved, and quilted. Daisy wasn't quite as eager to share details about her life, other than that she was in Marigold to help Grace and her mother. She definitely didn't want to talk about Maynard. She was already missing him.

Would she and Maynard have love in their eyes fifty years from now if God willed for them to have that much time on earth together? Of course they would, even if she couldn't imagine them as an old couple right now. If she loved him now, she would love him forever.

Almost twenty minutes passed before a silver sedan finally pulled into the parking lot and stopped in front of her. The passenger side window rolled down. "I sure hope you're Daisy Hershberger."

She nodded.

The man heaved a sigh of relief and put his car in Park. He

scrambled out of it and jogged to the other side. "I'm sorry I'm late. There was some confusion about what time I was supposed to pick you up." He held out his hand. "I'm Jackson Talbot. I run a taxi service in Birch Creek and Marigold."

Daisy shook his hand, and he took her suitcase and put it in the trunk. He opened the back passenger side door, and she got in.

Jackson hopped into the driver's seat and soon they were off. "We should be in Marigold in forty-five minutes or so. I apologize if I'm making you late."

"That's okay." *Mamm* and *Daed* didn't say anything about Grace or her parents needing her to be in Marigold at a specific time.

She glanced at Jackson as he maneuvered the car out of the lot. He looked to be in his late thirties, possibly early forties. She really couldn't tell age when it came to English men. He had short hair with graying sideburns and a mustache and beard with threads of silver through them. She also noticed he was wearing a thick, black wedding ring.

"My wife, Megan, is training our oldest daughter to take appointments," he said. "She's fifteen and every bit the distracted teenager. She wrote down that you were coming this evening. Fortunately, Megan noticed and texted me."

Daisy tried to pay attention to what he was saying, but she couldn't stop looking out the window. What she saw filled her with awe. Dover was flat, and while Pickering Beach was less than half an hour from her house and a great place to spend time relaxing, the beach didn't compare to what she was seeing now. Lush rolling hills covered with green grass, tall budding trees, and as they traveled farther from Mount Eaton, white Amish houses, black buggies, and pastureland. So much pastureland. Lots of woods too.

"It's so pretty here," she said.

"You should see it when everything is in full bloom." Jackson flipped on his turn signal. "Fall is gorgeous too. Even winter is nice, if you like lots of snow."

"I don't know if I do or not. We don't get much in Dover." She leaned closer to the window, as if it would bring her nearer to the beautiful landscape. No wonder Grace and her family liked living here.

"Have you always lived in Delaware?" Jackson took a left turn down an asphalt road where the Amish houses were spread out.

"Yes. This is the first time I've been out of the state."

He turned into a gravel driveway and pulled up to a modest Amish house with a wraparound front porch.

"Thank you." Daisy opened her purse and started to pull out her wallet.

Jackson shook his head. "Your father took care of it." He grinned and got out to retrieve her suitcase from the trunk.

Daisy slipped her wallet back into her purse and exited the car. Immediately she was hit with a fresh breeze, along with a whiff of livestock. While she and her parents had a horse and buggy, they only raised a few chickens in their small backyard that wasn't big enough to sustain any other livestock. They purchased their meat and vegetables from an Amish family who had a large farm, and they also visited Spence's Bazaar and Amish Market a few times a year. But the air here was very different. She took another big breath. Wonderful.

It was only after Jackson handed her suitcase to her that she noticed there wasn't a buggy parked in the driveway or near the barn. She assumed her *onkel* Howard was at work, but he rode in a van with a group of other Amish men to work their roofing jobs on construction sites, according to what Grace had told her. Maybe *Aenti* Rosella was out visiting friends or running errands. That was okay. It would give Daisy and Grace time to catch up alone.

"Enjoy your visit." Jackson smiled again and got into his car.

As he drove away, she walked to the front porch, glancing at the small house next door. It wasn't just small, it was tiny, and so was the barn next to it. She'd never seen such a diminutive residence. The gray-roofed, white-painted home was only a few yards from her aunt and uncle's property. She didn't see a buggy there either.

She reached her aunt and uncle's front door and knocked. Waited. When no one answered, she knocked again. A cow lowed in the distance, followed by a rooster crowing. After knocking a third time, she tried turning the doorknob. Locked. She sighed, left her suitcase and purse on the porch, and walked to the backyard. Maybe someone was out here and hadn't heard her arrive.

Other than their similar houses, her cousin's place was different than her home in Dover. There were the copious woods on the back of the property, for starters. Then there was the silence. While there were plenty of sounds around her—the cows, the rooster and hens in a coop by the back of the barn, the buzzing of a few errant flies—it was still much quieter here than in her busy neighborhood just outside the Delaware capital city limits.

To her left was a large pasture, and several silky brown cows stood by the fence, staring at her with large eyes as if they knew she didn't belong there. She'd make sure to get acquainted with them later. She went to the back door and rapped on the framed screen. Still no answer. Strange.

A butterfly landed on the back of her hand, and she smiled. She loved butterflies. They were such beautiful creatures, but they were also so skittish she could only view them from a distance. She stilled, expecting it to fly off. When it didn't, she took the rare opportunity to examine it. It's bright orange wings flapped slowly, and they were rimmed with black and white. She turned her hand so she could look at it from the side. "Lovely," she murmured.

As soon as she spoke, the butterfly took off.

Good thing, because she had to figure out how to get inside the house. When she tried opening the back door, she found it latched shut. Clearly no one was home. She put her hands on her hips and looked around. Now what was she supposed to do?

Daisy glanced at the neighbor's house again. A cool breeze kicked up, and she tugged her blue sweater around her. The temperature was about the same here as it was in Dover when she left early this morning, but the wind was chilly, and she'd put her coat in her suitcase, not wanting to have to deal with it on the bus ride.

Maybe someone was home next door even though the buggy was gone. In all the letters she'd received from Grace, her cousin hadn't mentioned her neighbors. Most of her news was about Kyle, and there were a few times when she felt a pang of envy when she read about all the different places Grace and Kyle went on their dates and the things they did. Nothing too personal or romantic, but Daisy had gotten the impression that Kyle was much more hands-on with Grace than Maynard was. Literally.

That was going to change when she went back home.

She headed to the neighbor's and scurried up the front porch. Just as she was about to knock on the door, it opened on its own. Another breeze cut through her, and the door swung open all the way. Daisy stuck her head partway inside. "Hello?"

When no one answered, she deduced no one was home here either. She stepped inside and reached for the doorknob, intending to close the door. When she tugged, the knob fell into her hand.

Oh no! Quickly she tried to put the knob back in place, but it fell out again. On the third attempt, it finally stayed. Carefully, she held the left side of the door and pulled it closer to her. When she heard it latch, she breathed out a sigh of relief, only to gasp when the knob fell out again, landed on her toe, and rolled off the front porch.

That'll leave a bruise. Daisy wiggled her big toe inside her black tennis shoes, then tromped to the end of the bottom porch step and snatched up the knob. Thank goodness no one was around to see her break the neighbor's door handle.

She went inside the house, intent on putting the knob somewhere easily seen. The living, dining, and kitchen areas took up one big room. She'd seen this type of layout before in one of her English friend's homes. An open floor plan, she thought it was called. The kitchen window was opened halfway, and plain white curtains billowed in the breezy air coming into the house.

She glanced around. The furnishings were sparse—one recliner chair and an end table with a gas lamp on top were to the right of the room near a wood fireplace. A small table with four chairs was farther inside, with one chair pulled away from the table. The kitchen counters were under the window along with the sink, and white cabinets were on either side of the curtains. There was no coffee table or couch, no rug on the floor, and nothing on the walls. It was the most un-homey home she'd ever been in.

Daisy blinked. She wasn't here to judge someone else's living accommodations. She walked toward the kitchen, searching for something she could use to leave a note. There was a full roll of paper towels by the sink, and a stub of a pencil by the stove. That would work.

She picked up the pencil, tore a paper towel off the roll, and started writing.

Dear Neighbor,

I'm sorry I broke your doorknob. I tried to fix it, but it wouldn't stay in place. See, I'm visiting from Dover because my cousin Grace—your neighbor—needs help planning her wedding. It's not until November, but for some reason she wants to do it early. I didn't really want to leave. I need to have "the talk" with Maynard. We have to make plans for our future . . .

Her palm pressed against her forehead. Whoever lived here didn't need all those details, especially the one about Maynard. And she'd already torn a little hole in her makeshift paper. Writing on a paper towel wasn't exactly easy, especially when it was quilted for fast absorbency. She tore off another towel, and with the stubby pencil poised above her writing surface, she—

A heavy thud sounded behind her. She whirled around to see an Amish man behind her.

"Hey!" he shouted. "What do you think you're doing?"

Chapter 3

When Perry pulled his horse and buggy toward the barn, he saw that his front door was open. He wasn't that surprised, considering he'd discovered that the doorknob was unfixable, and he went to E&J's Grocery, the store his brother Nelson's wife, Ella, ran with her father, to buy a new one. He thought he'd repaired the old knob enough to keep the door shut. Apparently not. Oh well, once he installed this one, he wouldn't have to worry about his door anymore.

He took his time putting up his horse, then headed to the house with the doorknob and tools he needed to install it. He walked inside, shocked to see someone standing in his kitchen. When he yelled at her, she whirled around and dropped something on the floor.

Perry took a few steps forward, ready to interrogate this woman he'd never seen before and find out why she was in his house. Then he halted, holding her astonished gaze with one of his own, his heart hammering in his chest. Her eyes were extraordinary. Honey brown circled the pupils in a starburst, and bluish-gray and green filled out the rest of the iris. She had long, amber lashes, and her round cheeks were the color of the pink-coral roses in his mother's garden.

He shook his head. He never noticed this level of detail about a stranger, or even someone he knew. He saved his observational analyses for butterflies and the flora that attracted them. And he could logically assign his rushing pulse to being shocked that she was here uninvited. "Who are you, and what are you doing in my—"

"I can explain." She held up her hands, as if warding him off. "My name is Daisy Hershberger, and I'm from Dover, Delaware."

"You've traveled a long way to break into someone's house."

"I'm not breaking in." She lifted her chin. "Your doorknob is broken."

"I'm aware."

"My family isn't home," she said, her hands twisting together as fast as she was speaking. "I came over here, thinking someone would be home. But *nee* one was, so I came in."

He stared at her, baffled. "What?"

She drew in a deep breath. "I'm from Dover, Delaware, and I'm visiting my cousin Grace."

"Oh." He nodded, relieved that she was finally making sense. "And she's not home."

"Neither is *Onkel* Howard or *Aenti* Rosella. I thought I would see if someone was here and if they knew where they were." She grimaced. "I don't understand why they're not here."

"They're on vacation." Perry picked up the bag he dropped and set it on the end table by the lamp. "I'm taking care of their animals while they're gone." Although he kept to himself, he did know his neighbors, and he didn't mind helping them out while they were out of town. Howard worked as a roofer, and his wife, Rosella, had a lot of friends in the district. He knew less about Grace, other than she was in her mid-twenties and a decent looking girl with a boyfriend named Kyle. As soon as his mother and Phoebe found out he'd moved next door to a single woman, he made sure to tell them she was taken.

"I don't understand," Daisy said, more to herself than him. "If they're out of town, why were Rosella and Grace in such a hurry for me to visit?"

"They're supposed to come back today."

"They must be running late then. I'm sorry about the doorknob. I tried putting it back a couple times, but it wouldn't stay."

"It's been broken for a while." He loosened up a little, now that he understood who she was and why she was here. "I'm putting in a new one today."

"*Gut.* Because anyone can just walk into your *haus.*"

He almost grinned. But she wasn't smiling, and she looked extremely uncomfortable. "You're welcome to wait here until your *familye* returns," he said, trying to put her at ease. He wasn't thrilled about unexpected company, but she seemed harmless.

"That's okay." She was heading toward the door. "I can wait on the front porch."

Perry was about to shrug and tell her to suit herself. Then he saw she was wearing a thin sweater, and the cold wind had been increasing throughout the day, threatening rain showers. *She'll be fine.* Surely the Hershbergers would be back soon, since they were obviously expecting her.

Daisy had almost one foot out the door when he changed his mind. "I don't mind if you stay here. It's a little chilly to be sitting outside."

"But you've got your kitchen window open."

"*Ya,* because . . ." He hesitated. This morning the painted lady had been flitting around his house, fully healed, and he opened the window, expecting her to leave. Instead, she sat on his table as he ate his bacon and eggs, her little wings slowly waving back and forth. He cut a thin slice of apple and put it on a paper towel next to him, and she ate while he polished off the rest of the fruit. Before he left for E&J's, he left the window open for when she decided to go back in the wild.

But Daisy didn't need to know all that. She'd think he was abnormal for having breakfast with a butterfly. Either that or pathetic. "I like lots of fresh air."

"I don't blame you." Daisy took a deep breath. "It smells wonderful here."

Like everyone else in Ohio, he appreciated the refreshing spring air after a long, snowy winter. But she was acting like she was inhaling the most fragrant perfume in the world. Did it stink in Dover? He'd never been there or met anyone from the settlement, so he had no idea.

He heard a growling noise and glanced at her. "Have you had lunch?"

She started twisting her fingers again, then put them behind her back. "I'm not—"

Growl.

"Hungry. All right, maybe I am, a little bit."

Although it was past two o'clock, he hadn't eaten either. "I was going to make a peanut butter and jelly sandwich," he said. "My *mamm* makes delicious preserves. Do you like cherries?"

Daisy nodded, her pretty eyes slightly widening. "*Ya.*"

Disregarding that he'd noticed her eyes again, he went to the kitchen and spied the stubby pencil on the floor. Before going to E&J's, he'd taken a few notes on the painted lady on the spiral pad he kept in the kitchen drawer by the sink. He had notebooks and pads of paper, along with pens and pencils in different areas of the house, and he thought he'd put it back in the drawer. Picking up the pencil, he said to Daisy, "Won't take but a minute to make the sandwiches."

She stood by the dining room table. "You don't have to *geh* to the trouble."

"I need to eat too, Daisy from Dover."

"I did say that a few times, didn't I?"

"Just twice." He got out the peanut butter and jelly from the pantry. "Must be a special place."

"It's—Do you know you have a butterfly on your shoulder?"

He glanced down. Sure enough, painted lady was sitting on his left shoulder, as if she belonged there. He extended his hand to her. "You decided to come back, huh?" he murmured as she hopped onto his finger. Although he tried not to get too attached to his butterflies, there was something special about this one, and he was glad she had decided to come home.

***

Ferman Eash scowled as he turned his buggy into Perry Bontrager's driveway. His foul mood was partly from pain. The anti-inflammatory the English doc had prescribed six months ago for his bum hip worked great in the beginning, but now it offered zero relief.

"*You need a hip replacement, Mr. Eash,*" the far-too-serious doctor had said. "*The sooner the better.*"

"*Well, Doc*"—Ferman had gotten up from the exam table, hiding his wince—"*that's not gonna happen. I was born with this hip and I'm gonna keep it.*"

Once the doctor realized Ferman wasn't budging, they had discussed medication to manage the pain. But now he was hurting as much as ever, and another trip to the doctor would be useless. He would just say the same thing—replace the hip. *No way.*

He pulled his horse to a stop and exited the buggy, trying to ignore the sharp, stabbing pain the movement caused. He stilled and closed his eyes. *Lord, help me get my aggravation under control.* He definitely needed divine assistance, because he couldn't talk to Perry while he was in a sour mood, thanks to being laid off from Wagler's Buggy this morning. Oh sure, Micah and Jesse had been nice about it, putting the reason more on themselves than on Ferman.

But he wasn't born yesterday, and he knew he couldn't keep up with the increase in work the shop had experienced over the past few months. He also had to admit that, way down deep, he was a tiny bit relieved, although he would miss talking to the customers. Standing all day wasn't helping his pain, and he had slowed down over the past six months. At seventy-five, he wasn't ready to be put out to pasture just yet, though, and despite his internal grumbling, he was glad Jesse had told him to talk to Perry about being his farrier assistant. He'd had plenty of experience with horses and had shod a few in his time, so he wasn't coming to the man empty-handed.

He just hoped Perry would hire him. And if not Perry, he prayed there was someone else willing to employ an old man with an achy hip and an occasionally dyspeptic disposition. His temperament needed improvement. Being testy wasn't exactly good for his Christian witness, or for customer service.

He opened his eyes and looked at the small, white house, took a deep breath, and tried not to hobble as he walked to the front door. His hands were oddly damp, and he could feel a ball of anxiety rolling around in his gut. Even though he was well set financially, he needed a job for his sanity. Puttering around alone all day in his three-bedroom home would drive him *ab im kopp*.

When he got to the front door, he was surprised to see it was partly open. He knocked anyway. "Perry?" he hollered, in case the young man was in the back of the house or otherwise disposed. "You home?"

"*Ya*. Come on in."

Ferman walked inside, a little taken aback by the lack of furnishings. His late wife, Lovina, had made sure their home was always cozy and welcoming. She had loved company, and if there wasn't enough room to sit and visit in the living room, she'd send Ferman to the basement to fetch the extra folding chairs. Even those were comfortable and had padded seats.

But Perry's house didn't have much at all. He knew the man had moved in two years ago, which was plenty of time to set up a house. Then he realized the main problem. Like Ferman, Perry was single. His place needed a woman's touch.

That's when he turned his attention from the almost empty living room and saw a young woman about Perry's age sitting at the kitchen table with him. Hmm, what a coincidence. Each of them had a plate in front of them with partially eaten peanut butter and jelly sandwiches and a few potato chips.

Ferman backed up a step. "I didn't mean to intrude."

Perry stood. "We're just having a bite of lunch. Do you want a PB&J?"

"*Nee*," he said, trying to hide his distaste. He never liked peanut butter, but his son loved it and peanut butter and jelly sandwiches, even now as an adult. "I can come back later."

"Are you here about the job?" Perry asked.

Ah, so Jesse had talked to his brother already. That was a good sign, because if Perry wasn't interested in hiring him, he would have said so. He nodded, then glanced at the woman again. She was quite pretty, if one fancied fair skin, blonde hair, a slender frame, and unusual eyes. His Lovina had been swarthy, with black hair and deep brown eyes. She was on the stout side, even before she'd had their son, Junior, and was a couple inches taller than he was. He was smitten at first sight. Even now, almost seven years after her death, he missed her intensely.

"*Ya*," he said, trying to keep his cool. "If it's still open."

Perry smiled. "If you want it, it's yours."

Praise the Lord. He didn't want to come across as too desperate, so he just nodded.

"*Gut.* Be here at four thirty tomorrow morning and we'll head out. Bring your lunch."

He almost gulped. He hadn't gotten up that early in a long time. Wagler's Buggy Shop didn't open until 7:00 a.m., and when he was working for a lumber company in Winesburg before he retired to Marigold, the van picking up him and the other Amish employees arrived at six o'clock. He made a mental note to wind up and set his alarm clock for three thirty. That would give him enough time to work out the kinks, get dressed, and arrive at Perry's on time. It wouldn't do for him to be late for work on the first day.

Perry shook his hand, sealing the deal. Ferman glanced at the woman again. She was staring at the sandwich, her expression uncertain. Whatever was going on here, he couldn't shake the feeling that he was intruding, regardless of what Perry had said. It was time to vamoose.

"See you in the morning then." Ferman nodded at the woman.

She gave him a small wave, accompanied by a slight smile.

He squared his shoulders, forced his hip to settle down, and walked out of the house. But when he carefully slid onto the buggy seat, he let out a loud whoop, startling his horse. "Sorry, *bu*," he said, lowering his voice. Then he turned the buggy around and headed home. He'd have to turn in early tonight, that was for sure. But he didn't care because God had provided him with a new job. *Thank you, Lord.*

Daisy nibbled on a potato chip as Perry sat back down across from her. He'd been right about his mother's cherry preserves. They were scrumptious. Better than *Mamm*'s, and her mother had won a blue ribbon for her raspberry preserves at the Delaware State Fair twenty years ago.

"That was Ferman Eash," he said, picking up his sandwich. "He's now my new assistant."

She was surprised she hadn't heard Ferman's buggy pull up in the driveway, especially since the door and kitchen window were open. Then again, she'd been caught up in eating her lunch. She was almost starving, and it took everything she had not to inhale the food. She was also watching the butterfly that was fluttering around the room. It looked exactly like the one that had landed on her hand at her cousin's house. Maybe it was the same one, maybe not, but it seemed happy to be inside the house.

Perry was ignoring it.

"What do you do?" she asked, before taking a bite of the sandwich.

He swallowed and took a sip of water. "I'm a farrier."

That was interesting. She'd always wondered about the job but didn't have the courage to ask John Henry, the gruff man her father had hired to shoe their horse. He never said more than hello and good-bye, and he was singularly focused on his job, almost as if he were in a hurry to get it done and move on. He did good work, but he was one of the most unapproachable men she'd ever met.

She opened her mouth to ask Perry a question about his occupation, then clamped it shut. Having lunch with him was awkward enough. She didn't need to pester him with questions.

Then again, she realized that sharing a meal with him wasn't all *that* awkward. He'd already asked her a few questions about Dover that she easily answered—how many people lived in their district, what the main jobs and industries were—and when she mentioned that many of her family members and friends liked to fish in the ocean, particularly the men, he seemed intrigued. Growing up near the Atlantic, she'd never thought that ocean fishing was all that enticing, and she'd never gone herself. Just as she was about to tell him that her father often went deep-sea fishing, Ferman showed up.

The butterfly was now hovering around Perry's head. He had taken off his hat before making lunch, revealing a head of thick, wavy black hair, the bangs slightly pressed against his forehead above straight eyebrows and hooded blue eyes with green flecks. He was also several inches taller than her, enough that she had to look up at him. She never quibbled about height, though. Maynard was quite short, and she didn't care.

The butterfly landed, perched right in the middle of the top of Perry's hair. He continued to eat his sandwich, apparently unaware.

Daisy lifted her hand. "Uh . . . you . . ."

He paused, a chip halfway to his mouth. "I what?"

"The butterfly is on your head."

Perry looked up, his eyes almost crossing, making her hide a chuckle. He gently felt around for the butterfly and made a delicate shooing motion with his fingers. The insect flew away, and he watched it fly out the kitchen window.

Daisy tried to come to grips with the contradictory man in front of her. Although she hadn't spoken to John Henry, she had watched him a time or two as he shod their horse. The man had large, rough hands, with long, thick fingers that handled the tools with ease. Not exactly the hands that would treat a butterfly as gently as Perry just had.

She glanced at his hands as he picked up a few broken chips and popped them into his mouth. They were large, like John Henry's. Strong-looking too. She couldn't tell if they were rough or not. Wait, she just noticed a callus on the knuckle of his pointer finger on his left hand. He was wearing a navy blue pullover, and he had pushed the sleeves up to the elbows when he had prepared their lunch. Naturally her gaze wandered to his forearms . . . and stayed there.

They were muscly. Tanned. Well formed. Maynard worked hard, but his forearms didn't compare to Perry's. A man didn't get that muscular without a lot of taxing, strenuous work. A flittery, fluttery feeling filled her stomach.

She reined in her thoughts. She shouldn't be noticing Perry's arms, or anything else about him physically, not when she was in love with Maynard. She was already missing him. *Sigh*.

"Something wrong?"

Had she actually sighed out loud? *Oops*. "I'm just tired from the trip." That was true. She was also eager for her relatives to come home. She'd imposed on Perry long enough.

He nodded and stood, picking up their plates. "You must be ready to unpack and settle in, *ya*?"

"I am." She took the glasses and followed him into the kitchen, just as another butterfly flew in the window. Wait, was this the same one? She assumed so when the creature settled on Perry's shoulder again. "Butterflies seem to like you."

With a shrug of his shoulder, he shooed it away again and took the glasses from her. The butterfly fluttered to the stove and perched on the edge of it. Perry turned on the tap and started filling the sink.

Daisy walked over to the stove and examined the insect. "I think this is the same one that was here earlier." It had the same coloring at least. Then she turned around. "I can do the dishes."

He shook his head. "It won't take long to finish these."

From his lack of beard and sparse furniture, she was fairly sure he was single. Maybe he had a girlfriend . . . oh, she hadn't thought about that. He didn't mention one, but then again, she hadn't brought up Maynard either. If he did have a girlfriend, Daisy was glad she hadn't showed up while they were eating lunch. Now that would be awkward.

But she didn't feel right just standing there while he worked either. "It's the least I can do," she said, moving closer to him. "You fed me after all."

He glanced at her. "Not exactly a gourmet meal."

The butterfly moved to the kitchen window, capturing Perry's attention. Daisy used the opportunity to reach over him and grab the bottle of dish detergent.

Perry shrugged and moved away. "I guess you're doing my dishes."

She smiled at him and squirted a few drops of soap into the hot water, then put the rest of the dishes in the sink.

"Daisy!"

She spun around, her hands still in the soapy water. Grace! She yanked her hands out of the sink as Grace dashed into the house. Perry handed Daisy a towel and she dried off, then rushed to her cousin. They quickly embraced.

"I can't believe you're here." Grace grinned, holding on to Daisy's elbows. "*Mamm* was in such a hurry to get home today, but she didn't tell me and *Daed* why until I saw your suitcase on the front porch. I'm so happy to see you!"

Daisy was happy too, but she was also confused. Why would her cousin be surprised she was here? Hopefully Grace would clear things up when they went to her house.

Grace dropped her hands and looked at Perry, who was still in the kitchen. "Thanks for keeping her company."

"I just have to finish the dishes," Daisy said, starting for the sink again. "Then I'll be right over—"

He intercepted her. "I'll do them. *Geh* be with *yer familye.*"

She smiled her thanks, and she and Grace left.

"I see you met Perry," Grace said as they walked the short distance to her house. "He's, uh, an unusual guy, isn't he?"

"He seemed normal to me."

"He's not *abnormal.*" They made their way up the porch steps. "He's just . . . I don't know how to describe him. He likes to keep to himself. I'm surprised he invited you inside."

Daisy glanced at his still-open front door. "He didn't exactly invite me in."

"Oh?"

She threaded her arm through Grace's. "It's a long story."

Chapter 4

I want to know everything about you and Maynard."

Daisy glanced around Grace's room. After they had gone inside, her *aenti* apologized profusely for being late. "I'm so sorry you had to wait on us, Daisy," she said, giving her another hug, then taking her to the other side of the living room while Grace and *Onkel* Howard fetched their luggage. "I don't know how I would manage planning Grace's wedding without you."

"I'm happy to help any way I can."

"Just do me a favor," *Aenti* Rosella said. "Don't let Grace know I asked you to come, okay? I wanted to surprise her. I'll tell her later that you're going to help with the wedding."

"Sure." But her request was baffling. If she was so desperate for Daisy's assistance, why was she hiding the whole reason for asking her to come here? Besides, Grace had older sisters who were married, and *Aenti* Rosella had managed their weddings just fine. Maybe it was because she and Grace were the same age and had grown up together. She could understand that reasoning. But there was also the strange fact that Grace and her family had returned home early from vacation for Daisy's visit. If they weren't going to be here, why didn't her parents get a ticket for another time? Even two days later would have been better.

She looked again at Grace, who was waiting for her to talk about Maynard. Their fathers were brothers, but she and Grace didn't resemble each other. Her cousin was tall for an Amish woman and had dark hair, not light brown like Daisy's. Their eye colors were different too, with Daisy having hazel eyes and Grace a deep brown.

Daisy regrouped and set aside the strange circumstances of her arrival in Marigold. She was here with her favorite cousin, she was going to plan her wedding, and that was that. "Maynard is wonderful," Daisy said, grabbing one of Grace's quilted pillows and hugging it. "So smart and hardworking. He's a very talented cabinetmaker."

"Yeah, yeah"—Grace leaned forward, a sly twinkle in her eye—"But is he a *gut* kisser?"

She froze, shocked at her cousin's intruding question. But Grace didn't seem self-conscious at all talking about such an intimate subject. And that wasn't a good thing for Daisy. Now she was regretting embellishing the status of her and Maynard's relationship. But Grace was always talking about how wonderful Kyle was, how great it was to be in love. Daisy was already feeling left out from her siblings and friends. Telling Grace that she and Maynard were a couple just . . . happened.

"Don't be shy." Grace grinned. "I won't tell anyone."

Clearing her throat, Daisy said, "Uh . . . is, um . . . Kyle *gut* at kissing?"

Grace sat back, a dreamy look entering her eyes. "Oh, *ya*. He's a very, very *gut* kisser."

Daisy gulped again. "Have you kissed anyone else?"

"Of course not."

"Then how do you know?"

With a cheeky grin, Grace said, "Because of how he makes me feel."

"And how is that?" Daisy was acting nosier than Grace, and even though the topic was making her a little uncomfortable, this was a prime chance to get some insight into romance, something she would need after she and Maynard had "the talk."

"Well . . ." Grace shifted positions on the quilt-covered bed that matched the pillow and sat cross-legged, her plum-colored dress covering her knees and bare feet. They had taken off their black socks as soon as they entered the bedroom. "I get this tickle in my stomach when we kiss. Then my whole body goes warm and cold at the same time."

Daisy wasn't sure how someone could feel two temperatures simultaneously, but she wanted to hear more. "And then what?"

"My heart starts hammering in my chest. Like someone is beating a drum inside me."

"Does it hurt?"

"*Nee*. Not at all. Don't you feel that when you're with Maynard?"

"Oh sure." She waved her hand. "All the time. I just wanted to know how you felt."

"Wonderful." Her smile was soft. "Kyle makes me feel wonderful. Not just when we're kissing—and we try not to do that too often because, you know . . ."

Daisy nodded. She did know, thanks to a book at the library and her mother's quick, red-faced "birds and bees" talk when she turned eighteen. Or was it sixteen? She couldn't remember, but her age didn't matter because she took to heart her mother's warning about saving herself for after her wedding. *"Being with a man is special—so special that God wanted intimacy to be under the covenant of marriage,"* Mamm had said. "You'll understand when the time comes."

And she was sure she would, eventually. With Maynard.

"So?" Grace said.

"So, what?"

"It's your turn." She leaned forward again. "How does Maynard make you feel when he kisses you?"

Daisy's neck heated, and her upper lip grew damp under her cousin's expectant gaze. How in the world was she supposed to answer this question? She didn't want to tell Grace to mind her own business, especially when she had been so open and quite helpful. She now knew what she should feel when she and Maynard finally did kiss.

She also didn't want to tell a lie. But the truth was too embarrassing. "Uh, well, you see . . ." Daisy wiped the back of her hand over her perspiring lip. "It's like this—"

"Grace! Time to fix supper!"

Daisy almost melted with relief at her aunt's voice from the bottom of the stairs. "We shouldn't keep her waiting," she said, bouncing off the bed as if her backside was on fire.

"To be continued, then."

Grace moved off the bed with much more *grace* than Daisy, and she didn't seem to notice that Daisy was in a hurry to go downstairs. Anything to get off the topic of kissing.

When they reached the kitchen, *Aenti* Rosella was hovering over a whole chicken sitting in a roaster pan on the gas stove and brushing the skin with oil. "Grace, why don't you and Daisy *geh* to the greenhouse and bring in some tomatoes and lettuce? We'll have a simple salad with the chicken and noodles."

They didn't bother to put on shoes before walking outside, and the grass felt soft and cold on her bare feet as she and Grace walked to a small greenhouse near the wooded edge of the yard. In her confusion about being locked out of the house, Daisy had missed seeing the small building the first time she was back here.

A cool breeze rustled the trees in front of them. Many of the branches had tiny green buds on the ends, and there were a few conifers among the many tall, mostly bare oaks and elms. The greenhouse was a square structure, made of old windows, including the roof. "I've never seen a greenhouse like this before."

"*Daed* and Tobias made it," she said, referring to one of her brothers-in-law. "This is the fourth year we've used it, and all my sisters have one now."

"Are they made with windows too?"

"*Ya.*" Grace opened the upcycled door. Daisy thought it was an excellent use of something people might thoughtlessly throw away or drop off at a dump.

They walked inside, the temperature much warmer than the outdoor air. "The lettuce is over there," Grace said, pointing to the back of the greenhouse. "We've got two kinds, so get a little of both."

Daisy walked past several pots with tomatoes, cucumbers, and cabbage, then a table that held smaller pots of parsley, dill, and coriander. "This is really wonderful," she said, touching the soft dill sprigs as she headed for the lettuce. "It must be great having fresh vegetables in the winter."

"*Ya. Daed*'s going to make one for me and Kyle, with Kyle's help, of course." Grace plucked two ripe tomatoes off a vine tied to a string attached to the ceiling of the greenhouse, the bottom of the plant sitting in a medium clay pot. "The hardest part is finding suitable windows no one needs anymore."

She was sure Maynard would be able to construct such a structure, but he'd have to do it without her *Daed*'s help. Her father was an excellent house painter, but *Mamm* was the one who did all the fix-it jobs around the house, and she had taught Daisy how to do them too. But Daisy wouldn't have to worry about that with Maynard. He was highly capable when it came to using his tools.

Once she and Grace had gathered the vegetables and Grace had decided to pick a couple of carrots for the salad, they went back to the house. Daisy couldn't help but glance at Perry's house again. His buggy was still in the driveway, but he wasn't outside. She had appreciated him making her lunch and keeping her company, but she couldn't forget that Grace said he was unusual, whatever that meant.

She shrugged and stepped on the patio, the flagstones even colder than the grass. But she didn't mind. She preferred being barefoot to wearing shoes. Maynard couldn't stand to take off his shoes, and whenever he visited Daisy, he always had a pair of protective overshoes covering his boots or sneakers. She initially thought that was a little odd, but she never had to worry about him dragging mud into the house.

After they finished the delicious supper *Aenti* Rosella, Grace, and Daisy made, Daisy walked down the driveway to the phone shanty at the end. It was between her aunt and uncle's house and Perry's, so she assumed they shared the phone. The sky was a dusky blue with layers of coral, lavender, and light pink from the descending sun. She opened the shanty door and stepped inside. Even though she trusted her mother to tell Maynard where she was, she wanted to give him the news herself.

Quickly she dialed his number, and after two rings she heard a clicking sound. "Hello?"

Disappointment filled her. "Hi, Neva," she said to Maynard's mother. She didn't call him all that often, and he never picked up the phone, but hope always sprang eternal.

"Daisy."

THE MARRIAGE PACT

She also hoped that one day Neva Miller would speak to her without sounding put upon. Maynard's father, Amos, was reserved too and worked at the same shop Maynard did. "Is Maynard there?" she asked.

"*Nee.*"

"Will he be home soon?"

"I don't know."

Daisy rolled her eyes. "Can you tell him I called?"

"*Ya.*"

"*Danki.* The number is—"

Click.

She flinched. How rude. Then she remembered she didn't leave her uncle's phone number. She started to dial Neva back, then changed her mind and called her parents. At least she could carry on a conversation with them, and she needed to tell them she was all right.

"Hi, Daisy," *Mamm* said as soon as she answered the phone. Because of her father's job, he had a cell phone that revealed the caller on the screen. "Did you make it to Marigold all right?"

"*Ya.* But no one was here when I arrived."

"Oh?"

Her mother sounded tense. "Did you know they were on vacation this week?"

Silence. Then, "There must have been a mix-up. I'm sorry about that."

"It's okay. I—" She was about to tell her that she had passed the time with Perry but thought better of it. It wasn't like her mother would ever meet him. "I managed."

"*Gut.* Enjoy yourself, Daisy. Your ticket is open-ended, and you can come back anytime you want to."

"But what about my job?"

"I forgot to tell you," *Mamm* said quickly. "I took your shifts.

Mr. Brickman didn't mind. Just while you're gone. It's nice to get out of the house."

"But—"

"Oops, your father needs me right now. Love you."

"Love you too—"

Click.

Hung up on twice in a row. Daisy frowned. Why was everyone acting so strangely? Well, not everyone. Grace seemed herself, albeit a little snoopy. And Neva would probably never change. But her parents and *Aenti* Rosella's behavior was more than a little off.

She put the receiver back in the cradle and left the phone shanty. Only one light was on at Perry's, and it was on the backside of his house. What was he doing tonight? Then she shook her head. It wasn't her business to be wondering about Perry Bontrager. She had more important things to ponder, like how to dodge Grace's kissing question when their conversation resumed. Her stomach knotted up. *Oh boy.*

─◦◦─

Perry yawned as he waited for Ferman to climb inside his buggy. The old man was trying to hide that his hip was bothering him, but his moan when he hauled himself onto the front buggy seat gave him away. Perry ignored the sound.

"*Gute morgen*," Perry said, grabbing the reins. "You're right on time."

"Of course I am," Ferman groused. "Even at this ridiculous hour in the morning."

"Not all jobs are this early." Or five miles away. That was the reason they left at this *ridiculous* hour. His client needed his horses to be finished by early afternoon, and there were several to shoe. One of them, Turbo, had a particularly difficult personality. Perry would have offered to pick up Ferman and save him the trouble of driving over, except that the job was in the opposite direction of his house.

Soon they were on their way. As sunrise broke through, he saw a familiar sign that announced they were only six miles to Birch Creek. That wasn't their destination, but it was a reminder that he still hadn't decided what he was going to do about *Mamm* and her letter-writing campaign to marry him off. He cringed. It was awful when he thought about it, and he'd tried not to. Fetching the doorknob and tools and fixing his front door had been a needed distraction. So was Daisy Hershberger from Dover, Delaware. He smiled. Daisy from Dover. Kind of cute how she kept repeating where she was from.

His mouth froze in place, then switched to a frown. That was the second time—okay, more than two times—that he'd smiled when he thought of her. After she left with Grace, he'd gone into the kitchen, Lady following him. He decided to shorten her name and she kept him company as he finished cleaning the kitchen. He was drying the last dish when he saw her land on a torn paper towel by the stove. He was about to throw the shred away when he noticed the writing and read the message.

So Daisy from Dover had a boyfriend named Maynard. No surprise there. Besides being pretty, she was a good conversationalist, and he enjoyed learning about a place he'd never been to. Noticing her pleasant looks and ability to chat didn't mean anything, though, and he was relieved she had a boyfriend. If she were single and his mother found out, no doubt she'd try to match the two of them up. Thank goodness he didn't have to worry about that, because he was definitely, 100 percent *not* interested.

"Are you gonna tell me about that *maed* you were eating lunch with yesterday?"

Perry jerked at Ferman's gruff voice. He'd been so lost in his thoughts he forgot the man was sitting next to him. Jesse hadn't mentioned anything about Ferman being nosy, and that had probably been on purpose. "She's Grace's cousin," he said, his tone clipped.

Ferman settled back in the seat and took a thermos out of his lunch cooler. When he opened it, the smoky scent of coffee filled the buggy. "Where's she from?"

"Dover. Delaware," he added, in case Ferman didn't know where Dover was.

"Nice place. Been to one of the beaches before. Years ago, with Lovina. Before we had Junior." He finished pouring his coffee into the lid and took a sip. "How long is she staying?"

"I didn't ask."

"Why not?"

Perry gripped the reins. "Digging into my personal life isn't part of your job."

"Well, excuse me for making conversation. I'll keep my yap shut from now on."

With a sigh, Perry said, "Sorry. I didn't get a *gut* night's sleep."

"Thinking about Daisy?"

He almost laughed in surprise. What was with this guy? And no, he hadn't thought about Daisy as he tried to fall asleep. Not too much anyway. "*Nee.* I just had trouble sleeping. It happens sometimes."

"You should try a little valerian. Or is it lavender? Lovina used to say that one of those was for menopause and the other for insomnia, but I forget which is which."

Chuckling, Perry said, "Lavender is for sleep. My sister-in-law Margaret is a naturopath, so I should probably get some from her."

"Get a pinch or two for me while you're at it."

Ferman drank his coffee in silence for the rest of the trip, and by the time they arrived at the horse farm, the morning sun was fully above the horizon. Before starting the job, Ferman admitted to having a little farrier experience, and Perry was glad he didn't have to train him. He gave him the lighter duties—conditioning the hooves and keeping track of the tools—leaving Perry to do the more physically demanding tasks of blacksmithing and shoeing. That gave Ferman plenty of time to chat with the owners, and Perry noticed he didn't mind conversing with the horses either. The man did like to talk.

By noon they had finished well ahead of schedule, partly because the usually persnickety Turbo was on his best behavior, but also because of Ferman's assistance. Perry had to admit it was nice to have some help.

After cleaning up at the wash station near the client's barn, they went to the buggy and put away their tools. When they were packed up and ready to go, once again Ferman struggled to climb into the seat. Perry could see why Jesse and Micah were concerned about him working in their shop. While he'd appeared to be fine on the job, he now seemed to have trouble masking his pain.

As Perry steered the buggy down the long driveway toward the road, he glanced at Ferman. His eyes were closed, a slight grimace on his face. He wondered if he'd given him too much to do. The man knew his way around horses and farriers, but if the work was too strenuous, he needed to know. "Ferman?"

His eyes flew open, and he straightened up in the seat. "*Ya?*"

"How bad is the pain?"

"I'm fine," he snapped.

"Look, I think you're going to be a *gut* assistant, but I need you to be honest with me. If you're hurting or too tired, you gotta tell me. You don't have to keep up with me, and I don't mind if you take breaks." Or even work at all, but he didn't say that. Other than apprenticing with Andrew, Perry had always worked alone. While Ferman was helpful, he could do the job without him.

Ferman pressed his lips together, and Perry thought he'd offended him until he started talking again.

"Having a break or two would be *gut*."

Perry nodded, glad Ferman agreed to some moderation. "Would you consider using a stool to get into the buggy? Just at my house. You don't have to use it unless you need to."

Ferman nodded, almost imperceptibly. Then he picked up his lunch cooler and opened it, signaling the conversation closed.

Perry saw a single sandwich and an apple inside his cooler, along with the coffee thermos. Perry also brought his lunch, as he always did when he was working. Unlike Ferman's, though, his was more substantial—three protein bars from the box he'd picked up at E&J's grocery last week, the last piece of zucchini bread Charity made for him a few days ago, a plastic baggie full of dried fruit, and the rest of the chips from the bag he'd shared with Daisy yesterday. Instead of coffee, his thermos was full of ice water. The lunch wasn't fancy or even all that balanced, but it was enough to get him through the day. He couldn't say the same about his new assistant's meager meal.

As Ferman unwrapped his sandwich, Perry hesitated. He wasn't keen on going out to eat. Growing up on a farm and with his mother being an excellent cook, he preferred eating at home and bringing his own lunches. He also didn't like crowded restaurants. Or crowds, period. Church was the only exception, but that was because he wasn't there for the people, but for the Lord. Otherwise, he found big groups exhausting.

All the eateries in the area were usually busy, so the chance of them finding a quiet, low-populated restaurant was almost nil. Good for them, but not so great for him. Still, Ferman needed more than a cheese sandwich and a piece of fruit to get him through the next job.

"What do you think about going out for lunch?" Perry asked. "We've got time before we see our next client."

Ferman stared at his sandwich as if considering the offer. Then he shoved it back in his cooler and shut the lid. "You know that new restaurant just outside Marigold? The one with the train theme?"

He didn't, but he nodded anyway.

"They make these bite-size potato square thingies. Crispy on the outside, tender on the inside. Melt-in-your-mouth *gut*."

"We'll *geh* there then." Perry thought he saw a faint smile on the old man's face. While he knew better than to hope the diner wasn't packed, he was hungry and crispy potatoes did sound good. It was only lunch anyway, and he'd get through it even if it was crowded. *How bad could it be?*

Chapter 5

"Have you decided?"

Daisy looked at the English waitress who appeared to be around her own age, then at her cousin, who nodded. "We'll both have the special."

The waitress scribbled on an order pad, a blonde curl escaping the large bun on top of her head. "Two orders of country fried steak. You each get two sides and a roll."

Daisy and Grace picked their sides—black-eyed peas and mac and cheese for Daisy, grilled asparagus and yams for Grace—and gave the waitress their soft drink orders. As the waitress left to turn in their ticket, Daisy looked around the Railway Diner, taking in the uniquely themed restaurant and the busy crowd. Train memorabilia covered almost every inch of the walls, and on the front page of the menu was an explanation of the very short history of the diner that had opened last year, plus the owner's affinity for all things train related. Even the tables had old train and railway photographs on the top, covered with a transparent protective coating. "I like this place," Daisy said as the waitress returned and placed her drink in front of her.

"I've only been here once." Grace unwrapped her straw. "I didn't know there were so many things related to trains."

"Is it always this busy at lunchtime?"

"Last time it was. They've had steady business since they opened."

Right before lunch, *Aenti* Rosella had suggested that Daisy and Grace go to the diner while she repaired several of *Onkel* Howard's pants and socks. "I've put off the sewing long enough," her aunt said to Daisy. "You and Grace *geh* enjoy the afternoon."

"And talk about the wedding?" Daisy said.

"Uh, of course." *Aenti* Rosella scratched the side of her neck, ignoring Grace's puzzled look.

But Daisy had seen it and was also confused. Last night after supper, Grace had been too tired to even talk about Maynard and had gone to bed early, but this morning she and her mother had made breakfast together before Daisy had gotten up. Why hadn't *Aenti* Rosella said anything to Grace then? It was all so bewildering.

Grace pushed her chair away from the table. "Be right back."

After she left for the restroom, Daisy looked at the train photos on the table, but those soon blurred as she thought about last night again. With Grace retiring early and her aunt and uncle asleep in their chairs in the living room, that left Daisy on her own.

Surprisingly, she wasn't that tired, despite spending most of the day traveling. She fetched her stationery from her suitcase and went back to the kitchen to write Maynard a letter. She wrote a few lines, telling him about Grace's upcoming wedding, even though she was sure *Mamm* had already told him. Then she wrote:

The wedding is in November. Hopefully by that time you and I will—

Quickly, she ran her eraser over the last half sentence. It was too impersonal to bring up "the talk" in her letter. Instead, she mentioned the weather before signing off. After affixing one of the stamps to the right corner of the envelope she'd brought from home, she placed the letter on the counter near the back door, ready for her to mail it early in the morning.

For the next half hour, she worked in the living room on her sister's cross-stitch Bible verse, finishing it by the time she stopped. She'd started stitching Bible verses to help her with memorization, and she found herself also contemplating the words as she worked. So far, she'd stitched ten verses and designed the patterns herself with graph paper and a pencil. She needed to frame this one now, and she would when she went back to Dover. Her next verse would be a wedding gift for Grace and Kyle. She was still looking for the perfect scripture about love and marriage.

"I'm back." Grace sat down and adjusted her navy blue cardigan that she wore over a light blue dress that matched her eyes. "You looked deep in thought. Were you thinking about Maynard? We still need to continue our *talk*." She grinned.

Daisy inwardly cringed.

"I'm sorry I fell asleep on you last night. I didn't realize how tired I was until after I'd eaten supper."

"It's okay." The longer she could put off discussing Maynard and kissing, the better. Maybe she could avoid it altogether by continuing to change the subject. "Have you and Kyle finalized your guest list yet?"

Grace shrugged. "We haven't really talked about it."

"Not at all?"

"There's plenty of time to figure out the wedding."

"*Aenti* Rosella doesn't think so."

Her cousin's brow furrowed. "When did she say that?"

Daisy gripped her hands under the table, unsure how to respond. Since her aunt hadn't said anything about the wedding plans to Grace yet, then that meant Daisy still needed to keep her secret. *Ach*, the subterfuge was making her head hurt. "She didn't. I just figured—"

"Huh." Grace tilted her head toward the front of the restaurant. "I'm surprised to see Perry here."

When Daisy looked over her shoulder, she saw Perry standing by the front door, Ferman next to him. Perry wasn't wearing his hat, and once again she noticed his thick, wavy-bordering-on-curly hair. Even though it was chilly outside, he was wearing a short-sleeved shirt, suspenders, and blue pants that had some dust on them, but they weren't all that dirty. He hooked his thumbs underneath the suspenders by his waistline, drawing Daisy's gaze to his well-built forearms. *Sigh.*

Grace waved Perry and Ferman over. "You don't mind if they eat with us, do you? That way they won't have to wait for a table."

"Not at all."

"I don't think they see me." Grace got up from the table and weaved through the crowd until she reached them. She started talking to Ferman, while Daisy continued to look at Perry as his gaze darted around the room. He seemed a little out of sorts. When his gaze met hers, she gave him an encouraging smile.

His expression relaxed a little. Ferman tapped him on the arm and they both followed Grace to the table. "Daisy," Grace said, gesturing to the older man. "This is—"

"Ferman." Daisy smiled. "Nice to see you again."

"Likewise." His throat sounded like it was permanently lined with sandpaper, and he took the chair next to Grace, leaving Perry the empty seat by Daisy.

The moment they sat down, the waitress showed up with the

women's meals—large pieces of chicken fried steak covered in white gravy, the vegetables in separate cups, and fresh, fluffy, yeasty rolls. Daisy's mouth started to water. The food looked and smelled delicious.

"I'll have what they've got, plus some of those potato square thingies," Ferman said. "With an iced tea."

"Same," Perry said in a low, quiet voice.

The waitress nodded. "Two more specials coming up."

"What have you two been up to this morning?" Grace asked.

Daisy glanced at Ferman, his brown eyes deeply set, with heavy etched lines around them. "Just finishing the first day of my new job," he said.

"I thought you were working at Wagler's." Grace took a paper napkin and put it in her lap.

"Nope. Got fired the day before yesterday."

"*Fired* is a strong word," Perry said.

Surprise registered on Grace's face, and Ferman explained what happened.

Daisy glanced at Perry, who was looking somewhat tense again, one of his knees bouncing up and down. They didn't say anything for a few minutes while Grace and Ferman talked about community news, and she went back to looking at the train pictures.

He leaned toward her. "*Geh* ahead and eat."

"I don't mind waiting."

"But your food will get cold. He glanced around the diner again. "We probably should have gotten ours to go."

His leg bounced faster under the table. She wondered if he was even aware of it. "How was work this morning?"

"*Gut.* Turbo decided not to give us any trouble this time."

"Who's that?"

"A gelding who thinks he's boss of the world." Perry smirked, but his leg wasn't bouncing any more. "Ferman calmed him down while I worked on shoeing him. How's your day been?"

"Not as exciting as yours. We just did some household chores this morning." She didn't bother to tell him which ones, not wanting to bore him to pieces over a list of household duties. She also left out that she had mailed Maynard's letter before sunrise.

"I wouldn't call my job exciting."

"Then it's predictable?"

"Wouldn't say that either. More like steady. And stable. There are always horses to shoe around here."

Daisy smiled, glad to see he wasn't as uptight as he'd been a few minutes ago. Their conversation was basically small talk, but it wasn't strained. In fact, it felt surprisingly comfortable, considering she barely knew him.

When the waitress brought their meals, Perry thanked her, then cast a quick look at the front door. "Oh *nee*," he muttered.

"What?" She slid her fork into the delicious mac and cheese and lifted her head. Two women were by the front door, smiling and waving as they walked toward their table. "Do you know them?"

"*Ya.*" But he didn't sound happy about it.

Perry held in another groan as *Mamm* and Phoebe headed toward him, *Mamm* grinning and waving. Of all the people to run into when he was sitting next to a young woman. For a split second, he entertained the ludicrous thought of ducking under the table. Pointless, since they'd already seen them together. And it didn't matter that Grace and Ferman were also there. He could tell his mother and sister were already homing in on the unsuspecting Daisy from Dover.

"*Hallo*, Perry," *Mamm* said, raising her voice above the diner noise. "What a lovely surprise to see you here."

He nodded and glanced at Phoebe, who was talking to Grace. The whole Bontrager family had visited Marigold at one point or another, just not all at the same time, so his sister already knew her. She and *Mamm* had probably met Ferman during a church service, or maybe at Wagler's Buggy Shop.

But neither of them knew Daisy, and before they drew any conclusions, he quickly made the introductions. "She's visiting Grace for a . . ." He didn't know how long she was going to be here. She hadn't mentioned it.

"Two weeks." Daisy smiled at them.

"Only two?" Grace frowned. "I was hoping you'd stay longer."

An odd look flashed across Daisy's face, only to quickly disappear. "I have to get back to . . . *mei* job."

And Maynard. Perry almost mentioned him, considering the way *Mamm* was sizing up Daisy. He could practically read his mother's mind, not that she was bothering to hide her interest in the woman. Any minute now she would start peppering her with questions.

"I don't want to interrupt your lunch, but . . ."

Here we go.

"Can I talk to you for a minute? Outside?"

He reluctantly nodded. Then he realized that regardless of what she said, he would tell her to halt her latest matchmaking scheme and he would be firm with her, much more so than he had been in the past. He followed her out the door and they sat on one of the empty benches under the diner's awning.

"It's *gut* to see you, *sohn*." *Mamm* took his hand and squeezed it quickly, then let go. "It's been a while since you've visited us."

"I'm sorry. I've been busy with work." True, although he should have made more of an effort to see his parents and the rest of his family. He couldn't tell her that she was part of the reason he was avoiding Birch Creek. He wasn't that cruel. After today's conversation, he anticipated he wouldn't have to worry about this marriage nonsense anymore.

"Spring is almost here. Soon enough we'll all be too busy to think." She fished inside her large purse and produced a packet of letters. "Phoebe and I had planned to stop by your place after lunch and put these in your mailbox."

He decided to feign ignorance. "What are they?"

She patted his knee, like she used to when he was a kid. "Now I know you told me you were fine—"

"I *am* fine—"

"—being unattached for so many, *many* years."

Yeesh, she made it sound like he was a ninety-year-old never-been-married bachelor. Which would be fine if it were God's will and he lived that long. He'd already been burned once, and that was enough.

"So don't be mad at me. Please." She handed him the letters. "I thought you might find a pen pal or two in this stack."

"A pen pal." He looked at the girly script on the first envelope. "Right."

"Just give the letters a chance, Perry." She tapped the top of the packet. Your future *frau* might be closer than you think."

The diner door opened, and Daisy walked outside. She glanced at Perry and *Mamm*, giving them a small smile. "Grace left something in the buggy," she explained.

He watched her hurry to the row of buggies parked by a hitching post in the lot. Seeing her and Grace in the diner had been a surprise. So was Grace inviting him and Ferman to join them. He'd almost refused, feeling a little awkward. Then again, he was already feeling awkward in the crowded diner. In the end it didn't matter because Ferman made the decision for them, and it was a good one. Talking to Daisy had helped keep his mind off being around so many people.

"Daisy seems like a lovely *maedel*."

He turned to his mother, ready to tell her that Daisy was an acquaintance, and barely one at that. For good measure he'd also inform her that she had a boyfriend named Maynard back home in Dover.

But before he could get any of that out, an idea hit him. Hard, like a smack upside the head. And instead of taking a second to evaluate the wisdom or foolishness of said idea, he blurted out, "She's a *friend*."

Mamm's eyebrow went up. "A *friend*?" She peered around Perry to see Daisy bent over in the buggy, her feet hanging above the ground as she reached far inside. Then she sat back, her eyes wide with shock. "How long have you known each other?"

"A while," he said a little too quickly. But *Mamm* didn't seem to notice his overly swift answer. She was looking at Daisy again. "Grace, ah, told me about her, and I decided to, um, write to her."

"You're pen pals?" *Mamm* clasped her hands with glee. "Why didn't you tell me—wait, forget I asked. You're a grown man. You don't need me interfering in your personal life."

He gaped at her. That's all she'd done over the past several years, and it had only amped up since his youngest brother, Elam, got hitched.

Mamm leaned in close, lowering her voice to a conspiratorial whisper. "She's not only here to visit Grace, is she?" Grinning, she took the packet from him. "Obviously you don't need these anymore."

He dug his fingernails into his palms, his stomach heavy, like an anchor was dragging it down. This was bad. So, so bad, and he needed to clarify, or more accurately, tell her the truth.

Daisy walked past them, carrying a cloth tote bag. She waved her fingers at him and *Mamm* and went back inside the diner.

"Isn't she sweet."

He turned to *Mamm* and saw her huge grin and the happiness in her eyes. There was also something underlying her obvious emotions. *Relief.* He held his tongue. While his mother had overstepped her bounds more than once, she was well-meaning and loving. What would it hurt to let her think he and Daisy were *friends*? Just for a little while, and it would end her matchmaking for the time being. He'd burst her bubble soon enough.

"Can you do me a favor?" he asked. Despite rationalizing his decision, guilt was piling up by the second. Still, he plodded forward. "Keep this between you and me, okay? Don't let Daisy know I told you. We're still getting to know each other." Finally, he'd said something truthful.

"Of course." She shoved the letters in her purse and zipped her lips. "I understand completely. The fewer people who know, the better, *ya*? In case it doesn't work out." She stood. "I don't want to keep you from your *friend*," she said with a wink and walked inside.

Perry slumped against the bench. *What have I done?*

Chapter 6

Ferman hummed as he neared his house, his belly satisfied from lunch. The chicken fried steak at the Railway Diner had been moist and tender, the pinto beans well-seasoned, and the turnip greens tasty enough to knock anybody's socks off. The potato squares had delivered too. He even had a full meal packed up for supper tonight, courtesy of Perry suddenly losing his appetite after he and his mother and sister showed up.

The ride from the diner to their afternoon job had been almost silent, with Perry giving him one-word answers to his attempts at making conversation. Perry was a quiet sort, unlike his more gregarious brother Jesse, and Ferman had noticed his new boss had tensed up when they entered the busy diner. That tension continued when they joined the young ladies, until Perry started to talk to Daisy. Although Ferman and Grace were discussing the latest happenings in Marigold, he kept an ear on Perry and Daisy's conversation.

Then Perry's mother showed up and his mood changed. When he came back inside after talking to Miriam, he seemed more out of sorts than when they first arrived. Miriam and Phoebe had left soon after, declining to join them. Ferman caught the flicker of relief in Perry's eyes, but it quickly disappeared. Grace didn't seem to notice anything amiss, but Daisy had gone quiet too. Perhaps because Perry had.

There was something about those two. He could feel it. Grace might be oblivious, but Ferman wasn't, not at his age and considering his predilection for plain ol' nosiness. Lovina had gotten onto him a time or two hundred about poking into other people's business, though his intentions were always good—or at least he wanted them to be. He didn't have to spend a lot of time with Daisy to tell she was a nice girl. Physically, the two of them made a striking couple—she was fair, he was darker complected, and he was tall while she was on the shorter side. But it wasn't their opposite appearances that caught Ferman's attention. He sensed some sizzle between them. They didn't seem to be aware of it, though.

He would do well to heed Lovina's past advice and stay out of his boss's personal matters. He liked the work, and talking to the clients and chatting up the horses was enjoyable—much more so than being cooped up in the buggy shop. He also appreciated Perry's honesty and inclination to make sure Ferman was up to the task. For a minute, he'd been offended, then common sense kicked in. If he injured or overtired himself, he'd lose the job anyway. Better to conserve his energy and be aware of his physical limitations. Since Perry was fine with that, Ferman would be too.

When he reached his driveway, he stopped humming as he looked at a familiar buggy parked on the gray gravel. He scowled. *What's he doing here?* He was tempted just to drive on by and find something to do until after dark. Surely his unwelcome visitor would leave by then. But he was tired and sore, and the thought of driving around in the jouncing buggy searching for something to pass the time didn't appeal. Besides, that was the coward's way out.

He drove past the buggy and parked underneath the barn awning, got out, unhitched his horse, and led her to her stall. Just as he started to open the door, he heard someone enter the barn. Ferman didn't bother to turn around.

"Need help?" the man asked.

Gritting his teeth, he remained silent and gave the mare some feed.

"You're being ridiculous."

Unable to help himself, Ferman said, "Funny. Those were your exact words after you took off and left me alone."

"That was your choice. Not mine." Footsteps crackled against the dry straw on the barn floor. "Are you going to give me the cold shoulder for the rest of our lives?"

Ferman tried not to limp as he exited the stall and latched the door. He also fought for calm as he faced the man in front of him. His and Lovina's only child, the one they'd had after years and years of asking God for children. *My only* sohn. "Why are you here? You and Polly Ann couldn't get out of Marigold fast enough when you left last year."

Junior shook his head and gave his father a long-suffering look. "We asked you to come with us."

"Pfft." Ferman shoved past Junior, who didn't bother to move out of the way.

When they bumped shoulders, Junior lightly grabbed Ferman's arm. "We've got to work this out, *Daed*. Eight months is a long time to *geh* without speaking to each other."

"Nine," Ferman said sharply, and continued to move on. But the more he walked, the tighter his hip became, until he couldn't hide the limp anymore. Somehow he managed to leave the barn and make it to the front porch before he nearly collapsed.

His son's strong hand supported him under his shoulder, and

they eased themselves down on the top step. Ferman was grateful Junior had kept him from toppling over, but he hated showing anyone how truly weak his hip was. From now on, he would take the anti-inflammatory bottle that sat on his dresser with him wherever he went. The early morning dose had worn off.

To his credit Junior didn't say anything, and for several long moments both men stared out at the small front yard that needed a good mowing. Birds twittered in the budding branches, and normally Ferman enjoyed the birdsong, but right now he just wanted his son to leave so he could go lie down on his bed and rest.

Finally, Junior spoke. "Polly Ann is asking after you. She'd like for you to come over for a visit." He cleared his throat. "She's expecting."

Ferman's heart leapt for joy. After sixteen years, his son and wife were finally having a baby. Like he and Lovina, they had trouble getting pregnant, although neither Junior nor Polly Ann ever discussed it in front of Ferman. And they shouldn't. It was none of his business.

He started to grin. *I'm going to be a grossdaadi.* But his smile quickly disappeared. Junior and Polly Ann had moved to an even smaller town than Marigold on the other side of Birch Creek. Familiar resentment rose up within him. There had been no reason for them to move away, other than Polly Ann not wanting to live in Marigold anymore. She said it was because Bishop Fry was too lenient. Ferman thought he was just right, balancing the job of the spiritual leader of Marigold and the business of running the community.

But Polly Ann was always a bit snippety. She and Ferman had butted heads more than once when she moved in with him, Lovina, and Junior after she and Junior married. Finally, at least according to Junior, Polly Ann had enough of both Bishop Fry and Ferman Eash.

Would that change once the baby was born? Ferman doubted it.

"You can't even congratulate us?"

He turned to Junior and internally winced when he saw the pain in his son's eyes. Dark brown eyes that were the exact shape and color of his mother's, along with her olive complexion and black hair. But he'd gotten his short, stocky build from Ferman. "Congratulations."

"Don't sound so excited." Junior jumped up from the step. "Polly Ann told me this was a waste of time. She was right."

Ferman looked up at him. "I suspect you didn't just come out here to tell me about the *boppli*. Or invite me to supper. Say what's on your mind already."

"You—" Junior's mouth formed a thin line. "We want you to move to Ash Valley and in with us. You can't live here on your own anymore."

"I live here just fine."

"*Ya*, I can see that." Sarcasm dripped from his words. "You couldn't walk back to the house without falling over."

"Because I just got back from my job," Ferman shot back. But he didn't get up from the step. Not when he wasn't sure if he'd have to sit right back down. "I'm working as a farrier's assistant and doing just fine."

Junior rolled his eyes. "Talk about stubborn," he mumbled.

"If you were so concerned, you shouldn't have left."

"You still don't get it." Junior waved him off. "Or you don't want to. Doesn't matter." He turned and headed for his buggy. Halfway, he stopped, inhaled a big breath, and turned around. "You're welcome to our *haus* anytime, *Daed*," he said, his tone softer and contradicting his granite-set jaw. "I want you to know that."

Ferman punctuated his next words with his index finger pointed at the ground. "I'm gonna stay right here. Where I belong."

Junior threw up his hands and marched to his buggy, jumping inside with the same athletic grace Ferman had in his youth.

He watched his son leave, only attempting to get up from the step after he couldn't see Junior's buggy anymore. Ferman placed his hands on both sides of his body and pushed up. Pain shot into his hip, but he clenched through it. Quickly, he reached for the railing, missing it once and almost falling again. The second time he grabbed it, turned around, and made his way slowly back into the house.

Then he remembered the lunch in his buggy. He'd have to get that later. Right now, he needed to lie down. He would never leave his medicine behind again.

Limping into the room, he shut the door and made his way to the bedroom he'd shared with his wife for fifty-six years. He'd lived in Marigold even longer, before it had become an official Amish district and there had been only three families nearby. That had been when he was a young boy.

He'd grown up in this house. Married Lovina here. Junior was delivered by an Amish midwife in their bedroom. They'd raised him here.

And Lovina had died here.

Ferman couldn't leave. Too many memories. No, not just memories. Marigold was in his blood, and he couldn't imagine living anywhere else. He didn't want to. And when it was time for him to join Lovina in heaven, he wanted to die right here. Where she had.

With weakening steps, he made it to his room, downed his pills without water, and collapsed on the bed. Thank the good Lord above that Perry's client had canceled tomorrow's job at the last minute, right before Ferman had headed home. He needed the unexpected day of rest. He'd also have to come up with a better way to manage his pain so he could function. He had no other choice, despite how much his son tried to convince him otherwise.

Daisy gathered her cross-stitch bag and headed outside. She kicked off her flip-flops the minute she sat under one of the large trees in Grace's backyard. The budding branches didn't provide shade, and that was fine with her. The midmorning sun was warm, and the breeze was not nearly as chilly as it had been the first two days of her visit. She was comfortable wearing her navy blue cardigan over her pale green dress.

She leaned her back against the rough bark of the tree's trunk and crossed her ankles. This morning, Grace went to her job at an agency that cleaned English houses, explaining that if she'd known Daisy was coming, she could have asked for more time off. As for *Aenti* Rosella, she was spending most of the day shopping with one of her friends for supplies to restock her kitchen after being gone for more than a week. "Just enjoy yourself today," her aunt said as she left the house.

Daisy frowned at the cloth craft bag in her lap. She was feeling a little abandoned, even though she knew her cousin and aunt hadn't meant for her to. Once again, she still didn't understand why her mother and father had rushed her here when the wedding seemed to be the last thing on Grace and Rosella's mind.

Her confusion increased the night before. After she and Grace had cleaned up the kitchen, Daisy decided to call her mother again to make sure she'd told Maynard why she was in Marigold and had given him Grace's phone number. She thought she would have heard from him by now. They might not be romantically involved yet, but they were friends, and she had just upped and left him. Didn't he miss her a little bit? She sure missed him.

"I won't be long," Daisy told Grace, who was sitting at the table, looking through one of her mother's cooking magazines, a small file box and a stack of index cards close by. For the past several years, Grace had been gathering recipes for her own household, and she was also adding Kyle's favorites to her collection.

When she arrived at the shanty, the door was open, her aunt talking animatedly to someone. Daisy didn't mean to eavesdrop, but she couldn't help but hear part of the conversation.

"I think we should have planned this better," she said, waving her hand over her face. *Aenti* Rosella was going through the "change" and often had heat flashes, which was probably why the phone shanty door was open. "It's all so last minute, and I haven't had time to think of reasons to—I know, and I'm glad for the visit—"

Visit? Was her aunt talking about her?

"I understand. I'd feel the same way if I were in your shoes. We'll figure out how to make this work. You too. Bye."

Aenti Rosella hung up. When she left the shanty, her jaw dropped. "Daisy," she said with an uneasy chuckle. "How long have you been there?"

"Not long. I was going to call *Mamm*."

Her aunt stepped aside, her flustered expression diminishing. Then she gave Daisy a big hug. When she let her go, she studied her face. "You're happy, *ya*?"

"*Ya*." Daisy's brow furrowed. "Why wouldn't I be?"

Aenti Rosella smiled. "Grace works tomorrow, and when she gets home, we can talk about the wedding. I wanted to make sure the two of you had some time together before we dove into planning."

After hearing her aunt's explanation for postponing the wedding planning, she decided everything made sense after all. And as far as the phone call was concerned, *Aenti* Rosella must have been referring to a future visitor to whoever was on the other line.

When Daisy called her mother, she was relieved to hear that she had told Maynard where Daisy was. "I did give him Rosella's number," she said, sounding a little reluctant.

"Did he say anything about calling me?" She rubbed her thumb against the curved edge of the phone handle.

A pause. "*Nee.* He was busy."

Of course he was. He could have called her last night, though. Or the night before. Then she reminded herself that being married to a man who valued hard work was a good thing. Maynard would be an outstanding provider to her and their children. That was important.

Daisy smiled and picked up her cross-stitch. Maynard would call her when he had a chance, and she needed to stop fretting about it. With the sun beaming down, her toes free to wiggle in the grass, and having plenty of time to engage in her favorite hobby, she was content.

Although it would be nice if Maynard was beside her on a lovely day like this one. They would have a picnic basket, one filled with his favorites—fried chicken, broccoli salad, sweet-and-sour pickles, peach pie.

She'd only completed three stitches before she set down her work and closed her eyes, imagining Maynard fixing her a plate of food instead of the other way around, like it always was. He handed her the plate, a warm smile on his face. That smile turned passionate as he moved closer, letting his fingers run over her bare ankle. Mmm, that felt good. "Oh, Maynard," she whispered.

Chapter 7

Perry was in his backyard and about to start weeding underneath his clothesline when he saw Daisy walk outside and sit under a tree in her aunt and uncle's backyard. After his client had canceled his appointment for today, Perry had an unexpected day off. He'd hemmed and hawed before coming over to talk to Daisy about what he told his mother. Last night the reality of what he'd done sank in, and he struggled to figure out what to say to her. Even now he didn't have the right words to explain his stupid lie.

He ended up walking over without the words, asking God to help him out of the hole he'd dug for himself—not that he deserved it. He'd already prayed for forgiveness, and maybe the Lord would give him mercy for doing something so monumentally ludicrous.

When he reached Daisy, she was asleep. And smiling. Whatever her dream was, it must be a good one. He started to turn around and leave. They could talk later, and maybe by that time, he'd have come up with a plausible justification for telling *Mamm* they were seeing each other.

Then he froze.

There it was. *Limenitis arthemis*, otherwise known as the white admiral butterfly, his wings gently flapping as he perched on Daisy's ankle. And he was a beauty, with predominantly black wings, a half circle of white around the bottom and sides, and—whoa—cobalt and baby blue markings. Exquisite. And to top it off, the insect had red-orange dots above the bottom edge of the wings.

If Perry could capture him, the butterfly would be the apex of his collection. He wouldn't kill it, though. Like he'd done with Lady, he would put him in a glass jar with some food, make a few sketches of him, write down his color markings, and then set him free. After church on Sunday, he would spend the afternoon drawing him.

All he had to do was catch him. *Easier said than done.*

He crouched near Daisy's leg. Her ankles were crossed, the hem of her dress covering her knees. But his singular focus was on the white admiral, who seemed satisfied on his human perch. Rarely had Perry been fast enough to catch a butterfly without a net, and he didn't have time to rush off and get one from his stash. In the past he'd only managed to capture four of them with his bare hand. It required stealth, slow breathing, and quick reflexes. Any sudden movements and the admiral would flee.

He gradually reached out his hand toward the butterfly, his fingers almost within reach. *Less than half an inch away . . .*

The admiral unexpectedly switched its position, throwing Perry off balance while his hand kept moving. Instead of touching the butterfly, his fingers lightly brushed over Daisy's lower leg.

His heart rate began to gallop, and he wasn't looking at the admiral anymore. He didn't even know if the butterfly was still on Daisy's ankle. His focus was on his fingers—more accurately, the spot where he was touching her. Unable to resist, he once again lightly moved the tips of his fingers over her soft, sunshine-warmed skin. His spine tingled. *Nice. Very, very nice.*

"Oh, Maynard," she sighed.

He jerked his hand back, as if her skin shocked him. Wait, why had he touched her in the first place? Oh, the white admiral. He glanced at her ankle. The butterfly was gone, but he couldn't stop gazing at her ankle, then her feet, then back up, and up farther—

"What are you doing?"

Perry squeezed his eyes shut. With the admiral's disappearance, he couldn't blame the bug. "I, uh . . ." He opened his eyes and turned to her, expecting her to be furious.

Instead, all he saw was curiosity. Her question was genuine. He fell back on his behind and blew out a breath. "You're not going to believe this," he said with a clumsy quarter smile. "But I was trying to catch a white admiral."

"A white what?"

"Butterfly. White admirals are at risk of losing their habitats and they're becoming rare, and when I saw him on your, uh . . ."

"My what?"

He gulped. "Your ankle."

She tucked her legs underneath her dress, leaving only her feet exposed.

He didn't blame her for covering up, considering what he'd just done. Actually, he could think more clearly now that her knees and ankles were out of sight.

Glancing around the yard, she said, "I don't see any butterflies."

Perry frowned. "I said you wouldn't believe me."

"I believe you." She faced him again. "I just don't see any."

"He flew away. Unfortunately." He muttered the last word and was thankful she wasn't upset with him. Still, he owed her an apology for invading her personal space. "I didn't mean to touch you."

Her hazel eyes widened. "That was you?"

"*Ya.* I accidentally did while trying to get the admiral."

"I thought . . ." Her cheeks, already rosy from sitting in the sunlight, turned crimson.

"You thought I was Maynard."

"H-how do you know about Maynard?"

"He's your boyfriend, *ya*? I found the note on the paper towel."

"I thought I threw that away." Her knees were bent, and she was staring at the grass at her feet. "I guess I forgot to."

Her feet were small and so were her toes, including the big ones. Cute. Wait, he didn't need to notice her toes, or her feet, or her eyes, or anything else. He shifted his gaze to the unexciting view of the side of his house.

"Did I, um, say anything while you were catching the captain?"

"Admiral," Perry corrected, looking at her again. She was fiddling with her *kapp* string. He debated if he should tell her he heard her whisper Maynard's name. "I couldn't tell." Lie number two, but surely this wouldn't count against him since he was sparing her some embarrassment.

Daisy leaned against the tree, her needlework falling onto the grass. "I didn't hear you come over. I didn't know I'd fallen asleep."

He bent his knees and rested his wrists on them. "I saw you sitting out here, and when I noticed you were sleeping, I started to leave . . . and you know the rest."

She crossed her legs and sat up straighter. "Did you need

something from my *aenti* or *onkel*? Nobody's home right now, but I can give them a message."

"*Nee*. I'm not here to talk to them." He bolstered himself and looked at her again. "I came to see you."

⚓︎

Daisy was still reeling from the shock that the Maynard in her dreams was Perry Bontrager. While she understood and believed him about the captain—wait, he'd said *admiral*, right?—all she could think about was how real his touch had felt. Because it was.

She suddenly felt hot. Then cold. Then hot again. And what was that tingling sensation going down her spine?

Perry rubbed the back of his neck, not looking at her. Was he still embarrassed? He shouldn't be. It was an understandable misunderstanding. Yet the more he rubbed his neck, the more stressed he appeared.

Yesterday she thought lunch had been nice, up until Perry returned after talking to his mother. She had seemed nice too, along with his sister, Phoebe. But whatever they had talked about outside had bothered him. In fact, right now he had the same expression he'd had yesterday during the rest of their meal. He barely touched his food and gave the rest to Ferman to take home. "Is everything okay?"

"I told my *Mamm* we were dating."

"What?"

He held up his hand. "Before you get upset with me, I can explain."

She listened as he talked about his brother Jesse putting a bride

83

advertisement in the paper fifteen years ago. "It was a practical joke," Perry said. "But there were enough women who believed it and wanted to get married that soon Birch Creek was overrun with single women."

Interesting. "*Geh* on."

He continued, telling her that all his brothers had either gotten married directly or indirectly because of the ad. Except for Nelson, who had met his wife when he moved to Marigold. "Even my youngest *bruder*, Elam, married the sister of one of the women who found a husband in Birch Creek."

"How many *bruders* do you have?"

"Ten. Phoebe is my only *schwester*. I also have a nephew, Malachi, who is married to Nelson's wife's *schwester*."

Daisy was used to complex families, so she wasn't surprised when he told her about his.

"Out of my large *familye*, I'm the only one who isn't married. I'm thirty-one, and *Mamm* can't stop worrying that I never will." He finished his clarification by telling her about the circle letter she'd started with other Amish women across the country. "Yesterday when she came to the diner, she had a stack of mail for me." He jumped up from the ground and started to pace. "Daisy, I don't want to get married. I've told *Mamm* that over and over, but she won't listen to me. She insists that I need a wife, and she won't stop trying to make that happen. So when she asked me who you were . . ." He scrubbed his hand over his face. "This is embarrassing."

Daisy stood and went to him. Considering the circumstances, she could see why he'd slipped up. "I understand she's concerned about you, but no one should feel pressured to get married."

"I really am sorry," he said. "Don't worry, I'll set things straight and confess to *Mamm*."

They both turned around as a red sedan pulled into her aunt and uncle's driveway.

"I'm the only one home right now, so I should see who it is," Daisy said. No one had mentioned that they would have a visitor today. Or it could be someone who was lost. That happened sometimes at her house—a car would pull up and the confused English driver would ask for directions.

Perry picked up her cross-stitch and handed it to her. "I'll let you know when I talk to *Mamm*. It will be this weekend for sure."

She took the cross-stitch from him and glanced up. While he wasn't as distressed as he'd been when he told her about his lie to his mother, he still looked troubled. "Don't worry, Perry," she said with a smile. "This will all work out."

His shoulders loosened up a little. "*Danki*, Daisy. I owe you one."

Perry headed for his house as she walked to the driveway. He didn't owe her anything, although she did wonder if she should be a *little* mad that he'd used her as an excuse to placate his mother. But she couldn't. All she felt was sympathy. And she'd made plenty of mistakes in her life. It was only right that she accepted his sincere apology.

As she neared the driveway, the car door opened. "*Mamm*?" Daisy said, shocked to see her mother step out of the vehicle. Then she rushed over to her.

"Hi, Daisy," *Mamm* said, pulling into her a tight hug.

"What are you doing here? Are you helping with Grace's wedding too?"

"Oh, *lieb*." *Mamm* cupped her face. "You're such a sweet, trusting *maedel*. And I'm so, so sorry."

Dread started to churn inside her as she took in her mother's troubled expression. "For what?"

Mamm sighed. "We need to talk."

Chapter 8

Daisy sat at the kitchen table, the dread in her stomach flipping to anger as her mother explained the real reason she and *Daed* had been so eager to send Daisy to Marigold. "You what?"

"I know it was a *dumm* idea." *Mamm*'s face contorted with shame. "And wrong. But your *Daed* and I didn't know what else to do."

She gaped at her mother, one of two people she trusted most in the whole world. The second was her father, and they had both duped her.

When *Mamm* reached for her hand, Daisy drew back.

"You have to believe me." *Mamm* put her hands in her lap. "We never would have lied to you—"

"And betrayed. Don't forget that." She crossed her arms over her chest, not bothering to curb her caustic tone. She didn't get mad very often, and she'd always been told she had a good-natured personality. But if there was ever a reason for her to be furious, this was it.

"I know you're angry." *Mamm* touched her temple. "You have to believe that we have your best interests at heart."

"How can you say that? You sent me here because you don't want me to be with Maynard."

"Exactly."

"But I love him—

"You don't know what love is." The remorse in her eyes changed to frustration. "If you did, you wouldn't insist on chasing after a man who doesn't care about you."

Her mother's words pierced her soul. "That's not true. You don't understand our relationship. It's special. God set him apart for me."

"*Lieb*, you shouldn't have to beg someone to love you."

Angry tears pricked Daisy's eyes. Bother, she always cried when she was livid. She fought them back. "I'm not begging."

"Have you talked to him since you left Dover?"

Ugh, she should have known *Mamm* would ask that question. "*Nee*, but—"

"If he cared about you, he would have contacted you by now."

Mamm had a point, but Daisy wasn't about to acknowledge it. Besides, once she told him how she felt, she was sure he would feel the same way. Maynard just needed some guidance, that's all. "He and I are meant to be together." She lifted her chin. "You and *Daed* will see."

"Daisy . . ." *Mamm* heaved a sigh. "He doesn't deserve you."

A chilling thought hit her. "Do you know something about him that I don't?"

"What do you mean?"

"Is he . . ." She swallowed. "Is he seeing someone else?"

Mamm shook her head. "As far as I know, he's as consumed with his job as he says he is. Although it might be better if he were dating someone else."

"How can you say that!" She shoved away from the table and left the kitchen.

"Daisy!" *Mamm* called, following her. "Where are you going?"

"To pack. Since Grace and *Aenti* Rosella don't need my help to plan the wedding—" She paused. "Are they in on this?"

Mamm blanched. "Grace isn't. Rosella has the same concerns I do."

So the phone call last night was about Daisy. Whirling around, she glared at her. "How could she? She's never met him."

"I told her about the problems with Maynard."

"Oooh." Daisy clenched her fists. She had never been this upset in her life. "There are no problems with Maynard!" She stomped toward the staircase and started to go upstairs.

"Daisy Hershberger."

Daisy stopped at the quiet fury in her mother's voice.

"You will come here, and we will sit down and discuss this like civilized adults."

She gripped the banister so tightly her knuckles burned.

"I know you're angry, and I've already admitted that your *Daed* and I were wrong to deceive you. But that doesn't mean you get to scream and stomp like a spoiled *kinn*."

Slowly, Daisy released the smooth wood railing. Everything inside her wanted to ignore her mother, pack her bag, and leave Marigold. But she couldn't. Not only was respecting her mother and father one of God's Ten Commandments, but eventually her temper would cool. If she behaved poorly now, there would be more problems for her later.

Whoever is patient has great understanding, but one who is quick-tempered displays folly.

She had cross-stitched the verse from Proverbs last year as a birthday gift to her sister-in-law, who had taken it a little personally until Daisy had said it was just a reminder, not a judgment. She turned around and walked down the steps to sit in her *aenti's* chair.

Mamm parked on the sofa across from her, her shoulders slumping. "We probably should have had this conversation a long time ago," she said.

"About Maynard?"

"*Ya*, but not just about him. I've never been one to approve of dating people indiscriminately."

Daisy frowned, confused.

"Promiscuously," *Mamm* said. At Daisy's shrug she supplied, "Shamelessly. Recklessly."

"Oh."

"But you've been completely focused on Maynard for so long, you haven't looked in anyone else's direction, or given them a chance."

She didn't bother to tell her mother that before Maynard had moved to Dover, there wasn't anyone else in her community who made her feel the way he did the first time she saw him. The absolute shock of certainty that sparked through her brain when he sat down on the pew next to his father. In that moment she knew there was no one else. He was the *one*. "I don't need to. I love Maynard."

"You *think* you love him."

"*Nee*," Daisy said, feeling her ire rise again. "I know I do, right here." She pointed at her heart. "We're meant to be together. In fact, I'm positive we'll be married by November." Uh-oh. That was a bold claim. But once she and Maynard started dating, there wouldn't be any reason for them to put off marriage.

Mamm didn't say anything for a long moment, just stared at the coffee table in between them. Then she lifted her head, a small smile on her face. "Let's prove it."

"Huh?"

"If it's God's will for you and Maynard to marry, it will happen whether you're in Marigold or in Dover. If you stay here for three months, you'll find out if you two are meant to be."

Daisy considered her proposal. Her initial reaction was to say no, because the whole idea was silly and a waste of time. But as she thought about it, she realized the only way her mother and father would believe her love for Maynard was true was if she proved it to them. Three months was too long to be separated, however. And even though she was upset with her parents, she would miss them too. "What if I stay for six weeks instead?"

"Two months?"

She folded her hands in her lap. "One month."

"Six weeks then." *Mamm* nodded, her smile widening. "And if your *Daed* and I are wrong, you and Maynard will have our full support."

Daisy couldn't help but return her smile with a small one of her own. She didn't like the idea of being away from Maynard longer than her original plan of two weeks, but she was warming to the opportunity to quell their doubts. "Deal." With the issue settled, she started to lament her behavior. She glanced at her lap. "I'm sorry I acted like a brat."

"Oh, sweetheart, it's okay. You have a right to be angry with us."

"I'm not anymore." She was grateful to see the relief in her mother's eyes. "And I do see what you were trying to do. But I promise when I go back to Dover, Maynard and I will be a true-blue couple."

Mamm nodded, her smile fading a little. "If it's God's will."

"It is."

"I just have one favor to ask."

Uh-oh. "What's that?"

"You'll keep an open mind and heart while you're in Marigold. And if you should meet someone here who strikes your fancy—"

"I won't," Daisy said firmly.

"But if you do," *Mamm* stubbornly continued, "give him a chance."

She was about to argue again, then thought better of it. Daisy was positive no one else but Maynard would "strike her fancy," as *Mamm* put it. She nodded, and when she saw her mother's joyful expression, she knew she'd made the right decision.

Her confidence back, Daisy got up and sat next to *Mamm* on the couch. "How long are you staying?"

"Just for tonight. I don't want to miss church on Sunday, and then there's work on Monday." She put her arm around Daisy's shoulders. "I must say, I do like your job. Mr. Brinkman is a joy to work for."

"He is a *gut* boss. Will he be okay with you substituting for six weeks?"

"I'm sure he will. I think he likes me."

"What's not to like?" She put her head on *Mamm*'s shoulder, and they sat in silence for a short while.

"I love you, *lieb*. And so does your *Daed*, of course."

"I love both of you too." *And Maynard.* Daisy closed her eyes, tired from the blowup with her mother. She didn't need to date anyone else to know her feelings for Maynard were real. And soon enough she would show her parents, *Aenti* Rosella, and any other doubters that they were absolutely, profoundly wrong.

***

Perry sat on one of two chairs on his back patio, swiftly sketching on his artist's pad in a race to beat the sunset. He could continue working on his drawing inside under the gas lamp in the living room, but the yellowish glow didn't compare to bright, natural light. He ran his pencil over the thick paper with small, short strokes, then glanced up at Lady, who was being a very cooperative model as she perched on the back of the opposite chair.

After he'd parted ways with Daisy, he spent the afternoon weeding and mowing, then went inside to prepare yet another can of soup for supper. He'd been busy but not distracted enough to stop thinking about what he would tell his mother tomorrow night when he got off work and drove to Birch Creek. He was also thinking how extraordinarily well Daisy had taken the news of his deception, even going so far as to reassure him.

There was also one other thing he couldn't get out of his mind, no matter how hard he tried. Her skin was so soft, and his fingers were still tingling from touching her.

When he'd finished eating, he got out his sketch pad and went outside. Drawing was always a good diversion, and he tried to draw the admiral from memory, but after two attempts he realized he had little recollection of what the butterfly looked like and too much recall of Daisy's ankle. That's when Lady had flown by and landed on the chair, as if an answer to prayer. He flipped over his pad and started drawing her. He had a growing affinity for the butterfly, and he needed to get her image down before—

He shook his head, not wanting to think about the inevitable and that it wasn't that far away. He guessed she was about a week old—no more than two—and butterflies didn't live much longer than that. Plus, there was always the possibility that she would fly away for good. It was strange that she hovered around his house so much since he hadn't planted his garden yet and there weren't that many butterfly-friendly plants around in early spring. He would have to start that project soon.

The last trace of usable light disappeared, and so had Lady, who had flown away a little before sunset. He closed his pad and took a moment to look at the beautiful, warm colors striping the sky, each hue melting into the other. Tree crickets, katydids, and a barn owl made their presence known in a blended, if cacophonic, symphony. He stayed until the sun dipped past the horizon, then went back inside.

Per his habit, he shucked his boots and socks, then stripped off his shirt and dropped it in the basket near the wringer washer. His pants would be okay to wear tomorrow, but after he got home from work, he would put them in the wash.

Bare chested and barefooted, he entered the kitchen to get a drink of water before going to his bedroom to finish undressing for bed—

"Hello."

He fell backward and gripped the doorframe to keep from falling. "Daisy!" He pressed his hand over his thumping chest.

She held up the doorknob. "It fell off again."

"Don't . . ." He held his palm toward her, his entire body sagging. "Don't ever do that again."

She pressed her lips together and carefully set the knob on the table. "I, um . . ." She folded her hands in front of her, her gaze shifting down to her bare feet, then back up again, stopping at his chest. Her lips formed a cute, coquettish, and fully irresistible smile.

He couldn't help but grin.

Then as if they simultaneously recognized that he was half dressed and she was quite appreciative of that fact, they scrambled.

"Be right back," he said.

She spun around. "Okay!"

He dashed to his bedroom and shut the door, aware that moving fast in his little house couldn't have made his heart race this much. He paused, searching for his senses. It wasn't that big of a deal if Daisy had nice ankles, and who cared if she didn't hide her admiration of his body. In fact, it felt kinda awesome—

Perry slammed the brakes on his thoughts, took several deep breaths, and put on a clean shirt. As his wits came back, he frowned. He'd tested that doorknob three times after he installed it. There was no way it could have fallen out again.

He shoved his feet into the pair of slippers Phoebe had gotten for him seven years ago and he'd worn exactly twice, then left his room. Her back was still to him and she was standing by the table.

"I'm sorry," she said, glancing over her shoulder. Then she turned around. "I saw that the door was ajar again, and the knob was on the porch."

"There's *nee* way."

She kept her gaze down. "All I know is that it was partly open when I got here."

Perry started to speak again, then noticed her neck was the color of sour cherries. Then he had the off-putting feeling that he had imagined her visual admiration and her sultry smile. Or his pride had imagined it. Either way, he'd embarrassed her.

"Hey," he said, bending down a little so he could see her face. "It's okay."

Daisy glanced up, her head barely moving, but it was enough for him to make eye contact. "I didn't mean to interrupt while you were . . ."

"Enjoying my privacy?"

"*Ya*. That." She was standing up straight now. "I came over to ask you something, if that's okay."

He leaned his hip against the kitchen counter, relaxing his stance so she got the signal that everything was fine between them. When it came to comparing embarrassing moments, she was coming out ahead. At least she hadn't lied to her mother about him. She hadn't touched him either. "Do you want a drink?"

"*Nee.* I won't be here long."

"Okay." Satisfied that they had put their most recent awkward episode behind them and could finally be at ease, he asked, "What did you want to talk about?"

She took a step forward. "Will you go out with me?"

Chapter 9

*O*h. No.

Daisy wanted to crawl into a hole. After supper tonight, she'd figured out the ultimate way she could placate *Mamm*, and it involved Perry, if he would help her. He did say he owed her one. Then when Kyle dropped by to visit Grace, and *Mamm* went with *Aenti* Rosella and *Onkel* Howard to the living room, Daisy took the opportunity to rush over and talk to him, excited that she didn't have to wait until tomorrow. She saw the doorknob on the porch, the door ajar. Without thinking, she barged on in . . . and got an eyeful of Perry Bontrager. *Good golly.*

As soon as she saw him without his shirt on, she should have left. She shouldn't have stayed and marveled at him the way she did. But her feet wouldn't move. She'd never seen a shirtless man before, and Perry was flawlessly proportioned. Wiry, muscular, with perfect shoulders, biceps, chest—

"I thought you had a boyfriend."

She blinked, his words expunging the image of his, um, assets from her mind and getting her back on track. "I do. Sort of." Uh-oh, that made her sound fickle, and she could tell he thought so too. Her brain went into a tailspin as he crossed his arms over his chest. *Sigh.* Wait, why was she sighing? "I mean . . ."

Her jaw clenched as her anger returned. If only her parents hadn't interfered with her and Maynard. She would be in Dover right now, planning her future with him, like she was supposed to be.

"Daisy, are you okay?"

She nodded. Half shrugged. Then suddenly she was very, very tired. "Not really."

He gestured to the chair in his makeshift living room. "Why don't you sit down."

As she did, he dragged one of the folding chairs by the table and sat across from her. He bent forward slightly and waited for her to speak.

She gathered her thoughts, and it took a minute. A lot had happened in the past few hours. "Maynard and I are friends. Good friends. And we're ready to take our relationship to the next level." She was, anyway. And he would be once they had "the talk."

Perry didn't respond, and his face was blank. But not cold. She couldn't imagine him being anything close to frosty. While his blue eyes weren't exactly warm right now, they were kind, despite his unreadable expression.

Ahem. She needed to focus. "My *Mamm* is here."

"She's the visitor who showed up earlier today?"

"*Ya.* I thought the reason my parents wanted me to go to Marigold was to help plan Grace's wedding. And I want to do that, but it's not until November and that's months away. When *Mamm* showed up, I found out the real reason. They sent me here to get away from Maynard."

"Why? Don't they like him?"

"*Ya.* Absolutely." At least she thought they did. Her mother didn't say that she didn't like him, only that Daisy was moving too fast. "*Mamm* thinks I'm rushing things. She said if we're apart for a while, we'll find out if we're meant to be."

He frowned. "I'm confused. If you like him, then why did you ask me out?"

Finally, she was at the point where she could tell him her perfect idea. "*Mamm* wants me to consider going out with other people. Or at least open my mind to it, even though there's *nee* point. But if I *geh* out with someone and it doesn't work, she can't say I didn't try. Then when I *geh* back to Dover, Maynard and I—" She almost mentioned "the talk," but she held back. She didn't need to tell him everything. "I figured since our mothers are interfering in our business and you already told your *Mamm* that you and I are—"

"*Friends*," he supplied. "I see where you're going with this. If we pretend to be together for a little while, then—"

"We can get both of them off our backs." She sat up and grinned. "What do you think?"

He ran his fingers over his chin again, and she wished he'd stop because it made her notice his dark five o'clock shadow. Maynard was so fair she could barely see his whiskers. Not that she'd been that close to him a whole lot. Just a couple of times, like the other night when she handed him his scarf.

After several minutes of obvious deep thought, he muttered, "I think our mothers are *ab im kopp*. I don't know why they can't just let us make our own decisions. All right. We'll make a pact. You help me with my *mamm*, I'll help you with yours. By the end of two weeks—"

"Five and a half. *Mamm* wanted me to stay here for three months, but we settled on six weeks. I've been here three days already."

With a nod, he thrust out his hand. "Do we have a deal, Daisy from Dover?"

"Deal." She smiled. The nickname did have a nice ring to it. She slipped her hand into his to seal the pact. His skin was warm, strong, and a little rough, in a good way.

She recalled the one and only time she and Maynard had held hands. They were ice-skating with friends at a pond this past winter. It had been excruciatingly cold and the ice was several inches thick. She coasted past him, hoping he would see how gracefully she glided over the ice, having skated since she was three. Instead, she hit a rut, flipped up in the air, and landed on her backside. He'd helped her to her feet and even skated with her to sit on the bank of the pond so she could get her wind back. Once they both knew she was fine, he'd skated off. She savored holding his hand for those brief moments, despite wearing mittens.

Perry dropped her hand and stood, then picked the doorknob off the table. "Guess this is faulty. I'll get another new one tomorrow." He turned and looked at her. "I reckon we need to figure out how we're going to, um . . ."

"Get together?"

"*Ya*. That."

"We can talk tomorrow after supper. Or the next day. It doesn't have to happen right away."

"All right."

He seemed ill at ease, and she was getting that way herself. Maybe her plan wasn't as perfect as she thought. But they already shook on it, so they were committed. "I should head back to Grace's," she said.

"I've got an early job tomorrow."

For some reason, him mentioning work didn't bother her as much as when Maynard did. He walked her to the door. "*Gute nacht*."

She stepped onto the porch, then turned around. "*Danki*, Perry. I really appreciate your help." Not waiting for a response, she hurried back to her cousin's before she got cold feet and tried to go back on her word.

Since Kyle's buggy wasn't there, she assumed he'd gone home. Tonight was the first time she'd met him, and despite their brief interaction, she could see how much he and her cousin loved each other. Daisy couldn't wait for Maynard to look at her the way Kyle looked at Grace.

She entered the kitchen and intended to get a drink of water before going straight to bed, only to halt when she saw Grace sitting at the table. "Where have you been?" she said. "I thought you went upstairs after Kyle got here. But after he left, I couldn't find you."

She'd been gone longer than she thought. "Sorry. I should have told you I was going to Perry's."

"Perry's?" Her eyebrow arched. "Why?"

"We had something to talk about."

"Which would be?"

Daisy sat down at the table, unsure of what to say. Grace thought she and Maynard were an actual couple, and if Daisy told her she and Perry were going out on a date, she would think she was cheating on Maynard. *Ach,* she hadn't thought about that when she was formulating her plan. She never should have lied to Grace in the first place.

Time to tell the truth. "I have a confession to make. Maynard and I . . ." Her fingers twisted around each other. "We're not exactly dating." She launched into her explanation, telling Grace why she was in Marigold and the motive behind her mother's visit.

As she talked, Grace's frown deepened. "I can't believe you lied to me." Hurt flashed across her face.

"I didn't mean to." She had let her envy over Grace and Kyle's happy relationship color her judgment. "Maynard and I will be dating soon, after we talk."

Grace's light brown eyebrows furrowed. "Are you sure he even likes you?"

"Of course he does."

"I mean in a romantic way."

Daisy pressed her lips together. Why was Grace sounding like her mother all of a sudden? "He's shy and waiting on me to make the first move."

"Oh, Daisy."

When she saw the pity in Grace's eyes, she became frustrated again. She didn't need more discouragement. "Clearly you're on *Mamm*'s side."

"I'm on your side, Daisy. I always will be. If you say Maynard loves you, I believe you."

Daisy nodded, relieved and feeling foolish that she'd jumped to the wrong conclusion. "*Danki*. I needed to hear that."

She smiled. "Your *mamm* wants you to date other people, *ya*?" At Daisy's nod, she shook her head. "And you chose Perry?"

"He's, um, convenient."

"But he's so . . ."

Wonderful. And he was, helping Daisy out like this. "So what?"

She lowered her voice. "I don't think he's ever had a girlfriend. Or even a date."

"Does it matter?"

"*Nee*," Grace said. "I guess not. He's a nice *mann*, but he's aloof."

So was Maynard. "Not everyone is a social butterfly, Grace."

"I know." She sighed. "And I guess I'm being judgmental, aren't I?"

"A little."

Grace shrugged. "You could do worse."

Mamm *already thinks I have.* "Don't tell anyone about Maynard, okay?" Daisy asked. "It will complicate things."

"Your secret is safe with me." She got up from the table. "Do you really need to wait until you get back to Dover to talk to him?"

"What do you mean?"

"You could call him now. If he wants to start dating, then you don't have to go out with Perry because you two will officially be together."

It sounded like a simple solution. But getting him on the phone was always a challenge, and his mother wouldn't help even if Daisy begged her. Then there was Perry. She was committed to helping him, but she couldn't tell Grace why. That was his business, and he wouldn't appreciate Daisy telling everyone that his mother was desperate to marry him off. Lastly, she really wanted to have that conversation in his presence. "Something that important should be discussed in person, don't you think?"

"You're right. Then I guess you'll just have to *geh* out with Perry Bontrager. Ooh, how about a double date with me and Kyle?"

While that sounded like fun, she shook her head. "I think it would be best if we went out by ourselves. And it won't be an actual date, just something to make *Mamm* happy."

"Does he know that?"

Daisy nodded. "He agreed to help me."

"Huh. That's a surprise. Perry's the last guy I thought would get involved in something like this."

Daisy blew out a breath as Grace turned off the lamp in the kitchen. "I know this is all so convoluted, and I'm sorry I lied about Maynard in my letters. I was feeling so left out."

Grace slipped her arm around Daisy's waist as they walked to the living room. "I was pretty gushy about Kyle. I shouldn't have been so inconsiderate." They stopped at the foot of the stairs. "When you and Maynard get together, you can be just as gushy about him."

Gushy and Maynard didn't seem to go together. Not now, anyway.

After they went upstairs to their separate rooms, Daisy sat at the edge of the bed. She was still tired but too uptight to go to sleep just yet. While she was glad to have Grace in her corner, she felt foolish about lying to her. She also had no idea how everything had gotten so out of hand so fast. Only three days ago she had decided to make the first move with Maynard, and now she was pledged to go out with Perry. What a tangled web.

It would all be sorted out, though. After *Mamm* and Miriam found out about *the date*, Daisy could proceed with Maynard.

For the first time since she arrived in Marigold, she was able to fully relax, relieved that Grace knew the truth and they no longer had that lie between them. She was also grateful Perry was willing to help her, and in return she could help him. This was just a little bump in the road. Before long, everything would be back to normal.

Early the next morning, Perry gripped the reins as he drove to pick up Ferman. Before he left the house, he jammed the doorknob back into the hole in the door, expecting it not to work. To his shock, the knob and the lock were secure, even after he jiggled it several times. It didn't make sense, but at least he didn't have to get a new one anymore. He made sure to lock it, just in case Daisy stopped by.

As he headed to Ferman's, he tried to focus on the three jobs they had today. They probably wouldn't be back until after dusk, or possibly even later, depending on how cooperative the horses were. But all he could think about was Daisy's proposition and wondering if he had lost his mind. Why else would he have agreed to do something so nonsensical?

Except it did make sense in a way. She had presented a solution to their meddling mother problem, and he was the one who had set it in motion by leading his *mamm* to believe there was something between him and Daisy in the first place. She'd just taken the ball and run with it. Still, he was bothered by the deception, even though neither of their mothers would know their date was fake. But he and Daisy would know, and that didn't sit well.

Then there was the fact she was smitten with Maynard, although when she talked about their relationship, he got the impression it was rather one-sided. But he didn't have the right to doubt her words, and he believed that she believed there was something more between them than friendship.

Grimacing, he wished he'd told her no when she asked for his help. He should have stuck to his plan of fessing up to his mother about stretching the truth. Then he wouldn't be entangled in Daisy's problem. He barely even knew her, although he did think she was nice. *Like her ankles.*

He tightened his grip on the reins. He had to stop thinking about that, and about the way she'd looked at him yesterday when she barged in unannounced. But just like he was having trouble getting his mind off his and Daisy's pact, he couldn't forget the admiration in her eyes as she stared at him . . . or how much he liked it.

Maynard. Perry had to remember she only had eyes for her boyfriend back home. He also couldn't forget his own vow of keeping to himself.

He turned into Ferman's driveway and frowned at the totally dark house. Ferman wasn't on the front porch waiting for him either. Maybe he liked sitting in the dark. Perry got out of the buggy and walked to the front door to get him. But when he knocked on the door, there was no answer.

Alarm shot through him. "Ferman?" He grabbed the doorknob and turned it. Locked.

"Ferman!"

A weak voice came from the other side of the door. "The key is in the bushes."

Perry glanced around. There were no streetlights, and the sun wouldn't rise for another two hours. "Hang on." He ran to his buggy and grabbed one of his battery-powered buggy lanterns. Switching it on, he saw two groups of shrubbery flanking the porch. "Which side?"

"On the right. Under the flat brick."

He quickly spotted it since the brick wasn't exactly hidden. Perry grabbed the key and opened the door. "Ferman?" He held up the lamp and looked around.

"Over here."

Turning, he saw the old man crumpled on the floor a few feet from the door. He hurried to him. "Are you all right?"

"*Ya*," Ferman snapped, but his tone didn't have much force behind it.

Perry put the lantern on the floor, and it illuminated part of the room. "When did you fall?"

Ferman scowled. "An hour ago or so. Help me up already."

Perry complied, sliding his hand underneath Ferman's armpit and hoisting him to his feet. "Do you need to sit down?"

"*Nee*. Let's *geh*. We got work to do today." But his knees started to buckle, and he fell against Perry.

This wasn't good. "I'm calling an ambulance," Perry said.

"Don't you dare." Ferman glared at him. "I just need a minute."

"You need to sit down before you fall again."

"I ain't gonna fall!" He yanked his arm from Perry's and regained his balance. "See? I just had a little accident, that's all."

Perry shook his head. "If you won't let me call an ambulance, at least give me Junior's number—"

"Nee!" Ferman took three wobbly steps. "We're wasting time, boss. Let's get moving."

He took a step forward and sank to the ground.

Chapter 10

Shortly after sunrise, Daisy walked her mother to the taxi parked in the driveway. "Are you sure you don't want me to ride with you to the bus station?"

"*Nee*. Then you'd have to find a ride home." *Mamm* handed the driver her small suitcase. "This can ride in the back seat with me." As he put the case in the car, she turned to Daisy. "I'm sorry we had a fight," she said, touching Daisy's cheek. "But I'm glad we worked things out."

"Me too." She wondered if she should tell her mother about Perry but decided against it. It would seem suspicious if Daisy started "dating" him so soon after she and her *mamm*'s agreement. Better to wait a while so their encounter seemed natural. "Have a safe trip back."

"See you in six weeks." *Mamm* smiled.

"Five and—" Daisy stopped herself. "See you then."

Mamm got in the car, and Daisy waved to her as the taxi backed out of the driveway. She waited until the car disappeared down the road, then headed back to the house to help *Aenti* Rosella clean up from breakfast. Her aunt had prepared a simple, delicious meal of muffins and fresh fruit. She also packed *Mamm* a lunch for the trip—a ham and cheese sandwich, cut carrots and celery, another blueberry muffin, and some of the leftover fruit. Daisy told her *aenti* she would clean up the kitchen after she told *Mamm* goodbye.

But instead of going back inside, she stared at the phone shanty, tugging her sweater close to ward off the morning chill. More than once before she fell asleep last night, she pondered if Grace was right. One phone call and a quick discussion with Maynard and they would be an official couple. But she always came to the same conclusion—she had to wait until they were face-to-face to discuss their future so she could see his happy reaction. There was also Perry to consider. If she and Maynard were together before her "date," then she would be cheating on Maynard, and she would never do that. She also couldn't back out of their pact. For better or worse, she was sticking to her word.

She could call and briefly talk to Maynard, though. She missed hearing his voice. Hopefully he hadn't left for work. The shop wasn't open yet, but sometimes he went in early because he liked having the workshop to himself. She stepped inside the shanty and dialed his number.

"Hello?" A rigid voice responded on the other line.

Neva. "Hi," Daisy said, inserting a brightness into her tone that she didn't feel. "Is Maynard there?"

A pause. "Who is this?"

Daisy tapped her forehead against the shanty glass. Neva knew it was her. Was she trying to plant in Daisy's mind that other women were calling? Or was this just a dig? "Can I speak to him?"

The Millers kept their phone in the kitchen and Daisy heard the receiver clatter on the counter, then Neva calling Maynard's name in the distance.

A few seconds later, he picked up. "Hello?"

"Hi, Maynard. It's Daisy." She smiled, but for some reason it felt different than the other times she smiled around him. Less . . . eager. And she was surprised she announced her name to him. He knew it was her.

"Hi, Daisy," he said flatly.

His voice was naturally toneless. Kind of like his mother's, she suddenly realized. Then a question flew out of her mouth—one she'd always wanted to ask but never had. "Why does your mother hate me?"

"She doesn't hate you," he said, sounding surprised. "We aren't supposed to hate anyone, Daisy. You know that."

He was right, they weren't. "She dislikes me then. A lot."

"I'm on my way to the shop. Can we talk about this later?"

She inwardly sighed. She should have known better than to bring up such a testy topic with him right before work. "I'm sorry. I just wanted to know if you got my letter."

"Not yet."

That made sense. She'd just mailed it yesterday. "Will you read it as soon as you get it?"

"Yeah, sure. I've got to *geh,* Daisy. We're going to be real busy today."

"I miss you, Maynard."

He didn't respond, but he didn't hang up either.

"Do you . . . miss me?" she asked, cringing at the desperation in her voice.

"Uh-huh. I'll call you later."

"Okay."

Click.

She placed the receiver back in the cradle, disappointed. Then she looked on the bright side. He did say he missed her and that he would call her. And she didn't really care if Neva liked her or not. Once she and Maynard were married, Daisy would win her over.

Managing a smile that felt real this time, she left the shanty, glad she had his phone call to look forward to. Hastening her steps, she headed for the house to do kitchen duty when a buggy came down the road, the horse trotting at a quick clip. It turned into Perry's driveway and had barely come to a stop when Perry leapt out and ran to the other side.

Although she couldn't see his expression, she sensed something was wrong. Daisy dashed to him as he helped a glowering Ferman out of the buggy. "What happened?"

"I've been kidnapped," Ferman groused.

Perry rolled his eyes. "He fell at his house and is having trouble standing up." He looked at Daisy as he bent at the waist and hooked Ferman's arm over his shoulder. "Can you unlock the door?"

"It's working now?"

"*Ya*," he said, handing her the key but providing no other explanation.

She quickly opened the door and Perry half carried Ferman to the one comfortable chair in the house, gently setting him down.

Ferman rewarded him with a steely glare.

"He's cranky, but I think he's okay." Perry turned to Daisy. "I didn't want to leave him alone."

Daisy gave Ferman a once-over as he muttered something about young whippersnappers and their audacity. But his face was contorted with pain, and he was rubbing his right hip.

"I've got to call my clients and reschedule," Perry said, speeding to the door.

"You're not canceling on my account," Ferman protested and tried to get up. He moaned and sat right back down.

"I'm not leaving you here alone either," Perry said. "Not when you can't walk."

"Who says I can't walk?" Ferman's bushy brows flattened over his eyes. "Give me a minute or two and I'll be dancing out the door."

Perry crossed his arms and shook his head.

Daisy watched both men. They were at a standoff. "I can stay with him," she volunteered.

Perry paused. "You don't have to do that—"

"You certainly don't." Ferman harrumphed.

"But it *would* help me out," Perry continued. "You sure you don't mind?"

"Not at all. Grace and her dad are leaving for work soon and *Aenti* Rosella has plans today. I've got my cross-stitch to keep me occupied while he rests."

"I don't need any rest," Ferman insisted. "I need to work."

She turned to the elderly man, who wasn't hiding his disgust. She didn't take it personally. He was in debilitating pain.

Perry nodded, his relief clear. "I'll be back tonight." He looked at Ferman. "Don't give Daisy any trouble. Today she's your boss."

"Fine," he mumbled. When Perry asked Ferman to repeat himself, he yelled, "I'll behave!"

Perry's mouth twitched. Then he gestured for Daisy to walk out with him to the buggy. "I appreciate this," he said, reaching into the back seat for something. He handed her his card. "I keep a cell on me, so call if he gives you any trouble or if you need help. I'll get ahold of my sister-in-law Margaret and see if she can check on him. She knows a lot about natural medicine, and she might have something to help his pain. *If* he'll take it."

"I'll be on the lookout for her. Don't worry, Perry. I'll handle him."

He tilted his head. "I'm sure you can, Daisy from Dover." He hauled himself into the buggy. "See you tonight."

When she went back inside, she found Ferman trying to get up again. She walked in front of him and gently put her hands on his shoulders to make him sit down. She barely had to touch him, and he obeyed, or rather his achy hip wouldn't let him continue. Poor man. But she had to show him who was in charge, so she leaned in close. "You and I, Ferman Eash, are going to come to an understanding."

Shortly after Perry left, Ferman was fighting to stay awake. And fight he did, because he wasn't about to let Mr. and Ms. Bossypants get the best of him.

Deep down he knew Perry and Daisy were right. He did need to take it easy, and that scared him. He'd puttered around the house yesterday morning, and his only physical task was feeding his horse, which had taken minimal effort. Even though his hip was still a little sore, by midafternoon he decided to tackle his grass before the yard started to look seedy. Doing some physical labor would also help get his mind off Junior's visit and how that had ended in hurt feelings, yet again.

He'd taken the afternoon dose of his anti-inflammatory and figured it would kick in as he mowed the yard. He dragged the manual push mower out of the shed and went to work, ignoring the pain and stiffness in his hip. He was halfway done when his leg seized up, the muscles becoming so tight he couldn't take a step without pain. Somehow he hobbled to the house and collapsed on the bed, skipping supper and hoping he could sleep off his misery.

But when his alarm woke him up a couple hours ago, his leg was still achy and weak. He managed to get dressed, only to topple on his way to the living room to wait for Perry to pick him up. This time he couldn't get back on his feet.

He stared at Perry's white door, forcing his eyes to stay open. As soon as he was able to move again, he would go home, call his doctor, and ask for a stronger prescription. He didn't like taking drugs, but he disliked being dependent on anyone else even more. He wasn't about to impose on Perry or Daisy any more than necessary.

His eyes fluttered shut.

"Are you hungry?"

Ferman startled, and it felt like a hundred ice picks stabbed his hip. He tried and failed to stifle his moan.

"I'm sorry." Daisy crouched beside him, putting her hand lightly on his arm. "I have a bad habit of doing that lately."

"Scaring the life out of people?" he snapped, then grimaced and shifted, trying to find a comfortable position in the chair.

To her credit, she didn't shrink from his sharp tone. "I'll be more careful next time you're sleeping."

"I wasn't sleeping." He lifted his chin, not looking at her now. "I was resting my eyes."

"Then I'll be more careful next time you're resting your eyes." She stood up, her expression pleasant. "Would you like something to eat?"

He was tempted to say no, but his empty belly stopped him. "Just a nibble will do."

"I'll be right back with that nibble."

Ferman settled in the chair as she scurried to the kitchen. Behind him, he could hear her humming, cabinets and drawers opening and closing as she prepared his food. He inwardly smiled. He liked this young woman, particularly the way she stood her ground with him. But that didn't mean he was going to stick around here for any length of time.

A knock sounded at the door and it opened. A lovely Amish woman with dark hair and a confident manner walked inside carrying a wicker basket. She looked at him. "You must be Ferman," she said, giving him a warm smile. Then she glanced past him. "And you're Daisy?"

"*Ya*. Margaret, right?"

She nodded and went straight to Ferman. "Perry told me what was going on, and I got here as fast as I could. He said I could just come in."

Daisy placed a glass of water and a plate filled with cubes of cheddar cheese, a sliced apple, and a piece of bread with a delightfully thick smear of butter across it on the small side table near the chair. "I didn't hear your buggy," she said.

"I took a taxi." Margaret removed her cloak and black bonnet. "I live in Birch Creek, and I wouldn't have made it here until the afternoon. The driver is returning in an hour."

Daisy offered to take her outerwear, and Margaret handed it to her before turning her attention back to Ferman. "Perry said you might be a little resistant to my help."

"Just a *little*," Daisy murmured as she walked away.

Ferman gave a slight smile. He didn't want to show more weakness because, if he did, for sure one of these young people would call Junior, and he didn't want to deal with his son insisting that he move in with him. *Best I cooperate.* "How can you help me?"

She looked surprised at his agreeableness, and so did Daisy as she brought over a chair for Margaret, then stood nearby. "First I need you to tell me what's wrong," Margaret said.

"I got a sore hip."

"How sore? Where does it hurt?"

Ferman sighed, and for the next few minutes he answered

Margaret's questions. She sounded more like a doctor than he expected and seemed quite capable. "Bottom line is I overdid it yesterday. I need a little rest, that's all. Then I'll be right as rain."

She nodded, but he could tell she didn't agree. "Can you stand up?"

He pushed himself up off the chair, and praise the Lord, he was standing. His leg felt stronger than it had this morning. "See?" he said, taking a step forward. "I'm fine—"

Margaret jumped up to catch him before he crashed to the ground. Without a word, she helped him back onto the chair. Then she sat down and picked up her basket. "Here's what I'd like you to do," she said, pulling out a pad and pencil. She wrote on it, then handed it to him.

He read her neat handwriting:

Apply ice to the hip area at fifteen-minute intervals for up to twenty-four hours.
Switch to heat afterward.

He continued to read her list of tinctures and teas and the directions for taking them. Curcumin, elderberry, turmeric, and a lavender-chamomile mixture for sleep.

"I'm also going to give you a salve to put on your bursa area." She pointed to the outside of her hip. "Right here. You can put this on as much and as often as you need it if it gives you relief."

Daisy nodded. "I can help—"

"I'll handle it myself." He'd have to pull his pants down to put on the salve, and he was *not* doing that in front of Daisy.

"You need to eat well too. Nutrition is important."

"I'll make sure he does." Daisy gave him a pointed look.

"Most importantly," Margaret said, looking him straight in the eye, "I don't want you to be alone for the next few days. You're a fall risk and could injure yourself even more or break a hip. You'll need help moving around and getting dressed."

Blast it. He gripped the side of the chair. That was the last straw. "I'm fine—"

"Ferman—"

"I'll drink the teas and take the tinctures and put on the salves, but I don't need anybody's help." He crossed his arms. "And that's final."

"How about you sleep here?" Daisy offered, disregarding Ferman's proclamation. She turned to Margaret. "Do you think Perry would mind?"

"Considering the severity of Ferman's hip, I'm sure he won't." She got up and walked over to the kitchen. "What time is he getting back?"

"I don't know."

"You could call him," Margaret suggested.

Ferman twisted around the best he could in the chair, observing and listening to the women make plans for him without his input. "Doesn't anyone care what I think?"

"We already know what you think," Daisy said, giving him a sweet smile.

He turned back around and harrumphed again. The nerve of her, smiling while he was in crisis. And the impertinence of them leaving him out of the decision-making process. This was his life, his albatross of a hip. He felt helpless, and he didn't like that. Not one bit.

⌁

Daisy and Margaret went outside and let Ferman stew and eat his "nibbles," plus drink a special tea Margaret made to help him with pain. They waited for the taxi to return. *"Danki* for coming," Daisy said.

"You have your work cut out for you." She glanced back at Perry's house. "He's beyond stubborn."

"He's just upset and hurting." Daisy had a lot of sympathy for the old man, and she could see that Margaret did too. She was impressed by how thorough and intelligent Perry's sister-in-law was about the human body and herbal medicine. "My *grossvatter* is the same way. If you tell him the sky is blue, he'll insist it's brown just to argue with you. I think Ferman's a little like that. He and I will get along just fine." She paused. "I hope I didn't overstep by suggesting he stay with Perry."

"Knowing my brother-in-law, he'll want Ferman to be safe, however that ends up happening." A white van turned into the driveway. "There's my ride. I wrote my phone number on the instruction list. If nothing helps his pain, let me know. And if he's hurting too much, take him to the ER."

"I will." She wasn't sure how she'd manage that, other than to call an ambulance. Earlier, after Perry left and Ferman had promised to stay in his seat, she had run over to her aunt's and explained the situation. Rosella had been sympathetic and told her to stay with Ferman as long as she needed to. But none of Daisy's relatives would be home until around suppertime. Somehow she'd figure it out if Ferman had to go to the hospital before everyone arrived home. In the meantime, she would do everything possible to make sure he wouldn't have to.

After Margaret left, Daisy went back inside. The scowl on Ferman's face could melt a fireplace, but at least he was eating. Only two apple slices were left and he'd drunk all the water. She picked up the glass and refilled it, then set it back down on the table and grabbed the empty plate.

"Daisy . . ."

"*Ya*?"

"I"—his wrinkled face reddened—"have to use the facilities."

She nodded and helped him to the bathroom. It was only a few steps away, and when she looked inside, she saw there was a vanity sink he could hang on to. Whew. "Let me know if you need help."

He grunted his answer and shut the door.

Daisy waited a minute or two, deciding that after he finished up, she'd give him one of the portable ice packs Margaret had left, the kind that turned cold when broken in the middle. She had also provided some heat packs for tonight. While he was icing his hip, Daisy would make him some tea with the tinctures, then tuck him into bed. He was so tired, and she wanted him to rest comfortably. Being in the chair all day wouldn't do.

She walked down the short hallway. There were three closed doors—two on the left and one on the right next to the bathroom. She didn't like the idea of snooping around Perry's house, but she didn't have a choice. He wasn't there to tell her where Ferman could sleep, and she didn't want to interrupt his job to ask him. Not when she could figure this out herself.

Daisy opened the door beside the bathroom. That turned out to be a closet with a few towels, washcloths, sheets, and blankets on the shallow shelves. She also noticed some cleaning supplies, but the tiny closet wasn't close to being full. She closed the door. "Still okay, Ferman?"

"*Ya*," he yelled, still grouchy.

She turned to door number two and opened it, then peeked inside. A strange tingle went through her body as she saw Perry's bedroom. The bed was unmade, there were clothes on the floor, and one of the dresser drawers was left open. It wasn't sloppy. It just needed some tidying. Surprising since the living room and kitchen were always neat. At least they were the three times she'd been here.

Her face heated when she looked at Perry's bed again. Realizing she was dallying, she quickly left his room. Time for door number three. This had to be the spare bedroom. She opened the door. Peeked inside.

And gasped.

Chapter 11

Perry speedily pulled his buggy into his driveway after rescheduling his afternoon clients. He managed to finish the morning one, and fortunately he'd shoed those three horses many times over the years. They were gentle, and one of them, Mo, kept affectionately trying to nibble on his ear, something he always did when Perry shod him. But even Mo's antics couldn't stem his concern for Ferman. He'd been in bad shape when Perry last saw him. Hopefully Margaret had made it over there already, and he was just as hopeful Ferman didn't give her and Daisy a hard time.

He quickly put up his horse and buggy. Later he would let the gelding out into the small corral behind the barn to enjoy some fresh grass, but first he needed to check on the situation in his house.

When he walked into the empty front room, a thread of panic wound through him. Had they gone to the hospital? If so, why didn't anyone call him? He hurried the few steps to the back of the house.

"I'm done!" Ferman's weary voice came through the bathroom door.

Frowning, Perry opened the door and saw Ferman leaning against the vanity counter, his face contorted with pain.

"What are you doing here?" the old man groused.

"Checking on you. Is everything okay?"

"I'm . . . just give me a hand, will ya?"

The exhausted defeat in Ferman's eyes unsettled him, and Perry helped him back to the chair. "Where's Daisy?"

"Thought she was right by the bathroom." He leaned his head against the chair back and closed his eyes. "She can't have gone far. I was only in there a few minutes."

"Did she leave?" If she had, then Perry had her pegged wrong. Who in good conscience would leave a feeble old man alone like this?

"Doubt it. I heard her opening and closing the bedroom doors."

He froze, a cold knot forming in his gut. "Be right back."

Ferman's head tilted to the side. "Take your time . . ." He let out a robust snort.

Perry dashed to the back, praying that Daisy had only gone into his bedroom. Not that he liked the idea of her seeing his messy room, but he'd rather she did than discover his—

His stomach dropped. Only one door was open, and it was the one he always, *always* kept closed. And locked. He scrubbed his hand over his face, his anger rising. How dare she snoop around his house? Had she picked the lock? She would have had to, because he never left it . . . oh wait. He'd been in there last week, and it was possible he'd neglected to secure the door. That was on him.

He steeled himself, remembering the one and only time he'd allowed someone inside his private sanctuary and how that had backfired. Spectacularly.

His jaw clamped down and he entered the room to see Daisy standing in the middle of it, invading his privacy. *Again.* This time it wasn't endearing. Or pleasing. He cleared his throat, unable to trust that he wouldn't say something he might regret.

She whirled around, a surprised smile on her face. "Hi. You're home early."

He measured his steps as he approached her. "What are you doing in here?"

Her expression was the picture of innocence. "Looking for your spare bedroom."

His fingers flexed. "You found it," he ground out.

"*Ya*, but Ferman can't take a nap here, obviously. Is he finished in the bathroom?"

Unbelievable. She wasn't aware she'd done something wrong. Or she was pretending she hadn't. "He's asleep in the chair."

"*Gut.* I won't disturb him then."

"Daisy—"

"Is all this yours?" Not waiting for an answer, she walked over to a wall and stared at the long glass display case that spanned from one side to another.

He braced himself for her negative reaction.

"I've never seen anything so amazing."

His eyes widened. "Huh?"

She looked at the other wall covered in scientific posters, then up at the ceiling. "There are butterflies . . . everywhere."

Technically not, but his collection was unquestionably extensive. And weird and obsessive, according to Ruby—his ex-girlfriend.

Daisy stared at the four butterfly mobiles suspended from the wood beam across the middle of the ceiling. He'd ordered them from a hobby store, then painstakingly assembled and hung them up, the task taking him more than ten hours. They had been an incredible find, since most butterfly mobiles were either for babies or were unrealistic, nondetailed ones in girly colors. These were delicate and lifelike.

Until he moved to Marigold and purchased this house, he'd spent the past ten years keeping his collection in a storage unit between here and Birch Creek. It had taken him two weeks to unpack and display everything, and he always kept the door shut in case company dropped by. That only happened occasionally, and it was always family. Not a single Bontrager knew he had a room filled with everything and anything that had to do with butterflies.

When she reached up to touch one of the mobiles, he sprang toward her. "Don't!" He caught her arm, and with a light but firm touch, he brought it down by her side.

She took a step back, her expression sheepish. "I'm sorry. I'm sure you put a lot of work into them."

Perry frowned. For some reason she didn't seem disconcerted by his horde of papilio or that he had forcibly kept her from touching the mobile.

Her gaze shifted upward again. "They're so lovely. That one looks like the butterfly that was in your house."

"It's a painted lady," he said, moving closer to her and pointing to the one next to it. "And that's a red admiral."

"Oh, like the one you were trying to catch."

"*Nee*, that was the white admiral. He's a different species." Perry glanced at her again, feeling a little more at ease. She seemed genuinely interested in his collection.

"Which one is that?" She pointed at the spring azure, the wings a shimmering sapphire color. When he told her, she asked about several more.

He named every single one, resisting the urge to tell her their Latin designations, habitats, food preferences, and other trivial minutiae nobody but the most avid of butterfly enthusiasts would care to know.

Daisy moved away from the mobiles to the crowded wall full of framed butterfly portraits. "Who drew these?"

Perry hesitated. "I did."

"*Nee.*" She turned to him, incredulous. "Those look like they came out of a science book. You're a remarkable artist."

"I'm not that *gut*," he deflected. "I've just had a lot of practice."

"A whole lot." She walked around the room, continuing her observations.

He frowned. As much as Daisy seemed intrigued and appreciative, she would soon be aware that an Amish man having an entire bedroom dedicated to butterflies was beyond strange. Over the years, he'd questioned himself about his consuming interest in an insect that typically appealed to females. From his independent studies using science books and journals from the library, he knew there were plenty of male scientists and nature enthusiasts who exclusively investigated the beautiful insects. But he didn't know any Amish men who did, and he wasn't interested in finding one. He'd always been satisfied enjoying his hobby alone, and until now there was only one other person besides Daisy who knew about it. *Ruby.*

His family had assumed he'd never dated anyone, but they didn't know about Ruby King. He met her two years ago when her family started attending church in Marigold, shortly after he moved here. He'd never forget the day he decided to show her his collection, which he had neglected when they started spending time together. He could still remember his excitement when he opened the door to his room and invited her in.

"*How bizarre.*" She waved at his decade-long investment with a dismissive hand. "*When we get married, all this has to* geh.*"

Her words pierced him, but he anticipated she would come around. Because he thought—no, he *believed*—that Ruby was the woman God wanted him to marry, even though, like his collection, he'd kept her a secret from everyone. *"What do you mean,* geh?"

"In the trash." Ruby walked through the room, barely glancing at the display case. *"There's a lot of junk in here."*

He couldn't respond, his mind spinning that she would even consider throwing away his butterflies.

She'd glanced at the drawings. *"I'm sure we can reuse these frames, though. After we take out the pictures."* Then she looked up at the mobiles. *"Aren't these for* kinner?"

"Ruby, don't touch—"

Before he could stop her, she yanked down all four in quick succession. *"There. That's better."*

Perry shook his head, willing the memories away, but not before he recalled telling her he would expand the house after they got married . . . but this room was his. When he tried to explain how the collection started and how much it meant to him, she looked at him as if he were *ab im kopp*. Then she said it was either the butterflies or her.

He made his choice.

Looking back, it was the right one, because after they broke up, he realized she'd always been insistent on getting her own way during their four-month relationship. He dodged a miserable marriage, but losing her had been difficult at the time. Since he had kept their relationship under wraps, he'd had to suffer alone.

He was never going through that again.

"We should check on Ferman." He tried to covertly guide Daisy toward the door.

"I thought you said he was sleeping." She was looking at the drawings again, and she was almost nose to nose with his rendering of

Limenitis archippus—the viceroy butterfly. "I can't believe how lifelike this looks." She gestured to the other ones. "They all do. Did you copy them out of a book?"

"*Nee,*" he said, then unwittingly let down his guard. "I caught most of them. I would make notes on their appearance, do a preliminary drawing, and when I had the information I needed, I'd let them go."

"But you have some butterflies over there." She pointed at the display case with a slight frown. "They're pinned to boards."

"They were dead when I found them, or they were sick or injured and I couldn't revive them. I would never kill one to display."

Daisy turned, appearing more curious than before. "What about the admiral? You were trying to catch him."

"To draw him, Daisy. That's all."

"Then you would let him *geh.*"

"*Ya.* I don't see the point in ending a life, no matter how small, just for a collection. Others think differently, and that's their prerogative. I'd rather see them flutter about in the wild." That was more than he'd intended to say, and he wasn't going to say anything else. She might not think he was an oddball now, but he was certain if they spent one more second in this room, he would cave into temptation and go full-on butterfly nerd. *I have to get out of here.* "Want some lunch?"

"It's a little early, don't you think? I'd rather stay here and look around some more."

He took her arm and pulled her out of the room, almost slamming the door behind them. "I'd rather you didn't."

Daisy looked up at Perry's intense gaze, completely bewildered. His butterfly collection was the most amazing thing she'd ever encountered, and for some reason he seemed ashamed of it. Except when he answered her questions or explained his drawings and the various butterflies in the glass case. That's when his eyes lit up, like a giddy young boy at Christmas. So cute. And informative. Perry Bontrager wasn't merely a muscly, handsome man. He was really, *really* smart. A lot smarter than she would ever be. Which made his insistence that they leave the room even more baffling.

"I don't understand," she said.

"That's my collection, Daisy. I don't share it with anyone."

Oh. *Oh*. Remorse flooded her. No wonder he was upset. She'd intruded on his privacy . . . again. "I'm sorry," she said, her voice barely audible. She glanced down, unable to look him in the eye.

After an excruciatingly long moment, he said, "I should have told you this room was off-limits."

She looked at him again. "To Ferman too?"

"To *everyone*."

Despite knowing she needed to keep her nosiness in check when it came to Perry Bontrager, she wanted to ask why he was being so secretive. His collection was entertaining, educational, and impressive, particularly the drawings. And when he was talking about how he'd tried to nurse butterflies back to health and she saw the trace of sadness in his eyes when he admitted he sometimes failed, a warm thrill coursed through her. She hadn't expected this manly man to be so sensitive. Or to love butterflies so much. He was full of surprises.

"Don't tell anyone else either." He leaned forward, enough that she could see the tiny dimple at the left corner of his mouth. "Just forget it exists."

Oh, this was a shame, him hiding such a magnificent display from the world. But she had to respect his wishes. "I promise."

"I'll make sure to keep it locked from now on." He locked the door and started to walk away.

She remembered why she was there in the first place. "Wait," she said, jumping in front of him. "I need to talk to you."

"About what?" He crossed his arms over his chest.

"About . . ." He was wearing short sleeves and her gaze dropped down to his arms. Quickly she jerked her eyes back up. Ferman. Right. She needed to talk to him about Ferman. She explained about Margaret's mandate that Ferman couldn't stay by himself. "So I, uh, volunteered for him to stay here. With you."

He stilled. "Where am I going to sleep?"

"I thought you had a spare bedroom. Most houses do."

"Now you know mine doesn't."

His sharp tone irritated her. She was in the wrong, but he didn't have to be so testy when they were talking about their patient. "Excuse me, I was looking for a place for Ferman to nap."

"He looks comfortable in the chair."

"You can't be serious." Where was the kind man who didn't want to harm a butterfly?

Perry glanced away, then nodded. "He can have my room. I've got a sleeping bag in the attic. I can camp on the living room floor."

That didn't seem quite fair either. Perry had a job, and a physical one at that. He didn't need to sleep on the hard floor, even if it were for a few nights. "I won't allow that."

He smirked. "You won't *allow* it?"

At least he wasn't frowning anymore. "*Nee.*" She tapped her finger on her chin, trying to think of a solution. Then it came to her. "The couch."

"I don't have a couch."

She put her hands on her hips. "But you need one. And I know exactly where you can get it."

———

Ferman woke up to the sound of the front door flying open. "Hey," he said, two bodies and a sofa coming into fuzzy view. What had Margaret put in that tea? And how long had he been sleeping anyway? He hadn't slept so hard in months. Years, maybe. He'd have some more of that brew later. Yes indeed.

Finally, he recognized Perry and Daisy setting the sofa down several feet from him. "What's going on?" He followed up his question with a strong yawn.

"Perry's new bed." Daisy stood and brushed off her hands. "For the time being."

He shifted in the chair, and the movement surprisingly didn't hurt as much as it had before he imbibed Margaret's medicine. Daisy's statement cut through the haze. "Why is he sleeping on the couch?"

"You're taking my room." Perry sat down across from him. He leaned back and crossed his knee at his ankle.

"I'll get the throw pillows," Daisy said.

Perry lifted one index finger. "I—"

But she was already out the door.

"Don't think I need throw pillows," Perry mumbled. Then he focused on Ferman. "How are you feeling?"

"Surprisingly rested." And in need of the facilities. Again. At his age, that wasn't anything new. He started to get up, but Perry intercepted him.

"Not without my help." He put his arm around Ferman and helped him to his feet. "When you're steady, let me know."

"Confound it," he said, a little stunned that he only sounded—and felt—half annoyed. "I can get to the bathroom on my own."

"That's not what Margaret said. I read her notes. You don't want to cross her." Perry's grin dimmed. "She knows what she's doing. If you follow her directions and stop fighting me and Daisy, you'll feel a lot better."

Ferman wanted to grumble again, but he didn't have it in him. "Fine. Take me to the facilities."

After he finished and Perry helped him with the salve—which really brought relief, he had to admit—he allowed Perry to assist him to the bedroom. "Good gravy, *bu*," Ferman said. "What a mess."

"It's not that bad."

"My Lovina would have a conniption if I ever left our room in such a state." They were at the edge of Perry's unmade bed. He slowly sat down, and with Perry's help he settled against the soft mattress and firm pillow. Ah, that was better.

Perry closed the slate-blue curtains over his bedroom window, then swiped up his clothing and tucked the small pile under one arm. As he passed his bureau, he shut the drawer. "Do you need anything else?" he said as he opened the door.

Feeling tired again, Ferman shook his head. Being in pain took a lot out of him. "Wait. Maybe some more of that tea. Daisy knows the kind."

"Sure thing." He shut the door.

Plunged into semidarkness, Ferman closed his eyes, more than a little contrite. He didn't like the idea of kicking Perry out of his room, no matter what Margaret said. But even his ornery mind knew that if he wanted to get home ASAP, he would have to comply. For a brief moment he went against his grain and thought about calling Junior. He wouldn't feel as bad putting out family. But that would be more trouble than it was worth, and he would be alone with pregnant Polly Ann while his son was at work, and he didn't want to be a burden to her. Regardless of what Junior would say, his daughter-in-law would see Ferman that way. She already did, even before they moved away.

He sighed, feeling stuck. He was an intrusion, exactly what he never wanted to be. As he drifted off to sleep again under Perry's gray sheets and a thick brown blanket, he repeated a prayer that God so far refused to answer since his hip pain started long ago. *Dear Lord . . . please heal me.*

Perry worked outside for the rest of the day while Ferman slept. He cleaned out the barn and horse stall, sharpened and oiled his tools, then did some mowing in the backyard by the woods where he would plant his butterfly garden. By the time he was done and had put the horse up for the night, it was dusk, and he was famished.

When he entered the house, he was immediately greeted with the scent of fresh bread baking. He poked his head into the kitchen. Daisy was putting a tray of fluffy rolls on top of the stove before shutting the door. "Hi," he said.

She jumped, nearly upending the rolls. "You scared me," she said, her eyes wide. Before he could apologize, she held up her hand. "It's okay. This is the house where everyone ends up getting startled eventually."

He wasn't sure what she meant by that, and it didn't matter because he noticed the casserole next to the rolls on the stove, wisps of steam wafting from the top.

"You're timing is *gut*. Supper is done." She slipped off the red-and-yellow potholders *Mamm* had given him as a housewarming gift when he moved to Marigold, along with pots and pans, kitchen utensils—everything a bachelor would need for a stocked kitchen. He only used the pots for heating up soups, and the pan for cooking eggs or hamburgers. He had yet to bake anything.

Perry slipped off his boots, and since he was filthy, he refused to enter the kitchen. "You didn't have to make supper," he said, pulling off his socks and tossing them into the almost-full clothes basket. He'd have to do laundry early the next morning, and then he'd be off to see the two clients he rescheduled this morning.

"Margaret said to make sure Ferman ate enough. *Nee* reason why I can't feed you too." She smiled.

He paused, puzzled at the jolt of . . . something that went through him. When he and Daisy had retrieved the old couch from her aunt and uncle's basement—it wasn't that old, and it felt comfortable when he sat on it—he had calmed his emotions by the time they returned to his house. He was surprised by how strong she was, although he insisted they stop twice so she could rest. She didn't argue. The couch was heavier than it looked, and she was struggling by the time they brought it into his house.

Despite the exertion, Daisy didn't hesitate to get the throw pillows, and right after he put Ferman to bed, he went outside. As he worked, he wondered if he owed her more of an explanation for why he had banished her from the butterfly room. He decided he didn't. This was his house, his room, his collection.

"I need to clean up," he said, pulling his gaze from hers.

She nodded. "I'll check on Ferman. He's been sleeping all afternoon."

Perry entered the bathroom, stripped down, and took a hot shower, scrubbing the dirt and grime from the barn and yard off his body. When he got out of the shower and grabbed the towel hanging on the hook on the wall, he discovered he'd forgotten something very, *very* important.

Clean clothes.

Living alone and with the bathroom being in close proximity to his bedroom, he never worried about simply wrapping a towel around his waist and walking to the room after a shower, sometimes skipping the towel altogether. But now there were not one, but two people here, and he couldn't risk immodesty. It had been bad enough being shirtless around Daisy. He couldn't only wear a towel. And she said she would check on Ferman. She might still be in his bedroom right now.

Annoyed with himself, he looked at the smelly clothes on the bathroom floor. He could put these back on, but they were so soiled he'd have to take another shower and then probably end up explaining why to Daisy and Ferman anyway. For the first time he regretted that his house was so small.

"Daisy?" he hollered through the door.

Instantly he heard her light footsteps. "*Ya?*"

"Can you, uh, stay in the living room for a minute or two?"

"Is something wrong?"

"*Nee.*" He leaned his forehead against the door. "I just, um, need you to stay there. I'll let you know when you can come out."

"Are you sure you're okay?"

"I'm fine, Daisy," he said, trying to keep the impatience out of his tone. He started to dry off. "Just *geh*. Please."

"Okay."

He listened as she walked away and waited a few more seconds for good measure. When he was sure the coast was clear, he wrapped the towel around his lower body and started opening the door, only to spin around and grab the dirty clothes he'd forgotten. The way his brain was short-circuiting right now, he'd lose it if it weren't inside his head. His shirt slipped out of his grip, and when he bent down to pick it up, his towel slipped off.

"For crying out loud," he grumbled, setting the clothes in the sink and fastening the towel more securely this time. There. Now all he had to do was get to his room. He threw open the door.

"Land o' mercy, boy!" Ferman's brow flew to his hairline. "Put some clothes on!"

Chapter 12

Daisy was fluffing the pillows when she heard Ferman yell at Perry.

"Put some clothes on!"

She froze, mid-fluff. She was already wondering why Perry asked her to stay in the living room. Now Ferman was yelling at him, and it sounded like he was by the bathroom, not in the bedroom where he was supposed to be waiting for her to help him to the table.

Wait, Ferman wasn't supposed to be standing on his own, much less walking. She turned and started for the bedroom, then stopped. *Gulp.* Was Perry . . . *naked?* Surely he wouldn't walk around the house without—

"Daisy!"

She jumped at the sound of Perry's voice and inched away from the couch. "*Ya?*"

"Ferman's in the bathroom. I'll be out in a minute."

"So, ah, stay put?"

"*Ya.*"

All right. She'd stay put right here in the middle of the living room, which was technically the middle of Perry's house. Daisy hugged her arms. What a strange day.

Less than two minutes passed, and Perry showed up in the kitchen, dressed in a short-sleeved shirt and pants, combing his fingers through his damp hair. His bare feet padded against the hardwood floor.

It took some effort for Daisy to stop thinking about how it would feel to slide her hands through those deep brown locks. She forced herself to think about Maynard and his hair. What color was it again?

"Did you hear all that?" Perry asked, his expression unreadable.

She nodded. "It's a small house."

He walked toward her. "There's an innocent explanation. I forgot to take clean clothes to the bathroom—"

"I don't really need to know." She also didn't need any visuals that explanation would put in her head. She whirled around and ferociously fluffed another throw pillow, a white one with a lacy crochet overlay.

"I'm done!" Ferman hollered.

For an old man, he had a strong pair of lungs. "Coming," Daisy said, tossing the pillow on the couch.

Perry intercepted her. "I'll get him."

She nodded again. "I'll finish putting supper on the table."

Perry helped Ferman from the bathroom to the table and they all sat down, said a silent blessing, then started eating. Ferman picked at the *yumasetti* she'd made instead of eating. "Are you hurting?" she asked.

"A little," he admitted, not looking at her. "But *nee* where near as much as this morning."

"*Gut* to hear." Perry slathered butter on his roll.

Daisy agreed, but she was concerned about Ferman's lack of

appetite. "Would you like me to make you something else?" she asked. "Some soup? I saw a few cans in Perry's pantry."

He shook his head. "I'm not all that hungry."

She met Perry's uneasy gaze. Tomorrow she would prepare something a little less heavy for supper. When she went back to Grace's house for the pillows, *Aenti* Rosella was home, and Daisy told her that Ferman would be staying at Perry's and why they needed the couch. She also got the ingredients for the *yumasetti*.

"The poor mann,*"* her *aenti* had said, clucking her tongue. *"He's been favoring that hip for a while. I heard he needs to have it replaced, but he refuses to do so. I wouldn't mind if he stayed here, except all the bedrooms are upstairs."*

"He's settled at Perry's. But I agreed to keep an eye on him so Perry can geh *to work."*

"Oh? Then that means you'll be at his haus?*"* At Daisy's nod, her aunt grinned a little too much.

As she finished her roll, she remembered something—Maynard was supposed to call her back tonight! Okay, he didn't say tonight. He only said "later." But it was still possible that he would call.

She glanced at the clock. Six thirty. He would have been home for almost an hour by now. After she finished supper, cleaned the kitchen, and made sure Ferman was settled for the night, she would hurry back to her aunt's house and check the messages.

"Daisy?"

Blinking a few times, she saw Perry's face come into view. He was seated across from her, with Ferman in between them.

"Everything is *appeditlich. Danki.*"

His hair was nearly dry now, and several curls covered his forehead. The word *luxuriant* came to mind. Without warning she was feeling cold, then hot, then cold again. Bother. What was going on?

She jumped up from her seat and began clearing the table. Casserole dish in one hand and the breadbasket in the other, she hurried to the kitchen and set them on the counter.

While Perry helped Ferman to the bathroom again—he'd consumed a lot of tea today—she prepared the nighttime herbal blend Margaret had left and set out the salve for Perry to help Ferman apply to his bursa. She was grateful Ferman wasn't hurting as much, and the medicine in combination with lots of rest seemed to be the cure, for now at least. She said a prayer for God to heal him, cleared the rest of the dishes, and started washing them.

She was scrubbing the last plate by the time Perry entered the kitchen. Without a word, he took a fresh towel out of the drawer next to the sink and picked up the casserole dish sitting in the drainer.

"I can finish this," she said, glancing at him.

He dried the dish, still silent.

If he wanted to help, she couldn't stop him. She also appreciated the assistance. The faster she finished cleaning up, the sooner she could find out if Maynard had called. She pulled the plug out of the sink and the sudsy water gurgled down the drain. "I put the leftovers in the cooler. There's enough for two more servings. Hopefully Ferman will eat more tomorrow."

"I hope so too."

"Do you need anything else?" she asked.

"*Nee*. We're all set for tonight."

"What time should I be here in the morning?"

"I'd like to leave before dawn. I can reschedule, though. I don't want to take you away from your *familye*. I'm sure Ferman wouldn't want that either."

"Ferman wants to *geh* home." She rinsed out the soapy dishrag. "I'd like to help him get better. My *aenti* and *onkel* know about the situation, and Grace wouldn't mind spending more time with Kyle."

"Does that bother you?"

"*Nee.*" She wrung out the rag and laid it over the side of the sink to dry. "They're in love. Of course they would want to spend all their time together."

Perry ran the damp towel over the counter. "Are you missing Maynard?"

"*Ya.*" Although she'd been so busy today, he hadn't been on the forefront of her mind. In fact, she hadn't thought about him at all until a few minutes ago. Huh.

He stared at the sink for a moment. "I've been thinking about our pact. It's not sitting well with me." He turned to her. "I never should have given *Mamm* the wrong impression about us and I don't like the idea of compounding one lie with another. Pretending to *geh* on a date, even for a *gut* reason, isn't the right thing to do."

"*Ya.* I see your point." And she questioned why she didn't see it before. Maybe because she had lied so easily to Grace about Maynard. A sick feeling swirled in her stomach. *Forgive me, Lord.* "I'm sorry," she said, stepping away from the sink. "I know it was a lot to ask. Forget I mentioned it. I'll figure out another way to convince *Mamm* about me and Maynard." Although that seemed impossible, at least the part about being willing to give another man a chance. That wouldn't work—she would be lying no matter what. "See you in the morning." She hurried to the front door, filled with remorse and grateful that Perry had stopped them from being deceitful.

"Wait," he said, catching up to her as she touched the doorknob that had been working fine all day. "I think I have a solution to our mutual problem."

She spun around, surprised. "You do?"

He leveled his gaze at her. "We go out on a real date."

<hr />

Perry shut his mouth so hard his teeth hurt. It was official, he'd lost his marbles. Because he couldn't have told Daisy from Dover that they should go on an *actual* date. Nope. He never would have said that.

But he did, and he knew why. Earlier when he was outside doing the chores, he'd made the decision to end their pact, and he'd fully intended to do that tonight. Even as he was telling Daisy that he didn't want to lie to their mothers, he felt relief. He'd extricated himself from the predicament, and that was going to be that.

Until he saw her crestfallen expression, coupled with the note of remorse in her apology. It took less than a second for him to change his mind. But the only way they could avoid lying was to tell the truth. And that involved going out on a bona fide date.

Her eyes were filled with astonishment, and he could actually see her gulp. He had to explain himself. "It wouldn't be romantic," he said, wanting to make that exceptionally clear so there were no mis-understandings. "And we would only go out one time. But if anyone asked us if we went out together, we could tell them the truth."

"Perry . . . I . . ."

Then it hit him. How could he have forgotten about Maynard? He wanted to face-palm himself. A real date was out of the question—even an unromantic one—not when she wanted someone else. He held out his palms. "Sorry, that's a terrible idea."

She slowly nodded. "I can't."

"Because of Maynard."

"*Ya.*"

He leaned against the doorjamb. There had to be another way. Then he snapped his fingers. "Church."

"Pardon?"

"Birch Creek has church service this Sunday. You can come with me, and we'll be seen together by most of my *familye*. That should be enough to keep *Mamm* and anyone else from meddling for a while."

Daisy nodded, apparently mulling over the idea. "You think so? Or will she start up again when I *geh* back to Dover?"

"I'll make sure she doesn't. She needs to accept the fact that I'm happy being a single *mann*."

"Or maybe . . ." She folded her hands in front of her.

"Maybe what?"

"You could read the letters from those single women. Your future wife could be in that stack, and you don't even know it."

He was shaking his head before she finished speaking. "Not interested." He smirked. "Don't tell me you're going to start matchmaking now."

"Not interested." She grinned. "Attending church sounds like a great idea. Much better than being dishonest. It will be nice to meet the rest of your *familye*."

He laughed, relieved that they had come to an agreement that wouldn't compromise their principles. "Prepare yourself. They're a lively bunch."

<hr>

Daisy felt like a balloon tied to a cloud—light and free—as she left Perry's house and returned to Grace's. The sun had set over two hours ago, and she paused to gaze at the millions of twinkling dots scattered across the velvety sky. She was elated that Perry had come up with the solution to their dilemma—going to church together. Before she left, they shook on their new pact. Once again, she noticed how warm his hand was, and how wholly it enveloped hers. *Sigh.*

She caught herself and hastened her steps, pausing at the phone shanty and wondering if Maynard had called. Even if he did, it was past eight. Too late to call him back.

Daisy peeked at Perry's house in time to see the light in the window disappear. She was still reeling from his "real" date idea. For a split second, she thought he'd meant the typical kind of date, one where they liked each other . . . and not as friends. When he quickly confirmed that it would be a date in name only so they wouldn't lie about going out, a weird, not-so-pleasant feeling came over her. Disappointment? No, it couldn't be. Maynard Miller was the man for her, not Perry Bontrager. Besides, Perry couldn't have made it any clearer that he wasn't interested in dating anyone, especially her.

There the feeling was again. Like a pinch, right in her heart.

Ignoring the peculiar sensation, Daisy went inside. She thought about stopping in the kitchen where her relatives left notes and messages. She paused, then continued toward the staircase and yawned as she climbed the stairs. If Maynard had called, she'd find out in the morning. For once, he could wait.

"Rise and shine, sleepyhead."

Ferman shielded his eyes from Perry's portable lamp. "Morning already?

"*Ya.*" Perry set the lamp on top of his bureau, lighting up the bedroom. "How are you feeling?"

He almost snapped at the young man. He'd just been unceremoniously awakened from a wonderful dream. Lovina had been there, young and fresh as a spring flower, while he'd been his old, crusty self. She offered encouragement for his pain and predicament, along with a few kisses. Some were quite passionate. He leaned against the pillow and smiled.

"Glad to see you're doing better." Perry pulled out a navy blue pullover, white T-shirt, and a pair of pants out of the bureau and turned around. "These should somewhat fit you. After work, I can stop by your place and pick up some of your own clothes."

That dose of reality brought him out of his half-dream state. "Don't plan on being here after today," he grumbled. But when he sat up, he winced. The pain wasn't as intense, but it was there.

To his credit, Perry didn't say anything. He walked to the bed and waited for Ferman to slowly shift to a seated position. Well, look at that—he wasn't moving as slowly as he had yesterday. He'd take whatever progress he could.

Like he had yesterday, Perry assisted him with the salve and stood by as Ferman dressed, assisting only when necessary. He supposed if he had to get this personal with someone, he could do worse than Perry Bontrager. The young man managed to be helpful without hovering, and by the time Ferman was on his feet and ready to use the facilities—again—he really was feeling a little better.

Later, after he ate most of the oatmeal Perry fixed for breakfast, he was settled in the chair, another concoction of medicine and a glass of water on the side table.

"Daisy should be here soon." Perry folded the quilt he'd used last night and laid it haphazardly over the back of the borrowed sofa.

Ferman frowned, wanting to insist on sleeping on the couch tonight. He wasn't foolish enough to think Perry and Daisy would take him home this evening. But he didn't bother. Arguing with those two was almost as bad as quarreling with Junior and Polly Ann. He'd sleep in Perry's bed tonight, take all the medicine they gave him, and rest as much as possible. That was the only way he could return home. Margaret's advice was doing the trick, praise the Lord.

A soft knock sounded on the door and Daisy walked inside. A wicker basket hung over her elbow, and she was holding a piece of smooth wood that looked suspiciously like a cane. Fiddlesticks.

"Sorry I'm a little late." With a fetching smile, she set the basket and cane on one of the couch cushions.

He glanced at Perry, curious if Mr. Oblivious had finally started to notice what a pretty *maedel* Daisy was.

But he had his back to her as he took his straw hat off the rack near the door. "He's fed," Perry said, putting on a dark blue jacket.

"And dressed, I see."

"Humph," Ferman said. "I wish folks would stop conversating about me like I'm not here."

Ignoring him, she turned to Perry. "Anything you need me to do?"

He finally looked at her, although he made no indication that he noticed her looks—or heard Ferman's bellyaching. "Just make sure he doesn't leave the premises."

"Leave the premises?" What a laughable notion. He couldn't walk more than a few steps without assistance. Although if he could, he would have hightailed it home already. Perry had him pegged.

"Got it." She opened the basket lid and held out a small paper bag. "I brought a few treats to *geh* along with your lunch."

He paused, then took the bag with a small smile. "*Danki.*"

Ferman rubbed his stubbly chin with one finger. Hmm, maybe the *bu* wasn't as oblivious as he thought.

"See you later." He walked out the door.

Daisy picked up the quilt and started refolding it, her smile sunny. "How's our patient doing this morning?" she asked Ferman.

Our patient? Interesting way to put that. "I'm—"

The door opened again, and Perry poked his head into the house. "Daisy?" He gestured for her to come to him.

She laid the now neatly folded quilt on the back of the couch and went to him. When he leaned over and whispered in her ear, she nodded. "Of course."

Then he disappeared.

What were those two up to? "What was that about?" Ferman asked.

Daisy picked up the cane. "This is for you." She presented the rod to him as if it were a cherished treasure.

Confound it, disregarded again. "Figures," he mumbled.

"*Onkel* Howard said you could borrow it as long as you need to. He used it after he broke his ankle standing on the back of a horse last year."

"What?"

Daisy placed the cane in between the side table and his chair. "Talk about harebrained. Grace said he used to stand on the horses all the time when she was little. He would balance on their backs and ride around the pasture." She dropped her voice to sound manly. "'*Several years and more than several pounds ago*,' he said."

Not a bad imitation of Howard Hershberger. But yeah, that was foolish. It also wasn't the story he'd heard when Howard showed up to church limping and using the wooden cane. Ferman had forgotten all about that. Word was he tripped over his front porch steps. Ferman didn't blame him for the cover story, though. No middle-aged man would want everyone to know that he injured himself *literally* horsing around.

Ferman glanced at the cane. "What if I told you I'm not gonna use that?"

Daisy's smile faded a little, but the stubbornness he was becoming used to seeing appeared in her eyes. "Then I would call *you* harebrained."

Point taken. If he used the cane, he wouldn't have to lean on Daisy and Perry. He took it from her and ran his fingers across the smooth wood. "It'll do."

"*Gut.*" Her smile back in place, she dug inside the basket again. This time she pulled out a crossword book and a sudoku magazine and handed them to him. "You can sleep all you want. I brought these so you won't get bored while you're awake."

He glanced through the books, noticing some of the puzzles were completed in both. "Are these Howard's too?"

"*Nee. Aenti* Rosella's. *Onkel* Howard doesn't do puzzles." She held out two objects. "Pen or pencil?"

"Pencil." He took it, dabbed the graphite tip on his tongue, and started filling out several of the sudoku squares.

"Wow, you're fast." She closed the basket and slipped off her shoes.

"Been doing these for ages." He peered at more of the number clues and made himself comfy in the chair. When he was sitting, the ache in his hip was almost nonexistent. He took a sip of tea and continued solving the puzzle. Not a bad way to spend the morning, and he realized he hadn't felt this comfortable and relaxed in a long time. Thanks to Daisy and Perry.

<hr />

Daisy stared at the overflowing laundry basket in the cramped mudroom. Perry's house didn't have a basement, something she thought was unusual for an Amish home, and this was the smallest house she'd ever been in. Even the bedrooms were tiny.

Her brow furrowed as she wondered if she should wash Perry's dirty clothes. He didn't ask her to, and that put her in a quandary. With Ferman feeling better and occupied with the puzzle books, he wouldn't need as much care as he did yesterday. This morning when she woke up, she put the books and her cross-stitch into one of Rosella's wicker baskets, and her aunt gave her Howard's cane. At the last minute she decided to make a snack for Perry, so she put two poppy seed muffins from breakfast, some sliced cheddar cheese, and several crackers in a bag and added it to the basket.

But gathering supplies for the day wasn't what made her late.

When she went to the kitchen this morning, she asked Rosella if there were any messages. "*Nee*," her aunt said, scooping fluffy scrambled eggs with bits of sausage into a large bowl. "*Nee* calls yesterday."

"Oh." She was disappointed Maynard hadn't called. She wasn't surprised either. Work must have gotten in the way again. But that excuse was wearing thin, and she only picked at the muffins, sausage-scrambled eggs, and fruit slush *Aenti* Rosella had prepared for breakfast. Grace had left early for work, and *Onkel* Howard's head was buried in the paper while Rosella was upstairs stripping the bedsheets. Now that Daisy knew the real reason she was here, there was no point in discussing wedding plans anytime soon.

She leaned her cheek on her hand and stared at the golden muffin on her plate. Were *Mamm* and her aunt right? Was she mistaken about Maynard? Back in Dover when he was swamped with work, she would stop by the furniture shop, bring him a sweet or two that he always accepted and ate on the spot, and they could talk for a few minutes before he had to go back to his job. Even if they didn't get together very often, they at least interacted with each other. But there had been so little contact since she left Delaware. When he did say he missed her, she'd had to ask him first.

Mamm's words entered her mind. *"You shouldn't have to beg someone to love you."*

Was that what she'd been doing? Granted, she did a lot of things for Maynard and was the one who made sure they spent time together. He was always appreciative. Or she'd thought so. For the first time since she fell in love with him, genuine doubt started to creep in.

What she couldn't do was sit at the table and dwell on it. She had Ferman to attend to, and despite his surly attitude, she enjoyed taking care of him. It wasn't his fault he was crabby. If she were in that much pain, she would be just as irritable.

She quickly finished eating, got ready, told *Aenti* Rosella and *Onkel* Howard goodbye, and headed out the door. If she rushed, she would be on time. As she scurried to Perry's, she heard the phone ring in the shanty and almost ignored it, but she was only a few feet away and she assumed it was for one of her relatives. She dashed inside and grabbed the receiver. "Hello?"

"Hi, Daisy."

Stunned, she pulled the receiver away and stared at it for a second before pressing it against her ear again. "Maynard?"

"I have a few minutes before work if you want to talk."

He called her! She could barely believe it. Her smile was so wide, it hurt her cheeks.

"*Mamm* said she was tired of you calling."

Her smile vanished, and an ache appeared in her chest. "I told you she doesn't like me."

He didn't respond, and she thought he'd hung up when he finally said, "She doesn't like anybody, Daisy. It's not personal."

That tidbit of information surprised her, even though she had suspected that Neva was an unhappy woman. "I'm sorry."

"It's okay. *Daed* and I are used to it."

Daisy's heart squeezed. This was the most intimate detail he'd shared with her since . . . well, since ever, now that she thought about it.

"When are you coming home?"

She grinned and twirled the phone cord around her fingers. He really did miss her. "In about a month."

"*Gut*. I can't wait for one of your peach pies."

Was that all he could think about? Pie? He'd had one just a few days ago. Her smile slipped a little. "Of . . . of course."

"I wanted to clear things up with you about *Mamm*. I don't want you to be upset."

With his mother, or in general?

"I've got to *geh*, Daisy."

"But we just started talking." She sounded petulant, but she couldn't help it.

"I, uh, guess we could talk a little more."

Gut. She tried to think of something to say, but her mind automatically went to the thing they talked about most. "How's work going?"

"Busy. We've got a commercial order for custom-made chairs. One of the inns in Holmes County wants them for their new restaurant."

"That's nice." She waited for him to ask her a question.

Silence. Unwieldy, excruciating silence.

Then she realized she was late to Perry's. Oops. "I've got to *geh*, Maynard," she exclaimed. She couldn't keep Perry and Ferman waiting.

"You do?"

There was no time to ponder his surprised reaction. "Talk to you later. Bye." She hung up and ran next door. Fortunately, she was only a few minutes late.

Daisy put her mind back on Perry's laundry and decided to risk overstepping her bounds. When he left for work, he'd only asked two things of her—to make sure Ferman didn't escape, and . . .

A shiver went down her back, clear to her bare feet. He'd whispered his second request in her ear: *"Stay out of the butterfly room."* Which she would have done anyway. He didn't have to ask, and she shouldn't be thinking about his low and, dare she say, captivating voice.

"Laundry, laundry, laundry," she muttered. *Onkel* Howard had mentioned it would be windy and sunny all day. Perfect weather for drying clothes. Daisy figured she had a fifty-fifty chance of Perry being annoyed, or even mad at her for taking care of his clothes, and she decided to worry about that later. She also decided not to launder his unmentionables. He could take care of those himself.

She quickly sorted the clothing and got to work. But soon her thoughts turned to the forbidden butterfly room and all the beauty she'd seen in there, and she was tempted to go inside again. Not that she would. She'd given Perry her word, and it was locked now anyway. But given the chance, she could spend hours looking at his precisely perfect drawings.

While she worked on the laundry, she checked on Ferman twice. The second time he was asleep in the chair, the sudoku puzzle and pencil at the edge of his lap. Carefully she removed them and put them on the side table, then picked up the empty glass of tonic he'd dutifully drunk. She'd been prepared to argue with him today. Thankfully he was being more cooperative.

Daisy piled the clean, damp clothes back into the laundry basket and carried it outside to the aluminum clothesline pole in the back-yard. As soon as she hung up the first shirt, a pretty painted lady butterfly landed on the line, right at eye level. When she lifted her hand toward it, the butterfly fluttered to her finger.

Gazing at the insect, she inspected it more than she ever would have before she met Perry. She knew this wasn't the same butterfly—it couldn't be, considering how many butterflies like this she'd seen before. And butterflies weren't like dogs, cats, and other animals that returned to the same place over and over. Or were they? She'd have to ask Perry about that.

"Sorry to disturb you," she said, wiggling her fingers, "but I have to hang up Perry's pants."

The butterfly flew to her shoulder, just like the other one had to Perry. *How cute.* After a few seconds the butterfly took off, and Daisy finished hanging up the clothes.

Carrying the empty basket back to the house, she stopped at the patio. Four plastic chairs were randomly placed on the concrete pad. Maybe she would help Ferman come outside after lunch and get some sunshine if he was up to it. She could do her cross-stitch, he his puzzles, and they would have a nice, quiet afternoon before she started supper—a simple one this time. Baked chicken breasts, lightly seasoned rice, and cooked carrots. Hopefully Ferman would have a stronger appetite this evening.

A stray thought entered her mind as she went inside. *I wonder if Perry likes peach pie.*

Chapter 13

It was dusk by the time Perry neared home. Work had been harder than he anticipated, mostly because he didn't sleep well last night. The couch was decent enough, but the flat throw pillows weren't comfortable. He also wanted to make sure he didn't miss hearing Ferman if he needed anything, particularly help going to the bathroom. He wasn't going to let him fall on his watch.

He needn't have worried. Ferman slept through the night. Even if Perry was in a dead sleep, he would have heard him holler. He'd been the recipient of the old man shouting right in his face. That had been embarrassing, although after the fact, he chided himself for feeling that way. Modesty was important, but they were all adults. *Daisy had handled it well.*

The reins went slack in his hand. She kept surprising him, having turned out to be the ideal caretaker for Ferman. She refused to put up with any of his guff, and when he didn't eat much of her delicious supper, she wasn't put out at all. She didn't bat an eye while helping Perry move the heavy couch to his house so he would have a place to sleep. She'd even fluffed the pillows. And later when he'd fumbled through adjusting their pact, their discussion went well.

But what impressed him the most was the look of awe and wonder on her face when she was in his butterfly room. He'd expected her to think he was off his rocker, but she hadn't. Her reaction was the exact opposite of Ruby's, the woman who supposedly loved him. He shouldn't compare them, but he couldn't help it. And that's what caused his emotions to turn into tumbleweeds.

He could easily see himself letting Daisy back in the room, the two of them poring over his collection. He could even ask her to help him with the one-thousand-piece "Butterflies of North America" puzzle sitting on the bottom shelf of the bookcase, gathering dust. The puzzle was more for decoration than scientific information, and he'd purchased it on a whim but never got around to doing it. If they did the puzzle together, he could discuss the different butterflies and their habitats with her.

He halted his rambling thoughts and forced reality to set in. There was no point in sharing his hobby or doing puzzles. Daisy wasn't sticking around. She was going back to Dover in a few weeks, and then she would be with Maynard, the man she loved.

Besides, Perry wasn't interested in her. Or attracted. He had two goals in mind—get Ferman on his feet and his mother off his back. Daisy was assisting with both, and once those goals were met, they had no reason to be around each other. More importantly, he had no business interacting with a taken woman.

He'd do well to keep reminding himself of that.

Perry turned into the driveway and went to the barn. Then he groaned. He'd forgotten to go by Ferman's to get his clothes. Now he'd have to stop by after church tomorrow afternoon. Once the evening chores were done, he went inside through the back door. He'd taken off his boots and was walking into the kitchen when he smelled . . . furniture polish?

Daisy glanced up as he walked farther into the living room. She straightened, a small rag and a can of polish in her hand. She wiped off the leg of the side table and rose, her lips curving into a soft smile.

The most extraordinary and mystifying feeling traveled through him. Pleasurable too. He was home . . . and it felt more like a home than it ever had before. *Because of Daisy.*

The faint sound of a toilet flushing broke his stupor. He couldn't help but chuckle. "Let me guess?"

She grinned. "Supper will be ready soon."

Perry nodded. "I'll get him."

"*Nee* need, *bu.*"

He spun around to see Ferman shuffling with a cane. "Where did you get that?"

"From the harebrained Howard Hershberger," he quipped, then winked at Daisy before looking at Perry again. "Better get yourself cleaned up for our evening repast."

"Repast?"

"He's been doing crossword puzzles today." Daisy set the polish and rag in her basket on the floor next to the sofa.

"I'll take a quick shower." As he walked past Ferman, the old man leaned toward him.

"Remember your clothes this time."

Perry rolled his eyes, and Daisy's feather-light giggle made him smile. He started for his bedroom, but before he got to the door he was frowning. He'd forgotten about washing his clothes last night. He did have a clean pair of sweatpants and several T-shirts, along with his Sunday clothes for tomorrow. But he didn't have any work clothes ready for the following week. He'd have to wash and hang them tonight or wait until Monday after work to get it done. He wasn't going to break the Sabbath because of bad planning.

But when he opened the top dresser drawer, he saw clean work shirts next to the T-shirts. Then he opened the other drawers. All his clothes were freshly laundered and smelled great, although he noticed he was still low on underwear. He grinned. *Thanks, Daisy.*

Supper was a quiet affair, and Perry insisted Daisy join them. She was pleased that Ferman had eaten most of his meal, and perhaps that signaled his appetite was returning. Even though the food was on the bland side, Perry ate all of it. He also seemed deep in thought.

"May I be excused?" Ferman's eyes shifted from Daisy to Perry.

"*Ya,*" they said at the same time.

Perry met her gaze with a slight smile.

Uh-oh. She was getting that hot and cold feeling again. She jumped up and started clearing the dishes as Perry accompanied Ferman to help him with his bedtime routine.

As she cleaned the kitchen, the sensation went away, and for the first time since his call this morning, Maynard came to mind. It wasn't lost on her that this was the second day in a row that she hadn't ruminated on him or even wondered how he was doing at work. He'd even sounded a little surprised and disheartened when she had to cut their conversation short.

Now he knows how it feels.

She stilled. She shouldn't be petty about the man she loved. Giving her head a quick shake, she settled herself and finished the kitchen chores. When she was done, she went to the living room and started packing her basket.

"That was easy," Perry said as he entered the room. "I hardly had to help him tonight. If he keeps improving at this rate, he'll *geh* home soon."

She hid an unexpected stab of disappointment. Ferman wanted to go home. He'd made that abundantly clear. She'd only been taking care of him for two days, but she would miss coming over here. In a way, she was also tending to Perry by cleaning house, doing laundry, and cooking meals. He was fine on his own, but making his house a home had been nice. No, more than nice. It was satisfying.

"Before you *geh*," Perry said, "would you mind if Ferman went with us to church tomorrow? He's doing well, but I don't want him to be alone."

She smiled, setting her disappointment aside. "That's a great idea."

"There's one other thing." He shifted on his feet. "I've been thinking about our pact again. It seems lopsided to me. I'm getting more out of it than you are."

"That's not true." She set her basket back on the couch. "Telling *Mamm* that I considered dating someone else is all I need. And now I can."

He tilted his head. "Have you heard from Maynard yet?"

"*Ya.*"

He blinked, as if he wasn't expecting that answer. "When?" he asked.

"Yesterday." She didn't give him the details of the call. That wouldn't be right, and Perry hadn't asked. "I'm thinking about writing him another letter." Until now the thought hadn't occurred to her. But since their phone calls were so dull, maybe exchanging letters would make their communication livelier.

Wait. What if the reason their conversations were uninteresting was because she was uninteresting? *What if I'm the problem?* "Am I boring, Perry?"

He did a double take. "Who told you that?"

Good grief, why did she keep blurting out embarrassing questions? But the notion was sinking in. When she and Maynard were together, their conversations were brief, the topics were surface level, and there were more silent pauses than actual talking. If she were more exciting or a better conversationalist or . . . something . . . then maybe he would be more eager to communicate. *And eager to be more than friends.*

Daisy started to pace. She was going to lose him if she didn't change, or at least gain some understanding about the opposite sex and romance.

Perry intercepted her, dipping his head to look her in the eyes. "Who said you were boring?"

"*Nee* one, but . . ." She looked away, embarrassed anew. "I'm not very experienced." There, she said it.

His brow furrowed. "Experienced at what?"

"Romance. How to, um, initiate it." She was certain her entire body was as red as a poppy flower, but she couldn't stop plowing forward. "What do men want, Perry?"

The thumping sound of Ferman's cane made her jump and Perry turn around. "Forgot my salve," he said, limping into the living room, his gaze landing on the side table next to the chair. "Ah, there it is, right where I left it."

Daisy took the opportunity to grab her basket and flee. "Bye!" she said and hurried out the door, slowing down when she reached her aunt and uncle's driveway. Halting, she closed her eyes, humiliation washing over her. She had no business asking Perry such a question. Grace would have been a better choice. Even her *daed* or *Onkel*

Howard would have made more sense, although she would never ask them such a personal question that would reveal her ignorance when it came to romantic relationships.

With a sigh, she opened her eyes and started walking again, the streetlamp down the road giving her enough faint light to guide her steps, although she didn't need it. What she did need was her head examined, and she prayed Perry had somehow misheard her ridiculous query. If he had, it wouldn't come up again. And if he hadn't . . .

Daisy groaned. She didn't want to think about that.

⌐◞◟⌐

The next morning, Daisy smoothed her white apron over her navy blue church dress as she paced in the living room a half hour earlier than necessary. She was jump-out-of-her skin nervous about going to church in Birch Creek with Perry, even though she was truthful when she said she wanted to meet his family.

"When are you going over to Perry's?" Grace asked, entering the living room. She was also dressed for church, but she and her parents were going to a service in Millersburg since Marigold wasn't having service today. Birch Creek and Marigold's services were on opposite Sundays, and Grace's family often went to different districts in the area when their home church wasn't in session. The taxi would be picking them up in a few minutes.

"In a little while." Daisy kept her answer vague. Her cousin didn't need to find out how nervous she really was.

"It's just you and him then?" she said with a teasing smile.

Daisy scowled. "Ferman's going too." She sounded a little snappy, but she wasn't in the mood for ribbing, no matter how good-natured it was.

"You're kind of touchy this morning."

"I'm sorry." Daisy sat down on the couch and smoothed her apron again.

Grace joined her. "You also seem nervous."

So much for concealing her apprehension. She was tempted to explain the source of her nerves—her conversation with Perry last night. But she needed to keep that embarrassing moment to herself. Instead, she admitted her other concern. "I'm worried how his family is going to react."

Grace put her arm around Daisy's shoulders and gave her a squeeze. "Just be yourself. Everything will be fine."

That was good advice. Managing a smile, she said, "*Danki.*"

Aenti Rosella came down the stairs, followed by a less spunky *Onkel* Howard. "Is the taxi here yet?" She went to the coat rack and put on her cape.

Onkel Howard took his black hat and plopped it on his head. "Rosella, I told you we weren't running late—"

Honk!

She shot her husband a victorious look as she grabbed her black bonnet. "Enjoy your day in Birch Creek," she said to Daisy with a knowing smile.

Grace gave her a quick hug. "I want details tonight."

And just like that, her nerves returned. "Details?"

"Bye!"

They rushed out of the house and Daisy heard the car exit the driveway. That left her alone with her thoughts, and she wasn't preparing her mind for church like she should be. In a few minutes she would leave for Perry's, and Grace's small pep talk faded away, replaced by increasing jitters. Her question to him didn't just reveal her inexperience with men, it also sounded desperate. *Because I am.* She was desperate for her and Maynard to be a couple, and while she'd been confident that after they had "the talk," they would be, now she wasn't sure that she had the skills or words to convince him that they should be together.

Daisy glanced at the clock. *Time to go.* Her stomach flip-flopped. Mortification wasn't an excuse for missing church, so she rose from the couch, took her jacket from the coatrack, and clutched her purse, deciding to pretend her discussion with Perry last night had never happened. She would figure out on her own how to talk to men and be an engaging conversational partner. *Somehow.*

Chapter 14

Perry managed to tune out Daisy and Ferman as he drove to Birch Creek, but it wasn't easy. They'd been continuously chatting since she climbed into the back seat of his buggy. Last night after she left, he put away his tools and cleaned out his vehicle, scrubbing down the seats. He didn't want Daisy's church clothes to get dirty. Oh, and Ferman's either. The old man was wearing one of Perry's church outfits, and while it was a little baggy and long on him, he was presentable.

Ferman was spirited this morning, and from the moment they pulled out of the driveway, he had plied Daisy with questions. Perry wasn't exactly sure what they were talking about. He'd been distracted since he saw Daisy approach from the Hershberger home wearing her navy dress, white apron, and matching sweater. *Whoa.*

He tried to ignore the sudden thumping sensation in his chest as she neared, stopping when she reached the buggy. And he couldn't stop staring when he should have jumped out and helped her inside. By the time he got a grip on his senses, she was already in the buggy and sitting next to Ferman.

Perry rubbed his eyebrow, irritated with himself. Ever since last night when Daisy had asked if she was boring—she wasn't, not even close—and followed that up with her unexpected question about the male psyche, he couldn't think straight. He couldn't sleep either. Not a single wink. He was no stranger to occasional insomnia, yet last night was different. Because it wasn't just her innocent questions that had him counting sheep.

He couldn't believe she thought she was boring. Even though she denied that anyone had said so, she'd somehow gotten that wrong idea in her head, and he wondered if Maynard was involved. He was surprised she'd heard from him. Perry didn't know the guy, but for some reason Maynard bugged him.

Then she admitted her lack of knowledge and experience when it came to relationships. It wasn't her admission that affected him, it was the discouragement and shame in her eyes. She shouldn't be so down on herself. The woman he knew wasn't boring, and she sure didn't need to be ashamed of being naive. For a split second he wanted to comfort her, and not just with words. He wanted to take her in his arms and soothe her. And that wasn't a good thing.

He recalibrated his thoughts, needing to concentrate on wor-shiping the Lord and not on how Daisy had made him feel. Or was making him feel. Wow, was he confused. When they were close to Birch Creek, Daisy's and Ferman's voices were distant as he was finally able to somewhat prepare his mind and heart for the upcoming service.

That ended when he turned into his brother Mose's driveway. His family was hosting the service in their barn, and he saw several of his brothers congregating outside the entrance. Reality hit him. Despite the fact that he and Daisy were just making an appearance, the thought that his family—all fifty-eight members of them—would see them together made his stomach spin. He reminded himself that they didn't have to pretend to be anything but themselves, and they especially didn't have to fake having feelings for each other.

Feelings . . . for Daisy . . .

"Hey!" Ferman hollered from the back seat. "Watch how you're parking this thing!"

The high wood-slat fence bordering Mose's yard to the left of the driveway came into view and he was nearly too close to it. The horse sharply halted on his own and Perry blanched. His mind was so scattered, he wasn't paying attention. "Sorry," he muttered, engaging the brake and giving himself a mental shake. When he turned around, Ferman was already halfway out of the buggy.

"Wait!" he yelled and jumped out. All he needed was for Ferman to splat on the ground. He could hear the man's long-suffering sigh. No doubt the entire county did. Perry couldn't stop a smile. Now that Ferman was feeling better, he was starting to act like a drama queen. After Perry helped him out of the vehicle and made sure Ferman was steady on his feet, he turned to see Daisy getting out of the buggy.

He froze. Should he help her down? She might not appreciate it, considering her feelings for Maynard. *Maynard.* Talk about a splash of cold water.

"Excuse me." Daisy, already out of the buggy, slipped past him and went to Ferman's side. The two of them headed for the barn without him.

Hold up. Wasn't the point of coming to Birch Creek for his family to see him with her? He secured his horse before catching up to them, making sure he was walking next to Daisy.

"There's Aden Troyer," Ferman said, peeling off to hobble toward the community's resident beekeeper. Aden's family also owned one of three small grocery stores in the area, Schrock Grocery.

"I didn't know you knew someone in Birch Creek," Perry said.

Ferman cast a look over his shoulder. "You didn't ask."

Daisy moved a little closer. "Should we let him *geh* by himself?"

Perry watched Ferman walk. His gait was fairly stable, more so than it had been day before yesterday. There was something about being around people that seemed to give Ferman renewed energy. Aden was only a few steps away, and he reached him just fine.

"Looks like we don't need to," she said, chuckling. It sounded sweet and light. *Just like her.* The tension on her face when he first picked her up had disappeared, and she seemed her normal self. That made him relax a little too.

"Ferman's quite the character," he said as the old man pumped Aden's hand.

"*Ya.*" When she looked up at Perry, her grin dropped, and she seemed apprehensive again.

Their height difference forced him to bend a little so she could hear him. "Are you okay?" he said, lowering his voice. Glancing around, he saw his relatives interspersed through the crowd of church-goers, but his mother wasn't in sight and his family didn't seem to notice he was there, much less with Daisy. "There's still time to back out. I can get Ferman and take you home."

Without hesitation she shook her head.

The fact that she was partly here for herself, but mostly for him wasn't unappreciated. Would Ruby have helped him out like this? He already knew the answer. A resounding no.

"Hi, Perry," Margaret said.

He startled. His sister-in-law seemingly appeared out of nowhere. Or he hadn't sensed her approach because he was so focused on Daisy. Wow, he'd never been this unsettled. "Uh, hi."

She looked at Daisy, a flicker of surprise in her eyes. "*Gute morgen.*

Nice to see you. I saw Ferman talking with Aden. I take it he's feeling better?"

"Thanks to you," Daisy said. "He's followed all your directions, and he's in a lot less pain."

Margaret's smile was soft. "That's wonderful."

"Daisy's been taking *gut* care of him," Perry added.

"We both have." She touched his arm, only to quickly pull away.

Nearing forty, Margaret was still one of the prettiest women in Birch Creek. She arched a perfect eyebrow at him, not bothering to hide her curiosity.

So it begins. Perry touched Daisy's elbow. "We should get inside," he said, nodding toward the barn.

"*Ya.*" Margaret's gaze bounced from his to Daisy's, then back again. "You don't want to be late."

Perry didn't wait for Margaret to say anything else, and the three of them headed to the barn, his hand still on Daisy's elbow. When he and Ruby dated, they had mutually agreed to pretend not to know each other at church service. Being this showy went against his grain. Besides, she touched him first, although by the way she drew back so quickly, he was almost positive she hadn't done it intentionally.

The only way for his and Daisy's pact to work—and to end— would be for everyone to see them together, and being this close to her might grab their collective attention. Thus far, only Margaret had noticed. Fifty-seven more to go.

"Would you like to sit with us, Daisy?" Margaret asked.

"That would be nice." She left with Margaret to sit on the women's side of the church.

Unable to stop himself, he watched her walk away.

"Hmm."

Perry spun around to see Ferman sidle up to him. "What?"

"Oh, nothing. Time for church." He strolled into Mose's barn as if he owned the place.

Perry started to follow him, then stopped short. Did Ferman see him holding Daisy's elbow? From the twinkle in the old man's eye, Perry was sure he did.

Daisy glanced at Ferman. His snores had filled Perry's buggy for the last half hour on their trip back to Marigold. She glanced at Perry, and he seemed tired too. It had been a long day for all of them.

She shifted on the seat and looked at the passing landscape. After a slightly chilly morning, the afternoon was warm. This was her first trip in a buggy since she arrived in Marigold, and she was entranced by the rolling hills and thick green grass. Ferman had been so chatty during the trip to Birch Creek this morning that she didn't have a chance to fully enjoy the scenery.

Smiling, she breathed in the fresh air. Today had gone better than she thought. At first when Margaret introduced her to her sisters-in-law—eight in all, plus Junia, who was a cousin-in-law and used to live in Marigold—she thought she might be in over her head. They were all friendly. And curious, that was obvious. When she saw Miriam, who was sitting at the end of the row leaning forward and giving Daisy an enthusiastic wave, she waved back but internally winced. There was no turning back now.

But after the service, the Bontragers put her at ease, and she enjoyed getting to know them. She was concerned that she might have to field some questions about her and Perry, and she planned to insist they were just *friends*, making sure to emphasize it the way Perry had whenever he brought up the word.

She needn't have worried. His family was more interested in hearing about her life in Dover. "Usually we vacation in Pinecraft," Miriam said. "Perhaps we should try Delaware next summer."

"The beaches are a lot of fun, but Dover isn't as pretty as it is here," Daisy said over a meal of cold sandwiches, chips, pickles, Chow Chow, and a variety of desserts. The lunch meat on the sandwiches was the best she'd ever tasted, and she discovered that it was from Perry's brother Nelson, who was a butcher in Marigold.

During lunch she couldn't stop sneaking looks at Perry. He didn't seem to be enjoying himself as much as Daisy was, and she knew it was because of their pact. She wished she had never come up with this idea or made the agreement. Not for her sake, but for his. He'd already had reservations with misrepresenting their relationship, and she noticed he stayed close to one small group of men—his younger brothers, Mose, Mahlon, and Elam. She couldn't tell the twins apart, and they looked very similar to his older twin brothers, Zeb and Zeke. Elam was easy to spot—he was the tallest and the most outgoing of all the Bontrager men. Perry was clearly the most introverted. *And the handsomest.*

She inwardly sighed. There she went again, noticing Perry's looks when she should be thinking about Maynard. He was good-looking too, in a different way. And when did she become so enthralled with outer appearances? Then again, Perry's personality was appealing too. And just because she noticed his attractiveness and fine character, it didn't mean she wasn't devoted to Maynard. He was the one God wanted her to be with, not Perry. The tension eased from her shoulders.

When they reached Perry's, she intended to exit the buggy and go straight to her aunt and uncle's house. Ferman was managing fine, and he and Perry didn't need her hovering for the rest of the day. Once she was at Grace's, she would write Maynard another letter, then spend the rest of the afternoon cross-stitching.

The horse halted, and the lurching motion woke up Ferman. It also made him groan.

Oh nee. She hadn't even thought about him overdoing it this morning. Now that he wasn't in excruciating pain, she could see how extroverted he was, talking and laughing with everyone. He hadn't expressed any difficulty getting into the buggy when it was time to leave Mose's either.

"Are you okay?" Perry asked him, looking as concerned as Daisy felt.

"I'm fine." He reached for his cane and winced. "All right, maybe not fine. I'm hurtin', to tell the truth."

Perry hopped out of the buggy and dashed to the opposite side to help Ferman out.

Frowning, Daisy followed the men into the house. Her personal plans could wait. She wasn't about to leave now, not until she knew Ferman was okay.

"Back in bed, once again," Ferman muttered as he stared at Perry's bedroom ceiling. His grousing didn't hold its usual punch, however. How could it when Margaret's concoctions and the anti-inflammatory he'd taken made his pain subside? And he had to admit, the boy had an awfully comfortable bed.

Closing his eyes, he relaxed underneath the soft sheets and quilt. He hadn't expected to enjoy himself today as much as he had, figuring his hip would get in the way of having a good time. It was great to see Aden Troyer again, having met him through his honey-selling business a few years ago when Lovina was still alive. He also had a chance to meet new people, and the Bontragers seemed to be a quality bunch. Not surprising, since he'd always thought well of Nelson and Jesse. They weren't perfect people—no one was. Lovina had come close. But even she had her flaws. *Lord knows I have plenty of them.*

He was discovering firsthand what an exceptional man Perry was, and Daisy already had a special place in his heart. Not that he would reveal that tidbit to anyone. Or even out loud to himself. He respected her backbone, her refusal to let his stubborn petulance get to her. But there sure was something going on with those two, and that had become fully obvious today.

When Daisy climbed into the buggy, the tension was thicker than a brick wall. He'd tried to diffuse the unease by talking to her, and that had helped somewhat, although he noticed that as soon as they pulled into Mose's driveway the awkwardness returned.

Then there was that business of the two of them acting so cozy before church, only for the chumminess to disappear on the way home. Ferman had already been surprised that she had joined them for church. It was almost as if Perry and Daisy wanted everyone in Birch Creek to think they were a couple, only to drop the facade as soon as they left.

Ferman's inquiring mind came to the fore. What kind of game were they playing? Even when they had helped him to the house and fussed over him, plying him with medicine and making sure he was tucked into bed like an overgrown baby—he was starting not to mind all that much—he hadn't sensed there was anything between them. No connection, and definitely not a spark of attraction.

The two of them had it all backward for some reason. Typically,

Amish couples kept their relationship a secret from the rest of the community, even their own families, until they were ready to announce their engagement. Sometimes the lovebirds weren't so covert, like Grace and Kyle. He and Lovina had been in the middle—when they were dating, they didn't exactly shout it from the barn roof, but they also weren't concerned if folks figured it out. Many of them had been aware they were together by the time they made their announcement in church. And they had spent plenty of private, enjoyable moments with each other out of sight of everyone else.

Not Daisy and Perry, though. When they weren't close to each other, like during the service, preparing for lunch, or separately visiting with others, he had seen them exchange ardent looks. And Ferman spotted Perry putting his palm on the back of Daisy's waist as he assisted her in the buggy. But after that? *Nix.* Almost like they were barely acquaintances.

So very, *very* strange.

"Mind your own business, you old coot." Lovina's firm but loving warning went through his mind. If he were smart, he would heed those words. He needed to focus on getting better, not wondering about his caretakers. He needed to go back home.

To an empty house. To memories, both happy and sad. To manage a household and yard by himself. *That's what I want, right?*

He didn't understand his hesitation. He usually didn't like being fussed over, not even by Lovina. But he hadn't realized how much he'd missed living with other people. The intense arguments he had with Junior before he and Polly Ann moved away were fading in his mind a little bit, and the knowledge that she always resented him didn't hurt as much. It was slightly possible that he may or may not have always been easy to live with.

There had been times when he and Junior had gotten along. Like those cold winter nights the three of them would be in the living room, the fireplace cloaking them in a cozy blanket of warmth, he and Junior playing checkers and drinking apple cider while Polly Ann played with her yarn—although she called it knitting. It wasn't as congenial as it had been when it had been only him, Lovina, and Junior, but it had been pleasant. Homey. Maybe even . . . loving.

He turned over onto his healthy hip. That was something else he hadn't done in a long time—lie on his good side. Margaret's fine doctoring was to thank for that. Their brief conversation right after church service came to mind.

"*You should really consider taking your doctor's advice,*" she had said after he told her he was on the mend. "*The medicine and rest are only temporary fixes. They aren't going to solve your problem.*"

"*Out of the question,*" he responded, then wished he hadn't sounded so defiant. She was only trying to help. Like Perry, Daisy, and his doctor.

"*Then you'll need to permanently retire from work. I'm glad to see you're using a cane, but you still might fall if you don't get your hip tended to. Do you have family you could move in with?*"

Ferman had hidden his frown, but he didn't have to in the privacy of Perry's bedroom. Moving in with Junior was also out of the question. He didn't want to go back to fighting with him or dealing with Polly's mercurial moods. He suspected those were worse now that she was expecting.

But what if he was part of the problem? *Or the whole problem.* Now that he wasn't hurting, maybe his perpetual state of pain was a contributing factor to the rift in his family.

His eyes fluttered shut, the herbal tea he'd drunk a little while ago taking effect. Even if his attitude was better and he would be less of a grump to live with, he wasn't going to be a burden to anyone. Not his son, or Perry and Daisy. He needed to get well and go back home.

Even if deep, deep down, a part of him didn't want to.

Chapter 15

Perry drummed his fingers against the dining room table. Once Ferman was properly tended to and put to bed, Daisy went back to the Hershbergers, barely saying goodbye. Over the next few minutes, he alternately paced, sat on the sofa, sat down at the table, and then paced one more time. He considered going into his butterfly room. Usually, he could relax there. But thinking about that stirred up thoughts of Daisy, so he didn't. Finally, he couldn't stand being in the house anymore and went outside.

Today couldn't have gone better, and not just from their pact perspective. He loved his big family and he liked everyone in the Birch Creek community. He just wished he didn't find large groups of people draining. For once, though, the church crowd hadn't bothered him, possibly because he'd stayed close to his younger brothers and didn't force himself to mix and mingle . . . and probably because most of his concentration was centered on maintaining the facade with Daisy. From what he could tell, he had succeeded.

"I should have trusted you all along," Mamm had said before he left Mose's. She was the picture of happiness. *"Daisy is a lovely* maedel. *"*

Misson accomplished. And he should be happy about that. Their pact was fulfilled, and everything was back to normal, or it would be when Ferman healed up and went home. Perry wished he'd paid more attention to him. If he had, maybe he would have picked up on the old man's fatigue and pain earlier in the day. Then again, it had been hard to pay attention to anyone except Daisy.

He headed for the back of his yard to pace out his butterfly garden that was overgrown with weeds and grass. The warm afternoon sun was welcome but did little to settle his confused mood. Due to Daisy's hasty departure, he assumed she'd changed her mind about wanting an answer to the question she'd asked him last night. Fine. He still didn't know how to answer it, so there was some relief there.

There was no relief from the strange feelings that kept popping up without warning. He knew the soft, yearning looks she gave him were fake. She was just keeping up her end of their pact. But he couldn't stop his very real reaction to them. He'd genuinely believed Ruby had killed any possible romantic desires, so why was he having them now, and for a woman who was in love with another man?

A painted lady fluttered around him. When she landed on his shoulder he couldn't believe it. *Lady.* He was sure it was her, and that was confirmed when she stayed put as he continued to walk. He hadn't seen her in a day or two and tried not to think the worst had happened, choosing the optimistic assumption that she had moved on to better food sources.

"Hello, Lady," he said softly. "Welcome back."

She flittered off in the direction of the Hershbergers' and he followed her trajectory and saw Daisy sitting under the tree again. Her legs were stretched out in front of her, and she'd changed from her church dress and white apron to a light blue dress.

Lady had disappeared, but that didn't mean she wasn't hovering nearby. He could go over to the tree and have a look around to see if she was still in the Hershbergers' yard. Yeah, he could totally do that.

While he walked over, he expected Daisy to see him coming. When she kept staring straight ahead, her cross-stitch project halfway off her lap, he assumed she was sleeping. It took everything he had not to look at her bare feet. *Or bare ankles.*

His footsteps crunched several dry leaves, bringing her out of her daze.

Her eyes widened and she jumped to her feet, the cross-stitch hoop hitting the ground. "Is something wrong with Ferman?"

"*Nee.* He's sound asleep." Perry shoved his hands into the pockets of his black church trousers. He hadn't even thought to change his clothes. He did leave his black hat on the table.

"*Gut.*" Her relieved gaze locked onto his.

Those eyes. Beautiful didn't begin to describe them. He also didn't understand how the more he was around her, the lovelier she became. They weren't friends, he wasn't interested in her, and she was in love with someone else. He repeated the words in his head. They made zero impact.

"Did you need something, Perry?"

Her innocuous question brought him back to the real world. "Have you seen Lady?"

"She's back?" He listened as she explained how a painted lady had landed on her hand while she was doing his laundry the other day. "Do you think that was her too?"

"Possibly."

"How can you tell?" She picked her cross-stitch hoop off the ground and brushed a few blades of stray grass off it.

"Years of studying butterfly wings. Lady has one less spot on her left wing than the right. That's what makes her identifiable."

"Really? I never would have noticed." Daisy looked around. "Do you think she'll come back again?"

"I don't know." He had to be honest. "I couldn't tell how old she was when I found her. Butterflies don't have a very long life cycle."

"Oh." She frowned, a touch of sadness in her tone. "So you think she might . . ."

"I don't think about it at all."

Daisy nodded. "Then I won't either."

They stood for a moment, and the awkwardness that had been between them off and on today returned. He thought about going back home without saying anything else. But that wouldn't be right. After what she had done for him today, he needed to address last night's topic. Suddenly, after hours of trying to figure it out, he knew what to say. *Thank you, Lord.* "About your question—"

"That's okay. Forget I brought it up." She started to walk away.

Perry lightly grasped her arm. "I have an answer for you."

Daisy wanted to shrivel up and tuck away somewhere. She started to ask him what question he was referring to, but that would make her look foolish. She would also be lying, and there had been enough of that today. She'd even lied to herself that the sultry looks he'd given her after church were real. A couple of times when their gazes met, she thought she'd have to grab an unused paper plate and fan herself.

Then there was the incredible way he simply *looked*. Pants slung low on his waist, his crisp white shirt was a little wrinkled, and one black suspender was slightly askew on his left shoulder. His *broad* shoulder. *Double sigh.*

"Daisy?"

Her wits returned. There was no disputing how fine Perry filled out a shirt, church or otherwise. There was also no question that the glances he'd given her were part of their pact. Nothing else. And that was good because she was in love with Maynard.

Maynard. Oh, last night's question. Right. "You don't have to answer it if you don't want to." She dug her two big toes into the grass.

"Do you still want me to?" He pulled his hands out of his pockets.

Say no. Say no. "*Ya.*" The word burst forth like it had been kept under pressure. So much for letting them both off the hook. For some reason she couldn't get out of her own way. And she was very, *very* curious. Oh well, she might as well ignore her self-consciousness and press on. This was the only chance she'd have to get some inside information about the male psyche without going to her *daed* or *onkel*. *Ew.* She sat back down on the grass and looked up at him. "So . . . what *do* men want?"

"You said you and Maynard are friends." He parked himself across from her. "How long have you known him?"

"Eighteen months." She used to know the number of days too, but she couldn't recall that right now.

"What do you usually do together?"

When she told him about their occasional suppers, her visits to his shop, and the few young adult activities they did with their service group, she inwardly frowned. She and Maynard didn't exactly have an exciting friendship either.

Thankfully, Perry didn't point that out. "Men can get into a rut. Or so I've been told."

She leaned forward, fascinated. This was valuable information. "By who?"

He glanced away, as if he were mulling something over. Then he said, "They also like a challenge."

She didn't acknowledge that he bypassed her question. Surely, he had his reasons. "What kind of challenge?"

"Depends on the guy." He leaned on his side. "Have you ever thought about playing hard to get?"

His answer surprised her. She'd assumed the direct approach would be necessary, thus her decision to have "the talk" with him when she went back to Dover. "*Nee*," she said. "I wouldn't know how."

"You could start by not writing to him. Or calling him."

"Oh, I couldn't do that. What if he forgets about me?"

"He won't, Daisy from Dover. You're pretty unforgettable." He cleared his throat, his gaze darting away. "If you have to write to him, then tell him about your life here and how much fun you're having." He glanced at her again. "You are having *some* fun, aren't you?"

She nodded and smiled. "I've enjoyed spending time with my *familye*, even though we've all been busy. Meeting Ferman has been a treat."

He laughed. "I wouldn't exactly call it that," he said. "But definitely tell Maynard he is."

"You've been so kind to give up your bed, Perry."

Shrugging, he said, "Anyone would do the same."

Would Maynard? Of course he would. Only the most selfish person wouldn't give up their own comfort for a high-spirited elderly man with a bad hip. Still, it didn't diminish what Perry had done for Ferman.

"What else should I tell him?" she asked, getting back on topic.

"You could talk about Lady and the Railway Diner, along with anything else you can think of. If he hears how you're enjoying life without him, he might—"

"Get jealous." She was starting to understand where he was going with his advice.

"Maybe—"

"Why didn't I think of this before?" She snapped her fingers. "If he misses me and thinks I'm having fun without him, he'll realize his true feelings. Perry, you're a genius!"

Perry was no genius, but he was out of his depth, and he wondered if him giving her romantic counsel was like the blind leading the blind. He had only seriously dated one woman, so he wasn't exactly an expert. He was also perplexed by her bond, or lack of it, with Maynard.

From her description of their relationship, it didn't sound like they spent much time together or had anything in common. Still, she was insistent that there were feelings on both sides, and he had to take her word for it. He didn't have the credentials to judge anyone else's relationship when his one and only had combusted. Yet Daisy shouldn't have to manipulate Maynard to miss her or be interested in her. He already should be.

Perry was right about two things, though. One—men certainly did get into ruts. Ruby had accused him of that several times when he spent more time with his butterflies than with her. He was also correct about men wanting a challenge. But somehow that morphed into Daisy thinking he was encouraging her to make Maynard jealous. Which he wasn't. Was he?

She clasped her hands together and smiled. "I should tell him about us too. That would make him really envious, *ya*?"

"Uh—"

"I'm going to do that right now." She leapt to her feet. Clutching her embroidery hoop, she started for the Hershberger house.

Scrambling to his feet, he quickly intercepted her, prepared to tell her his advice was stupid and she shouldn't follow it. "Daisy, I . . ."

He lost his words as she looked up at him, all wide-eyed innocence and naivete. Maybe Maynard deserved some discomfort for neglecting her. Just the thought of him hurting her in any way made anger flare inside him. "I'll help you write the letter."

"You will? Oh, Perry, *danki*! Can we do that now?"

"Sure," he replied, a bit dumbfounded at himself. *What am I doing?* "I've got paper and pen at my house."

She grabbed his hand and led him home, basically dragging him along. He didn't resist.

He also wondered if he was making the biggest mistake of his life.

Chapter 16

Dear Maynard,

Hi. How are you? I am fine. I am having a good time in Marigold. It is fun here. There are a lot of things to do. I like doing them. My cousin is fine. My aunt and uncle are also fine. Tomorrow it will be sunny and windy. The grass is very green—

Daisy tossed the pen down. Talk about boring. She was putting herself to sleep. "I've never been *gut* at writing," she admitted.

Perry leaned over and scanned the few words she had written. Ferman was still asleep, and after Perry had given her the paper and pen from one of the kitchen drawers, they sat next to each other at the table, and she went to work.

He pushed the letter back to her, his mouth slightly downturned. "It's kind of . . ."

"Uninspiring?"

"I was going to say bland, but let's *geh* with that."

She sighed. "I know you suggested things to write about, but I don't know how to say them."

He was looking at her, and she could tell he was deep in thought. Then he took the paper and pen and started writing.

Dear Maynard,

Daisy scooted closer to him.

I'm having the best time in Marigold! Hanging out with Grace has been amazing. I met her boyfriend, Kyle. He's really cute!

"Hey." Daisy grabbed the pen and scratched out the last line. "I never said he was cute."

"Maynard doesn't know that." He took the pen from her and continued:

But he's not the only mann I've met. There's one guy I've been spending a lot of time with. His name is Ferman. He's—

"If you say 'cute,' I'm going to bop you."

Perry wagged his index finger at her. "No more editorializing."

—an older gentleman who has a bad hip and I'm taking care of him. He tells the best stories! I could listen to him for hours!

She was prepared to seize the pen from him again, but she didn't have to. As he continued writing, he was somehow making her time in Marigold sound more exciting than it actually was. It wasn't exactly what he was saying, but the words and tone he was using, along with lots of exclamation points. He even added Lady in the mix, although she noticed he didn't say anything about his butterfly room. Or himself. Time to correct that.

"My turn." Daisy took the pen and started writing.

I haven't told you the best part! Grace has a neighbor named Perry. He's—

Her pen remained poised over the paper.

"He's what?" Perry leaned in close.

Mmm, he smelled good, like fresh air and cedar soap. He was also making her lose her train of thought. What was she about to write? Smart? Handsome? *Ravishing?*

Goodness, she couldn't write that. Not to Maynard. Although that might make him green-eyed.

Ravish—

Quickly she scratched out the word, hoping Perry hadn't seen it. She also obliterated the word *he's* and wrote:

I'm helping him solve his lady problems.

Perry face-palmed.

"What?" She looked at the sentence. "It's true."

"You don't have to put it *that* way." He reached for the pen.

She raised it above her head and grinned.

He chuckled and tried again.

"Ha!" She held the pen as high as she could.

"You do realize," he said, leaning forward with a smile, "that my arm is longer than yours."

"Maybe so, but are you faster than me?" Giggling, she popped up from the chair and darted toward the door. She'd barely made it two steps before he grabbed her around the waist, making her squeal with delight.

He pulled her down onto his lap . . . and they both froze.

Daisy's chest rose and fell as she realized she was touching his bicep. Unable to resist, she applied light pressure against him with her fingertips.

His hand tightened at the side of her hip, his eyes turning smoky blue.

"Perry?" she whispered, feeling strangely lightheaded. Then his hand slid to her other hip, making her breath catch. *Oh my.*

He promptly deposited her back on the chair, then shot up from his seat, tossing the letter in front of her. "You can finish it now."

"But . . ."

His back was already to her, and he was almost in the kitchen. Granted that wasn't far, but he seemed eager to get away. *From me.*

"Perry," she said, her voice sounding small. "Did I do something wrong?"

<hr/>

Perry gripped the counter, a muscle twitching in his jaw. No, she hadn't done anything wrong. This was his fault and he marveled at how quickly a little fun and games had turned into something else. Something that had felt good. Oh *so* good. And that was the problem.

His problem. Not Daisy's.

He blanked his expression and turned around. "*Nee.* Everything's fine. I just needed . . ." He grabbed a glass out of the cabinet, nearly fumbling it out of his hand before filling it with water and draining it dry. "A drink." He set it on the counter with a loud *clink*.

"Oh."

"Ferman will be getting up soon," he said, opening the pantry. "I'm sure he'll be hungry."

"I can help."

"*Nee*—"

"I think you're mad at me."

He blew out a breath. "I'm not mad."

"You're acting strange, though."

He was, and he needed to stop. She was so naive he knew she wouldn't understand what had just happened between them, even if he could explain it to her. He wasn't sure that was possible since he was so bemused himself. All he knew was, in that moment, when he had experienced her feather-light touch on his arm and felt how perfect she fit on his lap, he realized it wouldn't have taken much for him to draw her close and—

Get it together! The best way to do that was to pretend everything was normal. "You should finish your letter and send it to Maynard ASAP." There. Mentioning Maynard a few times would cool him off.

"*Ya*," she said, her eyes turning bright. "I have to recopy it, of course. He knows my handwriting."

Perry nodded. Maynard. This was about—ugh—him. "You can do that here if you want." Good. He was sounding more like himself. More in control.

"I should make Ferman some supper first," she said.

"I've got it handled, Daisy. *Geh* finish Maynard's letter."

The gleam in her eyes disappeared. "All right. But I'll be back early in the morning." She went to the table and picked up the pad of paper, tearing off a sheet.

"Keep the pad," he said, nosing into the pantry again, not just for Ferman's benefit but to keep his sanity.

"Are you sure?"

He squeezed his eyes shut. "*Ya*, Daisy. I'm sure." He opened his eyes and shuffled cans about.

"Okay. Tell Ferman *gute nacht*, and that I'll see him tomorrow."

Perry moved a can of baked beans to the side. "Will do."

When she finally left, he slouched against the pantry door. Hopefully she had an inkling about how to handle Maynard, at least in the short term. Which meant Perry had fulfilled his part of the pact. Time for everything to go back to status quo.

"Did ya run her off?"

Perry jumped at the sound of Ferman's voice. "Don't do that."

"Do what?"

"Sneak up on me." He nearly slammed the pantry door and stalked out of the kitchen. The pad and pen were still on the table, but the letter was gone.

"*Bu*, how could I sneak up on anyone using this?" Ferman held up his cane. "I thought I heard you and Daisy out here."

Perry stilled, then slowly turned around. "What did you hear?"

"Voices." Ferman hobbled toward him. "Loud voices. Couldn't make out what you were saying, though." He leaned on the cane, his expression surly as usual. By the barely perceptible lift of one gray bushy eyebrow and the glint of nosiness in his eyes, it was clear he was snooping for info.

Perry swiped the pad and pen off the table. "She was writing a letter to . . . folks back home."

"Ah." Ferman lowered himself onto one of the wooden chairs.

187

"Bet there's some homesickness settling in there. She's probably missing her beau too."

He spun around. "What?"

"Oh, I'm sure a *maedel* as pretty and kind as Daisy would have a *mann* back home."

"Doesn't matter if she does," Perry muttered, going back into the kitchen. "You hungry?"

"Famished."

Perry grabbed a jar from the pantry and banged it on the counter. "Peanut butter and jelly it is."

Ferman lowered himself onto the chair at the table, wincing a little. Although his hip was aching, the rest had done him good, and the pain was tolerable. While Perry rattled about in the kitchen, slamming cabinet doors and banging drawers as he made their supper, Ferman digested what he'd recently witnessed after waking up to use the facilities.

Perry and Daisy didn't hear him stirring about, and soon it became clear why. He'd heard Daisy say something about Perry and "lady problems," and when he poked his head around the corner to investigate, he saw them sitting next to each other at the table. Perry's back was to him, but he saw Daisy's flirty smile and sparkling eyes. Ferman almost laughed out loud when they started chasing each other around the table like a couple of *kinner*. It was good to see Perry happy and relaxed, and it was no surprise that Daisy could make him feel that way.

But he couldn't keep ignoring nature's call, so he hobbled to the bathroom. When he came back out, Daisy was gone, and Perry was in an unpleasant mood. Ferman wondered what happened in those few minutes to cause such a swift change in his attitude.

Still, he was firmly convinced that Perry Bontrager had finally, *finally* realized what a gem Daisy was. That was clear from Perry's reaction when Ferman had brought up the possibility of her having a boyfriend back in Dover. He didn't know whether she did or not, but he couldn't believe a lovely *maedel* like her wasn't the apple of a few young men's eyes.

Perry plopped a paper plate and a glass of water in front of him. Ferman almost chuckled at the sad state of the peanut butter and jelly sandwich. The top piece of bread was only half covered with peanut butter, and cherry jam oozed onto the plate. A few chips were scattered next to the PB&J, and one of them was partly stuck into the side of the sandwich. Clearly the boy was distracted. And smitten.

"Aren't you having supper?" Ferman asked, plucking the chip out of the sandwich.

"Not hungry," Perry mumbled. "Need anything else?"

Ferman paused. He should just let Perry be, but his meddlesomeness wouldn't let him. "Have a seat." He gestured to the chair across from him.

Perry's expression turned wary. "Why?"

"It's time we have a chat. About you and Daisy."

Crossing his arms, Perry said, "There is *nee* me and Daisy."

"There could be, though. She seems to have taken a shine to you—"

"She has a boyfriend."

Ferman's mouth fell open. "What?"

"You heard me."

Impossible. Although Ferman was sure Daisy had plenty of male interest in Dover, he couldn't fathom her liking any one of them. Not from the way she'd looked at Perry. That had been clear as a cloudless summer sky. And when they were running around the table, he'd caught the same enchanted expression on Perry's face. "Are you sure?"

Perry's withering scowl gave him his answer. He walked away. Seconds later, the door to the room across from Perry's bedroom slammed shut.

Ferman flinched at the sound. He didn't pin Daisy as the fickle type, and he never would have guessed she'd cheat on anyone. But Perry seemed absolutely sure she had a beau, and he wasn't happy about it. That also brought up more questions. If Daisy was taken, why were they flirting with each other? And why was Perry involved in her letter writing anyway?

He finished his supper, keeping his distaste of peanut butter and jelly to himself, not wanting to incur Perry's wrath. The man did go to the trouble of making him something to eat, and Ferman was hungry. Then he stood and tottered over to the chair, his steps slower than they'd been at church this morning but miles better than a few days ago. He was definitely improving, and he could probably go home tomorrow, despite Margaret not wanting him to be alone. She didn't fully know how well he was doing, and if he kept using the cane, even though he didn't want to, he would be okay at his house.

But he wasn't ready to leave. Not after today's development. He couldn't accept that Daisy was in love with another man after seeing her and Perry together earlier. And if she was, then she had a problem on her hands. A big one.

"*Ferman . . . stay out of this.*" Lovina's firm words echoed in his mind. "Sorry, *lieb*," he whispered, picking up one of the puzzle books and pencil. He had two big soft spots in his heart for Daisy and Perry, and he didn't like the idea of either of them being unhappy. "I should . . . but I can't."

Daisy stood in front of the mailbox and stared at the little red flag on the side. It was still in the down position. She glanced at the envelope in her hand, Maynard's address written neatly on the front. She'd finished the letter last night, or more accurately, copied down what she and Perry had written together so it was all in her own script. All she had to do was mail it. *What am I waiting for?*

A wet blanket of a thought entered her mind. Would Maynard even have noticed it wasn't her handwriting? Other than the first letter she wrote to him, she couldn't remember if she'd ever written anything else to him or in front of him. She never had a reason to. As of their most recent conversation the other day, he hadn't gotten her last letter yet. Maybe he still hadn't.

It also wasn't helpful that the entire time she was writing the letter, her thoughts were on Perry Bontrager. Last evening had been the first time she'd seen him genuinely smile, and she'd nearly melted in her chair. And then he pulled her onto his lap and—

She shook her head. They were just being playful, but in that moment her emotions shifted. When he set her aside, she wasn't just baffled. She was deeply disappointed.

And when she left, the guilt set in. She shouldn't enjoy being with Perry as much as she did. Not when her heart was with Maynard.

Daisy opened the mailbox and set the letter inside, then closed the lid and lifted the flag. She picked up her basket and went to Perry's, setting her muddled feelings and thoughts aside. Ferman was her primary concern, and even though he was improving, he still needed someone there to make sure he didn't fall and injure himself. This morning she asked *Aenti* Rosella if she could take a couple issues of *The Budget* for Ferman to read, and they were on top of her cross-stitch project.

A ripple of melancholy drifted over her. Soon her job as his care-taker would come to an end—perhaps in a day or two. He was getting around better and seemed to be in less pain. Her heart squished a little. She would miss him. *I'll miss coming over here too.* Once Ferman went home, there was no reason for her and Perry to interact with each other. They'd both fulfilled their parts of the pact.

Perry's horse and buggy were still in the driveway, and as she reached the front porch, he was coming out of the barn with his leather sack of farrier tools.

She hesitated, feeling awkward. Then she brushed it off. Perry had said he wasn't mad at her, and she should take him at his word. *"Gute mariye,"* she said, putting on a bright smile as she walked toward him.

He set the bag on the floorboard behind the front seat. "Mornin'."

"How's Ferman?"

"Grouchy as ever." He turned to her, and in the dim light of sunrise, she saw frustration on his face. "I don't understand," he huffed. "He seemed better yesterday."

Alarmed, she asked, "Has he had a setback?"

"I guess?" Rubbing his neck, he added, "He didn't eat much, I had to help him to the chair, and he barely touched his medicine. I wonder if I need to call Margaret again."

"Nee." She spontaneously put her hand on his forearm. When he glanced at it, she quickly pulled away. She'd also done that at church yesterday morning and had caught herself. Later she'd try to figure out why she kept touching him, but right now she had to reassure Perry. "If he's still in a bad way by tonight, you can let Margaret know. He could just be having an off day."

"I hope so." Perry climbed into the buggy. "I really thought he'd be well enough to *geh* back home. That's what he wants."

"Did he talk about leaving again this morning?"

"Come to think of it, *nee*. But he wasn't talkative either."

Hmm. That wasn't normal for Ferman. Not recently anyway.

He grabbed the reins. "I've got a full day. I won't be home until close to suppertime."

"I'll hold down the fort."

A faint smile appeared on his face. "*Danki*, Daisy. It's easier for me to concentrate on work if I don't have to worry about him." He tapped the horse's flanks with the reins. "See you tonight."

She waved as he left, relieved. She also hoped her assumption was true and Ferman wasn't regressing. Fortunately, her conversation with Perry wasn't strange or awkward. It was as if yesterday afternoon had never happened.

When she opened the door, Ferman had a pencil in one hand and the sudoku book in the other, his brow furrowed in concentration.

"Hi, Ferman." Daisy walked inside.

His head jerked up, the pencil and book hitting the floor. "Ugh," he moaned, grabbing his hip. "It hurts."

She stared at him for a moment, confused. "Your other hip hurts now?"

His eyes widened, and he put his hand back in his lap. "I'm in so much pain, I'm not sure of anything."

"Then you need to take your medicine." She set the basket on the couch and went to him. "Perry said you refused to."

"I gotta ache in my stomach." His lower lip poked out slightly. "Maybe I just need a little sodium bicarbonate."

"Baking soda?"

"Yeah. Just a touch in a glass of water." He placed both hands on his marginally protruding belly. At least he had the right body part this time.

"All right," she said, heading for the kitchen. She glanced at him again, positive he'd looked just fine when she walked through the door. But she wasn't here to question her patient, even if he was being a little daffy. "Baking soda it is."

Chapter 17

"Need help with anything else?" Perry slipped his hammer inside the leather bag.

Nelson shook his head. "Not that I can think of. *Danki* for coming out on short notice and fixing her hoof. I'm glad it's only a bruise and not an abscess."

"Me too." He stroked the mare's nose. "The pad I put on it will give her some cushion as it heals. Give her as much rest as possible. That will promote faster healing."

"Will do." He gave the horse a pat on the back and Perry stepped to the side as Nelson led her to her stall. "Ready for Saturday?" When Perry gave him a confused look, he added, "Don't tell me you forgot Devon is coming back to town. He's bringing the family too. *Mamm*'s got the whole day planned for all of us, including a huge meal."

He hid his groan. With all the distractions he'd had lately, he'd forgotten about his oldest brother's visit from Fredericktown. "Seems like he was just here."

"Two months ago."

"I still remember that cold I had." He'd been laid up for nearly a week, even after taking Margaret's foul-tasting concoction to help his coughing and sneezing.

Nelson exited the stall and walked over to him. "We all figured you're bringing that girl you're seeing."

Perry froze. "Huh?"

"Grace's cousin." He grinned. "Charity told Ella that Phoebe told her that *Mamm* can't stop talking about how you're finally not a bachelor anymore."

"Um . . ." He lifted his finger, then let his hand drop to his sides. "*Ya.*"

"We knew you could do it." Nelson laughed and punched him in the shoulder.

Perry rubbed his arm. Even though it was a playful thump, his brawny brother didn't know his own strength. And he should have predicted his mother would be talking about him and Daisy. *Now what am I supposed to do?*

"We're getting there early to help set up so the *kinner* can spend some time with *Mamm* and *Daed*. What's your *maedel*'s name, again?"

"Daisy," Perry said weakly. If he corrected his brother, that would trigger a bunch of other questions that he didn't want to deal with.

"Can't wait to meet her." Nelson grinned and headed to the front of the barn.

"Glad you're finding this so funny," he muttered.

He opened the door and let Perry go ahead of him. "Oh *ya*. Very funny. I'm just glad it's not me in the hot seat. Daisy must be a special girl if she's got your attention." He clapped him on the back, a little less forceful this time. "After all these years, Perry Bontrager's finally seeing someone."

Perry barely nodded, not wanting to bring up his past relationship with Ruby. He would never bring her up. She was a mistake—one that he would keep to himself. His pact with Daisy was a mistake too. So was holding her on his lap. He never should have allowed that to happen.

"I gotta get back to the shop," Nelson said. "I promised *Mamm* I would provide the meat on Saturday. I've got some quality hams in the smoker. I'm bringing ribs and steaks too."

Perry's mouth almost watered. "What about the pastrami?"

"Gotcha covered."

Perry finally managed to smile. His brother's pastrami was the best in the area, and he was gaining an excellent reputation for it. People traveled clear from Cleveland and Columbus to visit his butcher shop and deli for the pastrami sandwiches made with Ella's fresh-baked bread.

"See you Saturday." He gave Perry a short wave goodbye and walked across the street where his shop and Ella's family grocery store were located.

Perry climbed into his buggy. Time to head home. He wasn't as late as he thought he would be, mostly due to Nelson's panic over his horse's hoof being a false alarm. After finishing his scheduled job today, he met Nelson at his barn. His brother was worried it was going to be a bad infection, and at first Perry thought it might too. But when he took out his testers and examined the hoof, he discovered the bruise. If there had been an abscess under the hoof, it would have taken a little more time to figure it out and treat, but thankfully the injury was a quick fix.

As he drove, he thought about Ferman and hoped he was feeling better. This morning when he woke him up, he apologized to him for being so curt yesterday. Immediately Ferman had moaned and started acting strangely. Perry couldn't explain the sudden relapse, but he knew Ferman was in Daisy's good hands.

Daisy. Working on his drawing of Lady in his butterfly room had calmed him down, and he came to a decision. He wasn't going to help her anymore, for his own sanity. He couldn't keep denying he was attracted to her—that had been *extremely* clear yesterday. But she was off-limits, period. Even if she wasn't devoted to Maynard, he knew better than to get involved with her or anyone else. He needed to lock up his own heart and destroy the key.

Then Nelson reminded him about the Bontrager family gathering. His best-laid plan just went up in smoke.

The drive from Nelson's house to his was a short one and soon he was home. Dread filled him. He should tell Daisy about Saturday, but there was another option—go to the party and inform his family that they weren't seeing each other anymore. That would have a ring of truth once Ferman left.

He stopped a few feet from the house, his temple throbbing. If he told his mother he and Daisy were done, she would get right back to matchmaking. Also, if he neglected to tell Daisy about the party, she might be upset. She should at least know he planned to set the record straight with his family as soon as possible.

He entered the house, pausing at the cozy scene in front of him. Ferman was in his chair reading *The Budget* while Daisy was on the couch, her feet curled underneath her as she worked on a cross-stitch pattern. The scent of meat and vegetables cooking filled the small living area, blending with the fresh air coming through the open window by the dining table.

It's good to be home.

Ferman nodded at him, barely looking up from the paper as Daisy set down the cross-stitch and stood, a shy smile on her face.

Despite his vow to be unaffected by her, he returned her smile with a small one of his own. Then his unease returned. It wasn't suppertime yet, and he needed to get this over with. He glanced at

Ferman. *The Budget* was shielding his face. Perry craned his neck toward the front door and mouthed to Daisy, "Can we talk?"

Her eyes slightly widened, but she got up and followed him to the front porch. Ferman didn't say a word about them leaving.

As soon as they were outside and the door was closed, she asked, "Is everything okay?"

"*Ya.* How's Ferman?"

"Fine. He's hurting a bit more, and I made sure he rested today. *Aenti* Rosella came over and visited while I made the stew, and she had a great time visiting with him. He can be a charming conversationalist when he wants to be. Yesterday might have been too much for him, though."

Noted. "Should we let Margaret know?"

"I don't think so. He's been cooperative." She glanced to the side. "And a little nosy," she muttered.

He wondered what she meant by that, but he couldn't allow himself to get sidetracked. He slid his palms over his dirty pantlegs. "I saw my brother Nelson today." He explained about the horse's bruised hoof, then said, "I forgot that my family is getting together on Saturday at my parents' house. My *entire* family."

"That's nice. Do they have room for everyone?"

"*Ya.* It's a large compound. My oldest brother, Devon, and his family are coming for a visit. And my brother-in-law Jalon and his cousin Adam own the farm next door, and Adam's married to one of the bishop's daughters—" He halted his words. Too much detail.

"Sounds like fun." She smiled.

Cute. He inhaled a groan and forced himself to focus. "It will be entertaining. Somewhat." The thought of being around so many people was overwhelming, even though they were all family. "That probably doesn't make any sense. It doesn't to me anyway."

"*Nee.* I understand."

That was Daisy. She always understood, and he wanted her to again after he said his next words. "*Mamm* has been talking about us." His feet shifted. "She's really happy we're together."

Her cheeks turned rosy. "Oh."

"I'm sorry, Daisy. I didn't mean for things to *geh* this far."

"It's to be expected, *ya?*"

"But I thought she'd see us together one time, and then later on I would tell her we—" He shook his head. There was no point in going over what he thought would happen. "They're expecting both of us, but I understand if you don't want to *geh.*"

"Of course I want to *geh.* I like your *familye.* I'm just glad there's *nix* wrong."

He almost laughed at the absurdity of her statement. Everything about this was wrong, and now they were perpetuating a lie, one he would straighten out after Saturday was over. But he knew what she meant. The window by the door was open, bringing the scent of supper outdoors. "What are you cooking?" he said, eager to change the subject. "It smells great."

She beamed. "Beef stew. I got some ingredients from *Aenti* Rosella's while she was visiting with Ferman."

"Sorry the pantry is so bare." He hadn't had time to go to the store, or even get Ferman's clothing. The old man seemed fine wearing Perry's and hadn't asked for his. Or anything else from his house, come to think of it. Then again, he might have been expecting to go home tomorrow. Now with this small setback, he wouldn't be able to unless a miracle happened and he woke up healed enough to be on his own.

"What time is the party?" Daisy asked.

"I'll pick you up around ten if that sounds *gut.*"

She nodded and glanced over her shoulder, then back at him. "The stew is ready whenever you and Ferman feel like eating. If you don't mind, I'm going to get my things and *geh* home. I want to spend some time with Grace."

"Oh, *ya*." But it didn't seem right that she wasn't joining them for supper since she went to so much trouble to make it. Just as he was about to point that out, she moved closer to him and stood on her tiptoes.

"Spend some time in your butterfly room," she whispered. "Ferman will be fine." She turned and went back inside the house.

Perry didn't move. Ruby never would have encouraged him to spend time doing his hobby, and she supposedly had cared about him. Even said she loved him once. And here was Daisy who, only after knowing him a little more than a week, had realized he needed to be with his butterflies.

Maynard is an idiot.

⟜⟝

"I'm glad to hear Ferman's feeling better." Grace picked up several mancala stones and placed them in the wells.

"Me too." Daisy frowned. This was the third time tonight she and her cousin had played the game. Grace had won each match and it appeared she was going to do it again. She grabbed her two stones and played them.

"When do you think he's going home?" Grace asked.

"I'm not sure." That was the strange thing. For the first time since she'd been taking care of him, he hadn't mentioned leaving. And although he'd been in pain this morning, that had seemed to subside throughout the day. He'd even gone outside to sit on the patio and enjoyed the warm spring air while Daisy had fixed the stew. When she went out to check on him, he was asleep. Right before she turned to go back inside, she spotted a painted lady landing on Ferman's knee. Unlike Perry, she couldn't tell if it was Lady or not, and she'd forgotten to mention it to him when they were outside talking.

"I'm assuming he'll leave soon, *ya*?" Grace picked up her pieces and plunked them in the wells.

"You're so *gut* at this," Daisy grumbled, seeing she could only play one piece.

"It's Kyle favorite game." She rested her chin in her hand. "He taught me all his secrets."

Daisy smiled, wondering what Perry's favorite game was. Oh, and Maynard's. They'd never played a game together. That was something they would have to do when she went back to Dover.

"How's Perry?" Grace asked.

Talk about a loaded question. When he arrived home, she noticed his anxious expression. Then his face suddenly relaxed, only to tense up again before they talked on the porch. Throughout their conversation he seemed uptight, and when he told her about Saturday, she could see why. While she enjoyed going to parties and gatherings and she liked the Bontragers, there was that pesky problem of them all thinking she and Perry were dating. Even Ferman had been inquisitive about her love life for some reason.

When he woke up from his nap outside, she joined him for a little while. No sooner had her backside hit the plastic chair than he plied her with questions about Dover and her life back home.

"You have a lot of friends then, *ya*?" he said, angling his stocky body in the chair so he was looking straight at her.

"I wouldn't say a lot. Most of them are married, so we don't spend as much time together."

That must have been the magic phrase, because he then asked, "And how about yourself? Any marriage plans in the future?"

She almost couldn't answer him, she was so shocked. And how was she supposed to explain Maynard? She hadn't wanted to tell Grace or Perry about her complicated relationship with him, much less Ferman. She didn't want to lie to him either. "There's a possibility."

His expression fell, or at least she thought it did. He didn't ask her anything else after that, and in hindsight she should have told him to mind his own business. Then *Aenti* Rosella came over and that was the end of the conversation.

"Daisy?"

Her eyes focused on Grace, who was frowning at her. "*Ya?*"

"Is something on your mind? You kind of faded away for a bit."

She stared at the mancala board, trying to focus on her next move, only to think about Perry again, more specifically when she had whispered that he should spend some time in his butterfly room. She didn't want to risk Ferman eavesdropping, not knowing if Perry had told him about it or not. She doubted he did. He was clear about keeping that room a secret from everyone.

A flutter appeared in her stomach. He'd smelled of hard work—leather, dirt, sweat—but she didn't mind. Being close to him had been . . . *ahh*.

Grace grinned. "Thinking about Maynard?"

Daisy sat up straight. "Huh?"

She chuckled. "From the smile on your face, you must be."

"*Ya*. Maynard. That's who I'm thinking about." She jumped up from her chair. "Do you want some chips?"

"Sure. They're on the third shelf."

Daisy hurried to the pantry and looked, but for the life of her she couldn't see the bag. Grace was right—she should have been thinking about Maynard, not Perry. "There they are," she mumbled, grabbing the nacho-flavored chips and shutting the door. She poured them into a medium-sized bowl and set it down at the table. "Wait," she said, looking at the mancala board. "You won again?"

"Yep." Grace picked up a chip and nibbled on the corner. Then she got up. "I'll *geh* get Dutch Blitz."

"*Danki.*" She sat down. "I don't think I can take much more defeat."

Grace winked and left the kitchen at the same time *Aenti* Rosella walked in. "You *maed* having fun?"

"Grace is." Daisy chuckled and took a chip.

Her *aenti* went to the covered pan of chocolate chip brownies on the counter. "I know I shouldn't," she said, opening a drawer to get out a knife. "But I shall. You want one?"

"*Nee.* I had two for dessert. Those are delicious."

Grace entered the room with a forest-green pack of cards. She set them on the table and sat down. "Be gentle," she said with a smirk.

"After you destroyed me in mancala?" Daisy shook her head and opened the pack. "Never."

"It's so *gut* to see you two playing together again." *Aenti* Rosella slid a generous square of brownie onto a plate. "Like old times."

Daisy exchanged a smile with Grace, then looked at her aunt. "Do you want to join us?"

"Not tonight." She set the knife in the sink. "The latest issue of *The Budget* arrived this morning."

Her aunt didn't have to elaborate. *Mamm* was the same way when the Amish newspaper was delivered—they both read every word. Ferman had also enjoyed perusing the paper. *"Lovina used to read this,"* he'd said, a touch of sadness in his tone. *"I canceled my subscription after she passed. Polly Ann isn't much of a reader."* Daisy was about to ask him who Polly Ann was, but he lifted the paper in front of his face.

Aenti Rosella started to leave the kitchen, then stopped in the doorway.

"Oh. I almost forgot." She frowned slightly at Daisy, only for it to quickly disappear. "Maynard called right before you came home."

She stopped mid shuffle. "He did?"

"*Ya.* I told him you'd call him back. But there's *nee* rush," she said quickly and disappeared.

Grace pulled a face. "That's weird. It's almost like she doesn't want you to talk to him."

She doesn't. Daisy wondered if she should tell Grace that *Aenti* Rosella was in cahoots with her *mamm* about Maynard, then decided not to. Things were already too complicated.

"Have you told your *mamm* yet about your 'date' with Perry?"

"It wasn't a date. It was church," she reminded Grace. "*Nee.* I decided to let her know in a couple of weeks."

Grace nodded, then paused, the deck in her hand ready to be dealt. "Do you want to call Maynard? We can play another night."

She started to say yes, but something held her back. This was the second time he'd called her since she left Dover, and she glanced at the clock to check the time. It was only seven thirty and Maynard always retired for the night at eight. That would give them thirty minutes to talk, so it wasn't like she didn't have enough time for one of their short conversations.

Then she looked at Grace and the cards. Because she'd been with Ferman and Perry so much lately, she missed being with her cousin. Grace was the main reason she'd come here, and even though that initial reason had changed, she was enjoying hanging out with her. And she still didn't have a clue how to make conversation easier with Maynard.

Like it is with Perry.

But that was because she didn't like Perry the way she liked Maynard. Maybe that was it. Things were cumbersome between them because they hadn't reached their relationship potential. She shook her head. "*Nee.* I'll call him in the morning."

"Okay." Grace looked a little taken aback. "I just know if it were Kyle—"

"He's not Kyle."

She paused. "You're right. He's not."

Daisy touched Grace's hand, trying to soften the surprising harshness of her tone. "I want to play cards with you," she said. "Maynard's not going anywhere."

Grace smiled and started to deal. "You're going to see him in a month anyway."

She smiled. Then it hit her—a month wasn't that far away. Before she knew it, she would be leaving her cousin, aunt, and uncle. Ferman too. *And Perry.* She'd have to make the best of her time here, because once she went home, she and Maynard would start their new life together as an engaged couple. After they had "the talk," of course. And she'd call him tomorrow morning, first thing before she went to Perry's.

Right now, she just wanted to enjoy herself.

———

Ferman Eash was in a quandary.

It was Friday afternoon, four days after he'd decided to put off going home for the sake of Perry and Daisy. But now he was questioning his decision. Oh, he was still correct about the two of them having feelings for each other. Even though Daisy hadn't stayed for supper on Tuesday and Wednesday, she had last night, and he sat and watched as the two of them talked. It wasn't an exciting conversation. Or a flirty one. It was comfortable, like a *mann* and *frau* have when they miss each other after being apart for the day.

Those two stymied him. He'd managed to find out that there was *a possibility* for Daisy back in Dover, but that wasn't exactly confirmation that she was romantically invested. And as for Perry, getting him to disclose anything personal was like trying to open a can with a straw. There was only so much prying he could do without tipping his hand. Top that off with how fine his hip was feeling and that he was getting antsy just sitting around doing puzzles and snoozing in the chair, he didn't know if he could continue staying here, never mind if he should. Faking his pain and mobility wasn't the right thing to do, and he was being stingy by keeping Perry on the couch instead of in his own bed.

Still, not only was he trying to figure out the situation with his young friends, but he was also curious about what was in *that room*, as he now thought of it. After supper each night, Perry entered the room and shut the door, staying in there for an hour or two before retiring for the night. The door was always closed, and Daisy hadn't gone in there either—at least that Ferman had witnessed. More than once, he was tempted to find a way to unlock it and peek inside while Daisy was busy outside or running next door to Rosella's to get this or that.

Then again, it probably wasn't anything special. Maybe a storage room that needed cleaning and organizing. Perhaps Perry was a secret pack rat. That explanation didn't hold much water, though.

With Perry back at work and Daisy busy, either with house chores or her cross-stitch, Ferman unfortunately had plenty of time to think and it was becoming clearer that staying here wasn't just because he was curious about Perry and Daisy's true feelings for each other or his desire to find out what was in *that room*.

Truth was, he liked the company. Even though Perry spent time alone each evening, they did talk at supper and sometimes before Ferman went to bed. Again, nothing too personal, but he did find out about Perry's family, his numerous nieces and nephews, how long he'd been a farrier and how much he loved his job. In turn, Ferman talked about Lovina and growing up in Marigold, steering clear of discussing Junior and Polly Ann. Perry wasn't the only one who kept things close to his chest.

Going back home and letting Perry have his house back was an easy choice. But every time he leaned toward asking Perry to take him home, he balked, the idea of rambling around a house full of memories making his heart pinch. *I never expected to be in this pickle, Lord.*

Ferman got up from his chair. Daisy had left to get a few eggs from Rosella's coop, even though Perry had finally gone to the grocery store on Tuesday and picked up a dozen, which Daisy promptly used during the week. He went to the restroom, then paused in front of *that room*. He hobbled to the closed door. At least he could settle one thing in his mind if he found out what was on the other side. And he'd only take a smidge of a look. Perry would never know.

Ferman touched the doorknob, gripped the cold metal, and started to turn—

"Hello?"

He jumped at the female voice that wasn't Daisy's. All his weight shifted to his left hip and leg. "Ow!"

"Ferman?"

The pitter-patter of feminine footsteps headed his way, and he recognized the voice. Margaret Bontrager. What was she doing here?

His gaze darted back and forth. Too late to dash into Perry's room. Maybe he could hide in the bathroom? Nah, too obvious. He had no choice but to surrender. "I'm comin'," he groused, meeting her at the edge of the living room. "Let me guess. Lecture time, *ya*?"

She smiled. Like Daisy, she seemed unfazed by his testiness. "That depends," she said, going to the couch without being invited. She sat down. "Are you still following orders?"

"*Ya*." He limped to the chair and lowered himself down. His hip ached more than usual due to her scaring him.

"You're moving well." She untied her black bonnet ribbons and took off the head covering. "I was out and about today, and I thought I'd stop by and see how you're doing."

"We just saw each other on Sunday."

"And now we're seeing each other again."

A snug feeling went through him. She and Daisy reminded him of Lovina—caring, but with a backbone. "I, uh, appreciate you stopping by."

"Where's Daisy?"

"Gathering eggs at Rosella's," he said. "She'll be back soon."

"Have you given any more thought about our last conversation?"

He blanked his expression, even though he knew exactly what she was referring to.

"About you either moving in with someone or having someone live with you?"

Ferman scrambled for an answer. While he'd given plenty of thought about returning home, he refused to entertain her suggestion. He still didn't want to move in with Junior, and he had no idea who would want to live with him. "A smidge," he said. Maybe if she thought he was taking her seriously, she'd drop the subject.

She chuckled. "Well, that's something."

For the next few minutes, he answered her questions about his pain level, his mobility, and if he was having any side effects from the medicines he was taking. He fudged a little bit about how much his hip ached and stated that he was having some trouble walking. Then the guilt arrived. He should be honest with her, but he couldn't. Not just yet.

"I won't be giving you more tea," she said, rising from the couch. "You don't seem to need it anymore, and it's not something you should take long term. What you should do—"

"Is get a hip replacement." He rolled his eyes. "Don't need you telling me that."

Her mouth downturned slightly. "If you would have let me finish, you would have heard me say to spend as much time outside as you can. You're looking a little pale."

Ferman touched his cheek. "Really?"

She put her bonnet back on. "I would also say that you could help Perry with his garden, but I know you'll be going back home soon."

"*Ya*." Then he said, "Garden?" The few times he'd been outside, he didn't see anything that hinted that Perry had a garden. The only thing in his yard was grass and the clothesline.

"He had one way in the back of his yard last year. Small, with only a few vegetables. Lots of flowers, though." Margaret picked up her basket. "If you insist on living alone, I hope you don't mind if I check in on you from time to time."

His heart softened at her words, something he refused to let her see. If he showed too much weakness, she might be more insistent. "I'll be fine."

"I'd like to make sure of that if you'll let me."

Ferman was finding it hard to look this lovely woman in the eye. "Only if it's not too much trouble," he muttered, then lifted his chin halfway. "I don't want to impose on nobody." He inwardly cringed. He was imposing on Perry and Daisy right now.

She moved closer and patted his shoulder. "I'm happy to do it." Turning, she headed for the door. "You have a *gut* afternoon, Ferman."

"You too."

After she left, he slumped in the chair, his hypocrisy almost strangling him. *I'm being selfish.*

He slapped his thighs with his palms. No more imposing, and no more stalling. Perry was going to his family's tomorrow, and then there was church on Sunday in Marigold. But after the service, he was going straight to his house. If God meant for Perry and Daisy to be together, he was gonna do it without Ferman Eash. He glanced up at the ceiling. "You certainly don't need my help."

Chapter 18

Perry waited at the end of Daisy's driveway at ten o'clock sharp Saturday morning after agreeing last night that he didn't need to pull his buggy into the Hershbergers' drive when he picked her up. Daisy had offered to come over like she normally did, but for some reason picking her up seemed the right thing to do, even though this wasn't a date. He also wasn't as nervous as he expected to be. Part of that was due to his interactions with her this week. They had been comfortable and relaxed, as if they'd known each other a long time. He was still going to set his mother straight on their relationship next week and apologize for giving her and his family the wrong idea. Today, however, he was going to enjoy himself—or at least try, considering his low tolerance for crowds. Having Daisy by his side would help.

Howard offered to spend the day with Ferman, and none of the Hershbergers had batted an eye at Perry taking Daisy to a family gathering. He assumed they all knew about her mother's dating request, and even if they didn't, he was glad they didn't have to explain the situation to them.

Their front door opened and he watched Daisy making her way

down the drive, her feet light and movements graceful. She was wearing a butter-yellow dress with a navy cardigan over it, her *kapp* strings dancing on her shoulders as she moved. *Adorable.* Finally, he could mentally acknowledge her appeal without his emotions spiraling.

When she reached the end of the driveway, he heard the phone ring. She paused and held up one finger to Perry before dashing off and answering it. She stayed inside for a few minutes, and then exited and walked to his buggy, a slight frown on her face.

"Everything all right?" he asked as she climbed inside.

"*Ya.* I guess."

She didn't sound convincing, and he wasn't convinced. He waited for her to continue. When she didn't, he wanted to question her further but refused to pry. They were friends, and he had to respect her privacy.

Just as he started to pick up the reins, she said, "That was Maynard."

"Oh." He hid a frown. He'd managed to keep that guy out of his mind the past several days, and Daisy hadn't brought him up or asked for more relationship help, thank the Lord. "How, uh, is he?"

She smoothed her dress. "Okay. I guess. I haven't talked to him this week."

Seriously? "This the first you've heard from him?"

"*Nee.*" She glanced down, her hands becoming still. "I got a letter from him on Wednesday. He's also called every day."

Envy wound around Perry's gut and he tried to check himself. Other than what happened last Sunday afternoon, she hadn't given him an inkling that she considered Perry anything else but a friend, and he did the same. He should be happy Maynard was finally paying attention to her. "Do you want to stay and talk to him?"

She turned, and Perry was shocked at the bewilderment in her hazel eyes. "Not really. I've gone this long without talking to him." She looked back at her lap. "And I haven't read his letter."

Huh. He sat back in his seat, unsure what to think. "Are you mad at him?" he finally asked.

"*Nee.* I just don't want to talk to him." Daisy glanced at Perry again. "Is that bad?"

He didn't know. She'd been so eager to get his attention a few days ago, and now she wasn't interested. Strange. Or maybe there was another reason she was avoiding him.

"We should *geh.*"

"Daisy—"

"I don't want to talk about it anymore."

Suddenly Lady appeared. Perry couldn't believe it. He hadn't seen her for a couple of days. "Welcome back," he said, holding out his finger for her to land on.

"Lady?" Daisy asked, her eyes brightening.

"*Ya.*" He moved his hand toward Daisy, and Lady flitted to her shoulder. Daisy's smile practically glowed, her troubled expression vanishing. "Think she wants to come with us?"

"We'll find out." He tapped the reins on his horse's flanks, and they were off. As expected, so was Lady, who flew away before he finished passing the Hershberger house. He caught Daisy's downcast expression before she turned to look at the landscape, just like she did when they came home from church.

More than once this week, she'd mentioned the pretty scenery in Marigold, and she was excited to go to nearby Barton with Grace next Wednesday to do some shopping. During their conversations this week—some brief, others longer like on Thursday and Friday nights—she didn't mention Dover or her parents. Mostly they talked about Marigold, his job, and . . . butterflies. She was full of questions, and he'd been happy to answer every single one. In detail.

For the next half hour they drove in silence, something Perry didn't mind. He savored it, because soon enough they would be bombarded by his noisy, lovable family. He was curious about what she was thinking, almost sure it had to be Maynard, but he wouldn't push her.

They were nearing his parents' house when she eventually spoke. "Do you think Ferman is up to something?"

He turned left, barely guiding his horse. Not only did the gelding know his way around Marigold, but he also knew how to get to Birch Creek. "Now that you mention it, I was wondering myself."

Daisy turned around and faced him. "Has he been nosy with you?"

"*Ya.* But I don't take the bait." He glanced at her. "I just figured he was making conversation. What I have noticed is that he's moving just fine. I even caught him walking to the bathroom without his cane. And in the mornings, he doesn't need my help to get dressed anymore."

"Interesting." She tapped her chin. "Lately he hasn't said a word about going home."

"I noticed that too."

"What do you think's going on?"

Perry slowed the buggy, giving them a few extra minutes before the upcoming chaos. "I think he's lonely, Daisy. He won't admit it, though. I've urged him to call his son."

Daisy gasped. "He has a son?"

"*Ya.* Junior. He's married to Polly Ann."

"So that's who she is. He mentioned her once. But he never said a word to me about Junior."

"Junior and his wife used to live with him. They moved away

several months ago. Ferman's refused to call him, so I dropped the subject."

"Maybe we should call him."

Perry shook his head. "I don't think Ferman would appreciate that."

Daisy didn't say anything for a moment, then asked, "Aren't you ready to get your house back?"

He paused, unsure if he should tell her the truth—the longer Ferman stayed with him, the more he didn't mind him being there. Sure, he didn't have the privacy he'd become accustomed to while living by himself. He also hadn't realized how nice it was to have someone around, even someone as stubborn, talkative, and yes, nosy as Ferman Eash. He was also smart, unintentionally funny, and from his frequent mentions of Lovina, he'd had a long, happy marriage. "I imagine it might be hard going back to an empty house."

"Oh, I'm sure. He talks about Lovina a lot. He misses her very much."

His parents' house came into view. "I should probably tell him he's welcome to stay as long as he wants," Perry said.

"But that means you'll be stuck on the couch."

"That's fine. It's not a bad place to sleep."

"You're a kind, generous *mann*, Perry."

He almost blushed at her compliment. When it came to kindness, she had him beat.

They drove past a huge field, one of the Bontragers' pastures. His older nieces and nephews were playing volleyball on the adjacent grass court, the same one he and his siblings used when they were kids—and adults, admittedly. He glanced at Daisy. "Almost there. Are you ready to meet the crew?"

Her smile was like warm sunshine. "I can't wait."

～

For the next several hours, Daisy thoroughly enjoyed herself. She'd fail miserably if anyone asked her to name all the Bontragers and related family members, but she would always remember how open and friendly they all were. If any of them knew that she and Perry were an "item," no one let on, not even Miriam. And while visiting with the women, oohing and aahing over the young babies and little grandchildren—and in Phoebe's case, *her* grandchildren—then playing a game of volleyball with rotating members of the family, she kept one eye and ear out for Perry.

At first he seemed at ease with everyone, playing volleyball with the adults and teens and then baseball with the younger children. When it came time for lunch, he sat with Owen and Ezra—or was that Devon? She had no idea, but he was smiling and laughing as he ate his meal. That made Daisy smile too.

There was only one hiccup, and that was when Miriam pointed out Nelson and Ella's daughter, Neva. Which made her think of Maynard's mother, and that made her think of Maynard again. Young Neva Bontrager was nothing like Neva Miller, but for a little while she couldn't get Maynard, or his phone call this morning, off her mind.

She almost didn't answer the phone, thinking it was him. She'd avoided his calls this past week. But it might be for one of her relatives, so she picked up the receiver. "Hi," she said, peeking out the window at Perry waiting for her in his buggy.

"Finally." Maynard's normally mild voice held a trace of irritation. "I didn't think you'd ever answer the phone."

"I've been—" She almost said busy, and that would be the truth. She rose early every day to go to Perry's, and on Tuesday she started making the men breakfast in the morning, plus packing Perry's lunch—something he didn't ask her to do and up until Thursday had insisted she shouldn't. But she wanted to, just like she wanted to make him and Ferman hearty, home-cooked suppers. Ferman needed the nutrition, and she enjoyed seeing Perry enthusiastically dig into the meals she prepared.

"You've been what?" Maynard asked.

"Otherwise disposed."

"What does that mean?"

Daisy looked out the window again. "Someone's waiting for me, Maynard."

"Who? Where are you going?"

She startled. He'd never been this forceful before. *Or interested.* "A . . . friend. We're going to a party." Then it dawned on her. "Aren't you at work?"

"*Ya*, but I took a break. Are you ignoring me?"

"Of course not. I would never ignore you, Maynard." She winced at the fib.

"Then why haven't you called me back? Did you read my letter?"

This conversation was sounding eerily familiar. It was also making her feel bad. "I'm sorry," she said. They did need to talk, but she couldn't keep Perry waiting. "I'll call you back tonight."

He paused. "All right. I have to *geh* back to work anyway."

No surprise there. "Talk to you later."

"Bye."

They hung up, and as Daisy headed to the buggy, the truth hit her—regardless of her promise, she wasn't eager to talk to Maynard tonight and she didn't know why. Not only did that bother her, it scared her a little too. She used to yearn for him to pay attention to her. Now that he was, she wasn't sure what to do. It didn't seem . . . normal.

Then one of the wives who wasn't Margaret invited her to play a round of bag toss with her, and she did that after lunch. When she finished the game, she saw that Perry had disappeared. She was glancing around the huge Bontrager compound when Miriam came up to her.

"Looking for Perry?" she asked.

"*Ya*. Do you know where he is?"

"Probably in the back pasture. He tends to *geh* there when he wants to be alone. I never thought he'd be *mei* most introverted *kinner*," she said. "Zeb was always the quiet one, and Owen always had a book in his hand. The rest are more social. When Perry was in his late teens, he started spending more time alone." She rested her hand on Daisy's shoulder. "I'm so glad he has you for a *friend*." She gave her a knowing smile and walked away.

Uh-oh. For a while Daisy had been able to forget about their pretense, but now it had smacked her in the face. Ugh. She didn't want to upset Miriam or anyone else, or for them to think badly of her. She dragged her feet a little as she went to see Perry.

Sure enough, she found him in the pasture, staring at several horses grazing the grass. She paused a few feet from him, his expression unreadable on his handsome profile. Maybe she should just leave him be. He would come back to the group when he was ready.

He turned around, his dark brows lifting. "Oh, hey. I didn't know you were here."

She moved a few steps closer. "Can I join you?"

"Sure." He rested his forearms on the white fence.

Daisy tried not to stare at his sinewy muscles, but it was difficult when she was so close to him. She moved a few steps away. That didn't help, and she forced herself to look at the horses instead. Over the past few days, their dynamic had changed, and it felt like they were friends. Not in the Miriam sense, of course, but she believed there was genuine friendship between them. Still, she couldn't ignore his gorgeousness, and eventually she wouldn't notice it anymore. Right now, though, she was noticing aplenty.

"How did you find me?" he asked.

"Your *mamm* told me where you were." She drew in a breath. "She also thanked me for being your *friend*."

"Great." He grimaced.

"I don't want her to be mad at me," Daisy said in a small voice. "I really like your *familye*."

"She won't be. They won't be." He put one elbow up on the fence and faced her. "I'll take all the responsibility. It's my fault we're in this position."

"That isn't fair." He didn't have to be that gallant. "I agreed to it."

"*Ya*, but . . ." He held her gaze. "Let me handle them, okay?"

She couldn't look away. All she could do was nod.

He turned toward the pasture again. "You don't have to stay here."

"I don't mind." And she didn't. She breathed in the fresh timothy grass and saw several types of wildflowers bordering the pasture fence. A few butterflies flitted around, and she smiled. Now she knew why he'd spent so much time out here growing up.

"I can only take so much," he said, his voice so low she barely heard him. "I love my *familye*, but . . ."

"They are a lot."

His left eyebrow raised again. "You think so too?"

"*Nee*. But I understand why you do."

"I don't. A huge *familye* is all I've known. When I was little, it didn't

220

bother me. There was always someone to play with. And fight with, of course. But as I grew older, something changed. I guess that something was me."

She moved closer to him. "We can *geh* back to Marigold if you want. I'm sure we made our point."

"Aren't you're having a *gut* time?"

"*Ya*, but I won't if it's at your expense."

His mesmerizing blue eyes locked with hers. Then he mumbled something that sounded like *"What an idiot,"* but she wasn't sure and she didn't want to ask. She would do anything not to break this moment. The warm sensation humming through her was different than anything she had experienced before. She wasn't just attracted to him. She felt *connected*.

He stepped away, a muscle jerking in his cheek. "Why don't you want to talk to Maynard?"

Her heart dipped. Why was he bringing that up now? She supposed she did owe him an explanation, considering he was the one who had the idea of playing hard to get. It definitely worked. "I guess because I don't have much to say."

"Do you . . ." He grasped the top of the fence with both hands. "Do you still love him?"

"*Ya*." The word automatically flew out of her mouth, like a mechanical response. "I just don't think the phone is a *gut* form of communication for us. We need to talk face-to-face." Yes, that was it. Hadn't she believed that all along? She insisted that they needed to be in the same proximity when they had "the talk," and apparently also when they just . . . talked.

A car whizzed by, making the tall grass and flower border sway. "Are you going to tell him about our pact?"

She hadn't thought about that. "Should I?"

"It's not *gut* to have secrets."

Even with his reassurances about shouldering the blame for their agreement, she was filled with guilt over their slight deception. "You're right. I'll tell him when I *geh* back to Dover."

Neither of them moved or spoke, but she couldn't help glancing at his profile. His jaw seemed set in stone, and it was covered with a faint five o'clock shadow. Maynard was far from her thoughts as she wondered what it would be like to touch Perry's strong, whiskered chin, and that brought on even more guilt. She moved farther away from him. "I'm ready to *geh* back to Marigold."

"Okay," he said without hesitation, as if he'd been thinking the same thing.

They said their goodbyes to his family, climbed into the buggy, and headed back home, neither of them saying a word. For the first time, she didn't enjoy the scenery, and the stunning sunset was lost on her as she tried to drum up some enthusiasm for her return phone call to Maynard. She still didn't know what they were going to talk about. The weather? His job? *Perry?* No, she couldn't mention him to Maynard, even though they were only friends. That was another face-to-face conversation.

But telling him they shouldn't talk for the next month was extreme. *What if he forgets about me?*

What does it matter?

The notion shocked her. Of course it mattered if he forgot about her. How could she think such a thing?

To her surprise they were almost at Perry's house. When he stopped the buggy, she started to get out.

"Daisy?"

His deep voice stopped her. She turned around. "*Ya?*"

"Don't leave."

Chapter 19

Only after Perry turned into his driveway and parked his buggy did he realize he should have taken Daisy home the proper way. His mind had been so scrambled since their talk at the pasture fence, he was driving on autopilot. It was why he'd been silent on the ride home. What had started out as a great day had now become strained, and he was to blame.

He never should have brought up Maynard, but his curiosity got the best of him, and in all honesty, it had been a diversion. When she told him she was willing to cut short her good time for his sake, he couldn't stop holding her gaze, and his feelings of friendship flew out the window. He had to do something to chill the mood. Mentioning Maynard worked, only too well.

Now he needed to reset. He didn't want to go back to feeling clumsy and awkward when they were together. He swiveled to face her. "My advice about playing hard to get might have backfired," he admitted. "I didn't want you to pull away from Maynard or be worried about talking to him. I'm not exactly an expert when it comes to relationships."

"I'm sure you know more than me."

"I don't know about that."

"Then Grace was right?" Daisy flinched. "Oops. I shouldn't have said that."

He frowned. "Right about what?"

"You've never been on a date."

His jaw dropped. "Why would she say that?"

Sheepish, she held up her hands. "Because you keep to yourself."

"That's a big leap to make," he said, a little annoyed. "What else did she say?"

"That's it. She did say she was being judgmental. I totally agreed."

Daisy from Dover, his little white knight. He started to smile, then stopped. "Forget about Grace. I—"

"So you've been on a date before." Daisy leaned forward, her eyes filled with interest.

At least the tension between them was gone. He relaxed a little. "*Ya.*"

"With the same girl, or more than one?"

Before she thought he was some kind of womanizer, he said, "The same *maedel*. Her name was Ruby. We didn't work out."

"Why?"

"We thought we were compatible. Turns out we weren't." This was the first time he'd spoken about Ruby. Talking about this wasn't as difficult as he thought it would be, probably because this was Daisy he was talking to.

"Did you love her?"

"I thought I did." He hadn't expected their discussion to turn into a confessional. "The point is that I don't want my poor counsel to cause problems between you and Maynard."

"It's not." She scooted toward him a little. "Did you want to marry her?"

He hesitated. He should change the subject back to her and Maynard. They'd gone this far, though, so he ignored the inclination. "*Ya.* I almost asked her to. But she couldn't accept me for who I am. And after we broke up, I realized I didn't accept her either."

"Then why did you think you were in love?"

That was a good question—one he'd wrestled with after he and Ruby ended their relationship. The answer he landed on was the truth, although he wasn't proud of it. "I was infatuated with her. She was pretty, and I liked the attention she gave me when we started dating. She made me feel special, I guess."

Daisy glanced at her lap for a moment. When she looked up again, she said, "Did you kiss her?"

He stilled. Not in a million years had he anticipated that question, and it simultaneously made him feel hot and cold, excited and uneasy. She was looking at him with earnest, innocent beguilement. "Daisy . . ."

She shrank back. "I'm sorry, Perry. I don't know what's wrong with me. I don't think before I speak."

Her sincere regret moved him. "We're talking about romance, so it's bound to come up." Not really, but he wanted to make her feel better. By her still gloomy expression, it didn't work.

He moved closer to her. Yes, he was attracted to her, and he still thought Maynard was a *dummkopf* for not seeing what a great girl she was, but more importantly he wanted her to be comfortable around him, even if that meant they talked about a less than comfortable subject. "We're friends, *ya?*"

She lifted her head and nodded.

"Then you can talk to me about anything."

Daisy couldn't break her gaze from Perry's. She didn't just feel attracted and excited. She felt cared for. He could have scoffed at her for asking such a ridiculous and intrusive question. He could have gotten mad, and he would have been right to do so. When it came to Perry Bontrager, she couldn't stop from saying and asking embarrassing things.

Then he smiled. "What do you want to know?"

Her spine shivered, but she quickly regained her wits. This was a prime opportunity to gain some helpful intel. Because the time would come, possibly in a month or so, that she and Maynard would kiss, and she didn't want to disappoint him. "Did you . . ." Great, now she was clamming up.

"Kiss Ruby? *Ya*, I did."

Daisy wasn't expecting the feeling of jealousy that hit her when she heard those words. "Did you like it?"

"At first, *ya*. But as time went on and the feelings stopped, the kisses meant nothing. I felt . . . nothing." He rubbed his chin. "Now that I think about it, that might be the real reason we broke up. Whatever feelings we had for each other disappeared, even before she—"

"She what?"

"I showed her my butterfly room." He sighed. "Let's just say she wasn't impressed."

Daisy straightened her shoulders, offended on Perry's behalf. "She's just ridiculous then."

He laughed. "Agreed." Then he said, "Daisy, don't worry about kissing. When it's right, you'll know."

"But what if I'm a disappointment? What if—"

"You won't be. I can promise you that."

She grinned, and suddenly everything between her and Perry was back to normal after a short stint of tension. No, better than normal. He wasn't just a friend. *He's a good friend.*

The buggy jerked a little as his horse pawed at the ground with one hoof. "I should get him to the barn. He's ready to turn in for the night."

Only then did she realize it was almost completely dark, and when she looked at Perry's house, she didn't see any lights on. "Ferman must be at my *onkel's,*" she said.

He took the reins. "I'll give him a ride," he said, maneuvering the buggy out of the driveway and over to her aunt and uncle's house. "That will save Howard the trouble."

Daisy nodded. There was no way Ferman would, or should, be walking over to Perry's at the end of the day. He hadn't recovered that much.

Perry parked the buggy and got out, Daisy joining him on the driver's side.

"Wait," she said. This time when she put her hand on his arm, she didn't pull away.

Turning, he faced her, and she could barely see his facial features in the dark. *Aenti* Rosella and *Onkel* Howard's house was set back from the road, and the light from the streetlamp didn't quite reach all the way.

"*Danki,*" she said, taking a step closer to him.

"For what?"

"Being my friend." She stood on tiptoe and wrapped her arms around his neck, closing her eyes when he drew her close.

"Ditto," he whispered in her ear.

She stepped out of his embrace and walked away, feeling lighter than she had after Maynard's phone call, and even a little positive about talking to him later. She spun around and grinned, making a sweeping, overly dramatic gesture with her arms. "Ferman awaits!"

Perry was thankful it was dark and that the streetlight's bulb was on its last leg, because he didn't want Daisy to unexpectedly turn around and see his still outstretched arms. He quickly dropped them and forced a nonchalance he didn't feel as he walked to the Hershbergers' porch to get Ferman. Up until she hugged him, he was fine. Hunky-dory, even. Talking with Daisy and seeing her smile had felt good, in a platonic way. Getting his thoughts about Ruby off his chest was cathartic too. Until now he had thought their relationship bit the dust because of the butterfly room incident. The truth was that, once the strong desire of infatuation faded, there was nothing substantial between them.

He watched the sensor-powered light turn on when Daisy hit the top of the porch and went inside. His shoulders slumped. He thought he was firmly in friendship territory with her until he had her in his arms, and that all changed. He tried his usual mantra—Daisy was taken, and he was committed to singlehood. Then another thought hit him. *Maybe if the circumstances were different . . .*

Perry groaned and trudged up the porch steps. Circumstances were what they were, and nothing would change them. So whatever attraction and longing he had for her, he had to let it go. He got over his desire for Ruby. He could get over his . . . his . . .

The door opened, nearly crashing into him. "My apologies, Perry," Howard said, Ferman right behind him. "Didn't realize you were standing there."

Perry acknowledged the apology with a wave of his hand. "C'mon, Ferman," he said, eager to get back home where he could hopefully think more coherently.

"I'm comin', I'm comin'," Ferman groused like a little kid who was being made to leave his friend's house. "You know I move slow."

Perry stood at the ready to help the old man down the steps. Ferman managed to make it down them and limped toward the buggy.

"He's had a full day," Howard said when Ferman was out of earshot. "We hit all the Marigold hot spots."

Perry drudged up a half chuckle. "I'm sure that didn't take long."

"It wouldn't have, but you know Ferman. Never met a stranger. 'Night, Perry. *Danki* for bringing Daisy home."

Perry almost said "anytime" but caught himself. He walked to his buggy, his emotions in a freefall. There was absolutely no way he was falling for Daisy Hershberger. Impossible. Inconceivable. Never mind that he'd never experienced this intensity of feeling for Ruby, or anyone else.

She was taken. She saw him as a friend. And he saw her as . . .

A wonderful, amazing, beautiful woman.

Dear Lord . . . I'm in trouble.

—————

Ferman sat in the chair after Perry dropped him off at the front door and went to put up his horse. The *bu* had been gone for a long while, longer than it took to settle a horse in for the night. Ferman could tell he was highly agitated, and there had to be only one reason why—Daisy Hershberger. Thus, he waited patiently for Perry to finish his business so he could have a talk with him.

When Perry told him this morning that he and Daisy were going to a family event and Ferman would be hanging out with Howard Hershberger, he was confused. Not about Howard. He liked the man, and they'd had a great day running around Marigold visiting various businesses and people. They even stopped by Wagler's, and Ferman conversed with Micah for a while. The men were extremely busy, though, and he was grateful he wasn't working there anymore. Even if his hip hadn't gone sideways, he wouldn't have been able to keep up.

What he didn't understand was why Perry and Daisy had gone to the Bontragers if there was nothing going on between them. Sure, they could have gone as friends, but he couldn't wrap his mind around the two of them being completely platonic. There was too much chemistry between them, and eventually one or both would realize it. Maybe that's what happened tonight. Ferman was dying to find out.

Yes, he was a nosy old coot who couldn't stop meddling. *At least I'm acknowledging it.*

It wasn't long before his patience grew thin, and he got up from the chair to peek out the window. No sign of him yet—wait. A shadowy figure was heading this way. Like the Hershbergers, Perry had a porch lamp that was triggered by movement, and he was almost at the front door when the light came on. Only then did Ferman realize he'd left his cane by his chair. *Bother.*

He zoomed back to the chair—more like a hasty, inept hobble—and plopped down on the seat just as the door opened. Whew, that sudden movement took a little wind out of him. He folded his hands on his lap, attempting to appear casual and in control of his respiratory function.

Perry shut the door and turned to him. Then he tilted his head. "You okay?"

Ferman fought for breath. "Yep," he said with a strangled gasp.

Perry put his straw hat on the rack by the door. "I'll be in the back."

"I need a moment of your time."

Perry hesitated, and Ferman wondered if he was going to refuse his request and head into *the room*. Then he sat down on the couch, his posture uptight and his expression just as stiff.

Ferman had never seen Perry so out of sorts. Stoic, yes. Reserved, absolutely. But worked up? Nope. Hold up. He had seen him in this state once before—last Sunday afternoon when he and Daisy had been working on that letter. Something serious must have happened between them. "Everything *geh* all right today?"

"*Ya*. Just swell."

Sarcasm didn't suit Perry, that was for sure. "Doesn't sound like it."

"I'm not in the mood, Ferman. If you have something to say, just say it."

"All right." The boy had opened the door, and he was more than prepared to walk through. "You and Daisy—"

"There is no me and Daisy."

"You're wrong," Ferman said. He held up his hand when Perry tried to interrupt again. "I've been around the pasture a time or three and I know what I see. You have feelings for that *maedel*, don't you?"

Perry hung his head and nodded.

"That's nothing to be ashamed about."

"I'm not ashamed. I'm frustrated. She's in love with someone else."

"I don't think so—"

"His name is Maynard," Perry said. "Today I asked her if she was in love with him and she said yes."

Ferman almost fell out of his chair. "That doesn't make any sense."

"None of this makes sense." He slumped against the couch back. "I promised myself I wouldn't be in this position again. I would never fall in—"

"In love?"

"I can't be in love with her. I've only known her a little more than a week."

"Oh, I don't know about that." Ferman chuckled. "Me and Lovina? It was love at first sight. I saw her across the church pews—"

"Got it." Perry rolled his eyes.

Ferman would have been offended if he didn't know the situation was dire. "Are you *sure* she's in love with this Maynard fellow? It's possible she only *thinks* she loves him."

"That's not the case."

But Ferman saw the doubt in his eyes. Doubt and more than a little hope. "Maybe you should show her she's in love with someone else."

"Me?" Perry's laugh was full of bitterness. "Trust me, in her mind, we're only friends."

"What if you told her how you felt—"

"I can't do that." He shot up from the couch. "I won't. Not again . . . Never mind." He stalked to the back of the house and slammed the door to *the room* shut.

The house had never sounded so silent. Ferman winced. *That's a man who's had his heart broken.* Ferman had been fortunate enough not to go through that experience. Lovina was his first and his one and only. He could see why Perry was blind to his own feelings. What he didn't know was why Daisy was.

There was only one way to find out.

Tonight he had fully intended on telling Perry he was going home after church tomorrow. More than once this past week, he'd caught Daisy and Perry giving him strange looks whenever he faked the intensity of his pain or started to walk fairly normally. He was sure they suspected he wasn't being honest. But how could he leave when there was important, unfinished business here? And while he'd vowed to step back, stay out of the way, and let God do his thing when it came to Daisy and Perry, he had to wonder if maybe he was still here for a reason. Perhaps he was a part of God's plan. "Is that true, Lord?"

He rose from the chair, grabbed his cane, and headed for Perry's bedroom. Ferman Eash was about to engage in some long, intense prayer with his God.

Chapter 20

When Daisy headed to Perry's on Monday morning, she paused in front of the phone shanty. She hadn't called Maynard back on Saturday night, knowing full well she couldn't chat with him on Sunday. There was some time to talk to him this morning, but she still hesitated, despite her conversation with Perry the other night. She thought about asking Grace for advice or insight, but she had spent the afternoon at Kyle's and didn't return until after supper. Daisy decided that was a good thing. She couldn't bring herself to admit to Grace or anyone else about her continued reluctance to talk to Maynard. Not even Perry, and not after she'd made such a fuss over how they were 100 percent supposed to be together.

So she clung to her initial assumption—phone calls weren't for them. Still, she needed to at least let him know that. *Later.* She would call him after supper tonight and tell him her decision. As close to eight o'clock as possible.

As she walked over to Perry's, her mood lightened. Except for church, they didn't see each other yesterday. She wasn't surprised he'd left early, and that was okay. But she missed talking to him. He was so helpful Saturday night, even if she had changed her mind about reaching out to Maynard. And if, um, *when* she and Maynard kissed, she would be a little more prepared. She did think a lot about how good Perry's hug felt, but of course it would. They were connected now. *As friends. Only friends.* Strange how she was compelled to internally repeat that.

Perry had mentioned Friday that he had an early job on Monday and was going to make his own lunch, so Daisy had expected him not to be home when she arrived. She opened the front door, the knob working fine, as it had all week. Perry hadn't had to replace it after all. When she walked inside the house, she saw Ferman puttering around the kitchen, sans cane.

"What are you doing?" She dropped her basket on the couch and hurried to him.

"Making you breakfast." He glanced over his shoulder and gave her a cheeky grin. "How do you like your eggs?"

"Scrambled—wait. Why aren't you using your cane?"

"Don't need it in this tiny kitchen." He cracked two eggs into a bowl, grabbed a fork, and commenced scrambling.

Daisy stood there, observing him as he moved around the confined space, his limp only slight and using the countertop for balance, his face free of pain. Hmm. "You weren't moving as well yesterday at church. Or as fast."

"It's a Monday miracle." He poured the eggs into the sizzling hot pan and shooed her out of the kitchen. "Have a seat, young lady. You'll have your repast in a jiffy."

She did a double take, then followed orders. Sure enough, in less than five minutes he set a plate of fluffy scrambled eggs and buttered bread in front of her before taking the seat across the table. He winced slightly as he lowered his body, but nothing like he had before. Monday miracle or not, she was happy he was moving so much easier.

After a silent prayer, she tasted the eggs. Nice and peppery, the way she liked them. "*Danki*, Ferman," she said. "These are *gut*."

"They're my specialty." He folded his hands together on the table, his arthritic knuckles a little gnarled. "I'm going home tomorrow."

She almost dropped her fork at his sudden announcement. This is what he'd always wanted and what she and Perry had helped him achieve. Still, the abrupt way he said it caught her off guard. "That's . . . great."

"I think so." He grinned again.

"Does Perry know?"

"Told him this morning."

Daisy wondered if he'd had the same reaction. Probably not. He was generous and hospitable to Ferman, but he also treasured his privacy. He would be eager to regain it.

"You won't need to come over here anymore," Ferman said, sipping on his coffee. "Perry's got a lot of work lined up for us."

Her heart dipped. She'd expected to be a little disappointed about not being needed. But it hurt more than she thought. "I'm . . . happy for you."

"*Ya*," he said, stretching his arms out in front of him. "Now you can spend more time with your family and write all the letters you want to your fella in Dover."

Frowning, she said, "How do you know about him?"

He tapped his temple. "I put two and two together. You mentioned you had a 'possibility back home.'" He hooked his fingers in the air. "And Perry said you were writing a letter to 'folks back home.'" Another hooking motion. "Didn't take long to figure out you had a beau. What's his name?"

"Maynard," she mumbled, stabbing her eggs with her fork.

"I'm sure you can't wait to see him again. Tell me all about him."

She looked at Ferman and saw he was genuinely interested. "Well, he's . . . he's . . ."

The door opened and Perry walked inside.

The man I love.

Perry glanced at them as he went into the kitchen and opened the pantry. "I got partway to my first job and realized I forgot my lunch," he said.

"You could eat at The Railway Diner again," Ferman suggested.

Perry poked his head around the pantry door, a half scowl on his face. "No thanks." He took out a jar of peanut butter and a saltine sleeve.

He couldn't function on so little food. Daisy jumped up. "I'll make something for you," she said, going to the kitchen.

He shook his head and shut the door, brushing past her. "This is fine. See you guys later."

She stood there, unable to move as Perry left. Intense sadness filled her. *They really don't need me anymore.*

"Daisy?" Ferman turned around in his chair. "What were you saying about Maynard?"

"I . . ." She shook her head. "I have to check on the laundry." She went to the mudroom and looked at the basket in front of the wringer washer. There were barely enough clothes for a full load, but she put them in anyway. Since this was her last day at Perry's, she would spend it finishing up any chore that had to be done.

She picked up a single work shirt and held it for a moment, running her fingers over the fabric. She looked away and tossed it into the washer.

Ferman heard the wringer washer start and looked at Daisy's unfinished plate of eggs. He frowned, glad that he didn't have to force his good cheer anymore. He hadn't cooked breakfast in a long time, even before he moved in with Perry. Weeks, maybe months before that he had simply eaten easy breakfasts like cold cereal or instant oatmeal using hot water from the kettle. His hip was tweaking more than he anticipated. Still, not enough to keep him from going home.

He waited to see if Daisy would return, but when he heard the back door open and close, he pushed back from the table. He'd spent hours praying on Saturday night, not just about Daisy and Perry but about his hip, his relationship with Junior, even pouring out some pent-up resentment that Lovina was taken home before Ferman thought she should be. He repented of that, of course. God's timing was always perfect, although knowing that didn't make the grief any lighter. It did, however, give him more peace than he'd felt in a long time.

He also gained direction. He had to go home and face the empty house and memories. He also had to address his hip. While getting a hip replacement scared him, he would talk to the doctor about other options. And if that was his only one, he'd have to man up and get it done. He didn't want to be this dependent anymore, not when he still had years left to live, God willing.

Eventually he would have to talk to Junior too, and try to work things out. *One step at a time, though.*

As far as his part in Perry and Daisy's personal business? There was none, other than what he'd done this morning—verify that whatever her relationship was with Maynard, it paled to her feelings for Perry. The *bu* forgetting his lunch was fortuitous. Ferman was able to see the yearning looks they gave each other but didn't seem to perceive. But he was done meddling, questioning, and yes, doing a little manipulating too. It was hard enough seeing Daisy's disappointment when he said she didn't need to come over to Perry's anymore. The depth of it had caught him off guard. He just hoped that after he went home, they wouldn't do something stupid, like ignore each other.

And if they did? Then maybe that was God's will. His ways certainly weren't Ferman's.

Daisy was a whirlwind the rest of the day, and Ferman got tired just watching her. She not only finished up the laundry in the basket, she washed Perry's sheets and blankets, including the quilt he'd been sleeping with on the couch, scrubbed the floors, baked bread and cookies, and polished all the furniture until it gleamed. Near evening after she finished making a chicken potpie casserole and it was baking in the oven, she entered the living room as Ferman sat down in his chair after taking a nap on the patio. He was going to miss doing that.

He was going to miss a lot of things.

"Can you take the potpie out of the oven if Perry doesn't get home in time?" she asked, wearily picking up her basket.

"You don't want to stay for supper?"

She didn't look at him. "*Nee*. I can eat with my *familye*."

Bother, he was getting a lump in his throat. Why did this feel like goodbye? It wasn't like he wouldn't see her again. At church, and . . . well, that would be the only place unless he visited her or she visited him, and soon she would be returning to Dover.

Daisy headed for the door. "Bye, Ferman."

"See you later, Daisy."

She closed the door.

Goodbye, sweet maedel.

Daisy wiped her eyes as she hustled down the porch steps. She'd teared up while she made the casserole, knowing it was the last meal she would cook for the men. Ugh, she was frustrated with herself. She shouldn't be this disappointed or sad or teary. She should be thrilled that Ferman was healed and Perry's world would go back to normal.

Just like hers.

She paused in Perry's yard, gathering her emotions. She could see the Hershbergers' phone shanty from here, and that made her think of Maynard again. He had been on her mind all day, and it had been a while since he'd consumed her thoughts so much. Ferman was right. She would have plenty of time to talk and write him letters. She should be happy about that too.

Sniffing, she straightened up, her body aching from all the work she'd done today. Perry would have a sparkling house when he came home tonight. And she had to put that and him behind her. Other than spending the rest of her time in Marigold with Grace and her family, Maynard was her focus.

She started to leave when Perry's buggy pulled into the driveway. Talk about lousy timing. Her emotions were in shambles and she'd hoped to avoid him tonight. But she couldn't run off and not talk to him. That would be *seltsam*, not to mention rude.

He pulled the buggy to a stop in front of her, and she waited as he hopped out. He jogged to the other side. "Hey," he said, stopping in front of her but giving a wide berth. "I suppose Ferman gave you the news."

"*Ya.*" She clutched her basket to her. Over the past two days the weather had been warm, and spring was coming into full bloom. There was still plenty of sunlight and she could clearly see Perry's handsome face, unlike the other night when he'd dropped her off and picked up Ferman. His face was unreadable.

"I'll drop him off in the morning," Perry said. "Micah's going to bring Ferman's mare to him after work. She's been having a ball hanging out with his two horses. Oh, and I stopped and talked to *Mamm* today. She was upset with me for lying to her, but then she understood why. She promised not to interfere anymore. Don't worry, she doesn't blame you. She did ask when you were going back to Dover, though. She'd like to see you again if that's possible."

Daisy nodded, a lump in her throat. "Probably in a few weeks."

"I'll let her know."

She rocked back and forth on her heels as excruciating silence stretched between them.

He pulled down his hat brim, shielding part of his face. "Well—"

"There's potpie in the oven," she blurted.

"*Danki*, Daisy."

She hoped he would add "from Dover." He didn't. There was nothing left for her to do but go back to Grace's. With a nod, she walked away.

A butterfly flitted close to her, then flew off. It wasn't Lady. It wasn't even a painted lady. But it did remind her of something. She turned around to see Perry take the horse's lead to guide him to the barn. "Perry?"

He stopped and turned.

Rushing to him, she said, "Can I visit the butterfly room one last time?"

It seemed like an entire day passed before he finally spoke. "Tomorrow afternoon. I'll be home after three."

A spark lit up in her. She didn't understand why, but it felt so good after such a disappointing day. "*Danki*."

He nodded, then headed with his horse to the barn.

She didn't watch him walk away this time. Instead, she went

straight to her aunt and uncle's house, not giving the phone shanty a second look.

≈•≈

When Perry pulled into the driveway after work the next day, Daisy was on his front porch, and he assumed she was there waiting for him to let her into his butterfly room. Yesterday evening had been tough. The whole day was, with him thinking about Ferman's announcement that he wanted to go home and his baffling internal reaction to it. Instead of being happy for the old man, all he could think about was not seeing Daisy anymore.

He managed to face reality by the time he returned home. The conversation with his mother had gone better than he'd hoped, and she really did comprehend her role in his and Daisy's pact. *"I shouldn't have pushed you,"* she'd said, dabbing the corner of her eye with the handkerchief she always kept in her apron pocket. *"That's my fault."* Then she looked at him. *"So there's* nee *hope for you and Daisy?"*

"None," he said firmly, and she dropped the subject. But his strong tone hadn't just been for *Mamm's* benefit. After Ferman's insistence that Daisy had feelings for him, Perry had to shut down all the outside noise.

But he couldn't refuse Daisy's last request. That wouldn't be fair. She had demonstrated an honest interest in his collection, and butterflies in general. He couldn't say no to her, not in this case.

"Whoa," he said to his horse, slowing down the buggy. He'd intended to yell to Daisy that he'd be right there after he went to the barn, but she was running toward him, cupping something in her hands. When she reached his side, she looked distraught. "Oh, Perry," she said, her voice thick. "Tell me she's going to be okay."

242

When she opened her hands and revealed a barely alive butterfly, his chest almost caved in.

"It's Lady, isn't it?" She winced, staring at the immobile insect in her palms. "She appeared in front of me, and I thought she was okay. Then she landed on my shoulder and started to sway. I picked her up . . . she's going to be okay, *ya*?"

"Let's *geh* inside." His throat ached as he led her to the front door. If this was Lady, and he wasn't sure it was, he wouldn't be surprised if she was taking her last breaths. The butterfly had lived longer than any other he'd known since he started studying them. But there was no reason to jump to that conclusion. Not yet.

They went inside and he pulled out the chair for Daisy to sit down. "Be right back." He rushed to his butterfly room and got his insect emergency first aid kit, which consisted of tweezers, tape, and a few other odds and ends. He sat in the chair next to Daisy and held out his hand, glancing at the markings. Sure enough, it was female. "I'll take her."

Gingerly she put the butterfly in his hand, and instantly he knew it was indeed Lady. He also knew she was dead, although from how Daisy was staring at her, silently willing her to live on, he could see she still wasn't aware. He set Lady on a folded square of paper towel. "Daisy."

"She's okay, *ya*?" Daisy looked at him, tears in her eyes. "She's just taking a nap."

He shook his head. "*Nee.* She's gone."

Her lower lip trembled as she touched the butterfly's wing. "I'm so sorry, Lady."

Perry couldn't stop himself from taking Daisy's hand. "She lived a long time," he said, fighting his own sadness. He never liked to see butterflies or any other living thing die. Sometimes fatalities were necessary, such as controlling pests that killed vegetables and flowers, or keeping cockroaches and vermin out of the house, or putting food on the table. Death was simply part of the circle of life.

Daisy wiped her eyes with the back of her hand. "I know I'm being silly," she said in a thick whisper, gripping his hand as she stared at Lady. "I know she's just a bug."

"She was special." Perry swallowed. "I've known a lot of bugs in my life, and I knew she was special when I first met her."

Her fingers slipped out of his grasp, and she finally looked at him. "I don't know why I was so attached to her. I was always so happy when she showed up."

He smiled, unable to keep from wiping a stray tear from her cheek with his thumb. "Me too." When he started to remove his hand from her face, she stopped him, pressing his palm against her warm skin and closing her eyes.

Perry couldn't move. Couldn't breathe.

Her eyes slowly opened, locking on his. She pressed a tiny kiss against the heel of his hand.

A hot shiver went down his spine, and his already weak defenses were destroyed. "Daisy," he whispered.

"You said . . ." She swallowed. "You said I would know when it was right."

Perry stilled. She didn't have to define what "it" was. They both knew. He leaned forward until they were close, so close—

Knock. Knock.

They jumped apart and Daisy grabbed Lady before she was knocked to the floor.

Perry's heart slammed in his chest as they stared at each other, then at the door. Another knock sounded. "I've got to—"

"Answer it." She placed her hands primly on her lap.

He shoved his bangs off his forehead—when did his palm get so sweaty?—and opened the door to a short, unfamiliar man with red hair and glasses. "Can I help you?"

"Is Daisy here?"

Frowning, Perry glanced over his shoulder. Daisy was on her feet now, her face stark white.

"M-m-m—" She gulped. "Maynard?"

Chapter 21

*C*reak . . . *creak* . . . *creak* . . .

    Daisy stared blankly from her seat on the porch swing, the creaking sound hammering in her ears. She'd finally gotten over the shock of seeing Maynard on Perry's doorstep, but that was all she'd gotten over. She was still sad about Lady dying, despite knowing that butterflies didn't live long. Getting attached to a butterfly had never been a possibility, never mind shedding tears over her.

And then there was Perry. She could still feel the warmth of his rough palm against her cheek, see the tenderness and understanding in his eyes, experience the tingling sensation throughout her body as they kept their gazes locked. She shouldn't have kissed his hand. She shouldn't have wanted to kiss him either. Really, *really* kiss him.

But she didn't regret either one.

"Your *onkel* needs to fix this swing."

She glanced at Maynard sitting next to her, only a few inches separating them. They came out here after eating supper with her family, at Grace's suggestion. The swing was definitely made for two.

"It creaks really loud." He scratched behind his ear.

"*Ya*," she said tightly. After they left Perry's, Maynard explained that he had arrived in Marigold a few minutes ago by taxi. "You didn't call me back when I left a message yesterday morning, and you ignored my other calls. You've been acting *seltsam*, Daisy. I didn't have a choice but to see for myself if you were all right."

"You could have asked *Mamm*," Daisy mumbled, crossing her arms over her chest. She was keyed up, uncomfortably so, like she'd been robbed of something beautiful.

"Your *mamm* isn't very talkative." Maynard stepped onto the gravel driveway.

Talk about pot and kettle. During supper tonight, *Aenti* Rosella had been uncharacteristically quiet too. Daisy knew why. *Mamm* and *Aenti* weren't going to make things easy for her and Maynard.

Creak . . . creak . . . creak . . .

Daisy glanced at the sunset, at the two squirrels chasing each other around the yard, at the weeds growing at the edge of the driveway near the road—anything to keep from looking at Perry's house and wondering what he was doing right now. After he answered the door and she said Maynard's name, Perry had been friendly to him and hastily ushered the two of them outside. Which he should have, considering the compromising position they'd just been in. He also didn't seem the least affected by their almost kiss.

She found that most confusing of all, enough that she was sure she'd imagined he'd wanted to kiss her. That made more sense than him actually wanting to kiss her. He'd just affirmed their friendship Saturday night. Her cheeks heated. Of course he didn't want to kiss her. Now came the regrets. Oh boy.

"Well." Maynard ground out the word like he was a decade older than Ferman. "We should both get to bed. First bus leaves at six thirty in the morning."

She popped up from the swing. "I'll reserve the taxi for you."

He touched her arm, stopping her. His eyes widened as if he'd shocked himself with the gesture, and he quickly withdrew his hand. "Already took care of it." He got to his feet, the swing swaying behind him. "You should pack tonight."

"Pack?"

"*Ya*. You don't want to leave it to the last minute. We could miss our ride."

"Maynard, what are you talking about?"

He frowned. "Going back to Dover."

"*You're* going back to Dover," she said, still not following. "I have more than three weeks left of my visit."

His frown deepened. "But I thought you missed me."

"I . . . I do." Why was it so hard for her to say those words? "I'm just not ready to *geh* home yet."

Maynard took a step forward. "I'm ready for you to come home."

Daisy paused, waiting for a shiver, tingle, spark, something to happen inside her now that he was finally giving her undivided attention.

"I already took two days off to come get you. I have to get back to work." He put his hands on his hips, his eyeglasses slipping down his nose a little. He looked her up and down. "There *is* something wrong with you, isn't there?"

She lifted her chin. "*Nee*. I'm the same *maedel* you've always known. And honestly, Maynard, you haven't seemed all that worried, until you brought up work."

One reddish eyebrow lifted. "You've been gone a long time. How was I supposed to feel?"

"You missed me then?"

His brow furrowed.

"It's an easy question, Maynard. Did . . . you . . . miss . . . me?"

"*Ya*," he said, still looking befuddled. "I missed you. I want you to come home."

There it was. A small spark in her heart, a minuscule tickle in her tummy. She dropped her arms and moved closer to him. Perry had been right. Playing hard to get worked. Maynard was finally admitting some feelings for her. And although she should leave well enough alone and wait until they were in Dover where they would have genuine privacy to have "the talk," she needed more. She took his hand.

Maynard glanced down at their entwined fingers, seemingly terrified.

She moved closer to him, closer than she ever dared. "Kiss me, Maynard."

"What?"

"You heard me." She tilted her head to his. "Kiss me."

"Here?" He dropped her hand. "On the porch?"

"*Ya.*"

He stumbled, the swing hitting the back of his thighs as his gaze darted around. "But what if someone sees us?"

"So? Let them see."

He grimaced, lowering his voice. "This isn't appropriate, Daisy."

It wasn't, and she should back off right now. While she'd had eighteen months to pine for him, he was still sitting in the friend zone. But she couldn't stop as despair gripped her. What if she had misread their relationship all along? What if her confidence that God had brought them together was misplaced? *What if I was wrong?*

She took a step toward him. If he wasn't going to do it, she was. She had to know if she had made a huge mistake—

Maynard's arm shot around her waist. He pulled her against him . . . and kissed her.

Perry froze, his heart tumbling to his knees as he stood on the patio facing the Hershberger home. After Daisy left with . . . *him*, he was alone. He'd taken Lady to the butterfly room and set her on the glass case, his stomach in knots. He wasn't sure he would be able to mount her on a board and add her to his collection. Not now, possibly not ever.

And when he walked out of the room to his empty house, his mood darkened. When the silence he'd always craved became too much, he decided to sit on his back patio for a while, expecting that Daisy and Maynard would be inside the house.

Instead, he saw the exact moment Maynard took her in his arms and kissed her. Not just once, and not for a quick second. It was a full-on kiss.

Like the one he'd intended to give her.

He turned around, feeling sick. All this time he'd called Maynard an idiot. *I'm the stupid one.* He'd been wrong. Ferman was wrong. His mother was wrong, because he had caught the doubt in her eyes when he told her that there was nothing between him and Daisy.

And like the fool he was, he'd let his guard down.

Perry stalked back into the house, anger coursing through him. Not at Daisy, though. She'd always been honest with him about her feelings for Maynard. She'd even insisted she loved him when he asked her.

He stilled, standing in the middle of the dining room. She'd been honest . . . until today. Until the kiss on his palm, her soft, vulnerable words afterward, the desire in her eyes when she basically asked him to kiss her. Was all that a lie?

"*. . . She only* thinks *she loves him.*"

Ferman's words hit him like a battering ram. He knocked them away. They weren't true. She had no idea what a tiny kiss would do to him. The ache in his chest intensified as he thought about Ruby, or more accurately how their relationship started. In the beginning, she had looked at him the same way Daisy did. Like he was special. *Like she loved me.*

No. Ruby *almost* looked at him the same way. He knew now that she'd never managed to reach his soul.

Daisy had.

He jerked off his boots, then his socks and his shirt. He didn't have to worry about lack of privacy anymore, and he needed a shower for a variety of reasons. But no amount of mental scrubbing would erase Daisy from his mind and heart. That would take time. He knew that all too well. *I've been here before.* And it hurt worse the second time around.

His hands went to his waistband as a knock sounded at the door. He froze, seeing the doorknob fall to the floor with a bang. *What in the world?* Then the door opened . . . to Daisy.

Daisy stood in front of Perry, her chest heaving as she gasped for air, partly because she ran straight over here after Maynard kissed her, and partly because—triple whoa—Perry was shirtless again. Oh, and then there was the surprise of the doorknob falling out of its hole again, but that was the furthest thing from her mind as she battled to disengage her gaze from Perry. She seemed to have a knack for catching him without a shirt . . . and she wasn't about to complain.

"What are you doing here?" he growled, grabbing his shirt off the floor and yanking it over his head so hard she thought he would burst the seams. When he finished, he was glaring at her.

"I—" Her words disappeared at his ferocious look. She was here to tell him she was wrong and had almost made a horrible mistake.

When Maynard kissed her, she felt nothing. Less than nothing, if that were a thing. And when they parted, it was if scales had fallen off her eyes. From the ungainly way he moved away from her, he agreed.

"Um," he'd said, shoving his hands into his pockets. *"That was . . ."*

"Terrible," she supplied.

"Ya." His awkward expression eased. *"You should stay here."*

She nodded, relieved. *"I'll pay you back for my ticket."*

"Nee need. I'm sure I can get a refund." He paused. *"I really did miss you, Daisy."*

"Me, or my peach pie?"

"Both." He half smiled.

For the very first time, she was at ease with Maynard Miller. There was no wishing for things to be different. No forcing something to happen. Every single thought she had about her and Maynard being a couple vanished. Poof, it was gone. And she'd never felt better.

When he went inside to pack, she faced Perry's house, grinning. She had been totally wrong, wrong, *wrong*, about Maynard, but the incredible, delightful emotions now washing over her were oh so right. She loved Perry. She didn't have to kiss him to know, she just knew, deep in her heart. In her soul. And she couldn't wait to tell him. Even if he didn't return her feelings now, he might in the future if they spent more time together. Now that she was free from Maynard, they could do just that.

As sure as she was that God hadn't set Maynard apart for her, she was even more positive Perry was the *one*.

But now he was shooting visual daggers at her. His burly arms crossed over that incredible chest of his and he continued to stare at her. Hard.

"Maynard's leaving in the morning," she squeaked out.

Crickets.

She wanted to go to him, but his black look pinned her in place. "I . . . stop looking at me like that."

"Like what?"

"Like you're mad at me." The last time she had only thought he was upset with her. She was sure of it now.

He dropped his arms, and for the briefest of seconds his expression softened, only to turn icy again. "I'll ask you again. What are you doing here?"

"I came to talk to you. To tell you—"

"I don't care."

Her eyes widened. This was a side of him she'd never seen before, and she didn't like it. "What's wrong?"

"*Nix*," he said sharply and went to the door, his bare feet slapping against the wood floor. He picked up the doorknob and shoved it back, then opened the door wider. "Get out."

She couldn't believe what she was hearing. Or how harsh he was being. Something must have happened . . . oh no. Her whole body went cold. "Did you see—" She didn't have to say the words. His glacial demeanor said it all. "I can explain—"

"How could I have been so stupid." He scrubbed his hand over his face, his words muffled. Then he looked at her. "How could I have been so wrong about you?"

"Perry . . . I don't understand—"

"I think you do. Because I'm not buying your innocent act anymore. That's what it was, *ya*? An act to string me along so I fell in love with you? And now you're here after you kissed *another* man?"

She blanched. She didn't comprehend half of what he said, but she could easily clear up the Maynard part. "If you'll just listen to me—"

"Leave, Daisy. Now. If you won't *geh*, then I will."

He was serious.

And she was numb. She hung her head and dashed past him, hugging her arms, fighting tears as she ran back to Grace's. Not only had she been wrong about Maynard, but about Perry too.

That mistake hurt most of all.

"You can't leave."

Daisy folded the last of the three dresses she'd brought with her, ignoring Grace's plea. Maynard was in the guest room, and since it was almost eight thirty, she was sure he was asleep. That was fine. She'd wake up extra early and tell him she was going home with him. Not to be with him. Her horrendous interaction with Perry didn't change the fact that there was nothing between her and Maynard, and that included friendship. Once they were back in Dover, they would go their separate ways, and she was perfectly fine with that.

"Did you hear me, Daisy?" Grace took the dress from her. "Maynard isn't the man for you. That was obvious the moment I met him."

"I know that now."

Grace blinked. "You do? Then why are you leaving with him?"

She took the dress from her cousin and refolded it. Grace wouldn't understand, and she didn't want to tell her what happened with Perry. She couldn't stay here, not when she knew he detested her. She pressed the dress to her chest, her heart splitting in two.

"Daisy." Her cousin gently took the dress from her and led her to the side of the bed. "I'm sorry. Did you and Maynard have a fight?"

Tears spilled down her cheeks, and she neither confirmed nor denied Grace's assumption. Better to let her cousin think this was about Maynard and not Perry. Then her sorrow got the best of her. "Why am I such a *dummkopf*, Grace?" She bent over and sobbed.

"Oh, Daisy." Grace put her arms around her. "You're not *dumm*. Love is complicated."

"It's not for you and Kyle. Or your parents. Or mine, or—"

"Stop comparing your situation to anyone else's." She reached over and took a tissue off her side table and handed it to Daisy. "And just because something looks easy, doesn't mean it is."

Daisy sat up, honked into the tissue, and wiped the bottom of her nose. "It's nice of you to try to cheer me up."

"But it's not working."

She shook her head. "It's not just that I was wrong about Maynard." *And Perry.* It was apparent to her now that when she went to talk to Perry, she had started doing the same thing with him that she'd done with Maynard—assuming he was the one and rationalizing how she could make that happen. "I never should have presumed to know what God wanted for me. I can see that so clearly now. Why couldn't I see it then?"

"I don't know. God's ways aren't ours. We all know that."

Grabbing another tissue, she said, "At least *Mamm* is going to be happy."

"I doubt it. Not when she sees you like this."

"I'll get it together before I leave." She wasn't sure how, but she had to. She didn't want Maynard to see her cry, and she absolutely didn't want to tell him a single thing about Perry Bontrager. They would spend hours riding home together. If she was lucky, she could sleep during some of them.

"You could always stay," Grace said hopefully.

Daisy shook her head. Not with Perry next door. Even if she didn't see him every day, she would know he was there. She wouldn't be able to sit under the tree and do her cross-stitch without thinking about the time he had touched her ankle trying to catch a white admiral. And if she saw a painted lady, she would completely fall apart. *Poor Lady.* Oh no, she was crying again. "I'm sorry," she said, pressing her eyes with the heels of her hands, trying to keep her tears at bay.

"Don't be." Grace handed her the whole tissue box. "Cry all you need to. I've cried over Kyle a time or two." She leaned forward. "News flash. Guys can be insensitive sometimes."

Daisy managed a light chuckle, although she had no idea how. Perry was heartless earlier, but he had reason to be after seeing her and Maynard kiss. Before that, he was the kindest, smartest, and most generous person she'd ever met. "I just hope . . ." she whispered thickly.

"Hope what?"

She wanted to tell Grace, but she couldn't. Although she didn't mean to, she had hurt Perry deeply, and not long after he had told her about his breakup with Ruby. She knew how hard it had been for him when they broke up because he had cared for her at one time . . .

Daisy sat straight up, the tissue box falling off her lap. Pieces fell into place like snowflakes hitting the ground during a blizzard. Why would Perry be *that* upset to see her kissing Maynard? He was the one who had helped her with her Maynard problem, and he'd encouraged her several times to write and call him. He'd even given her the sage advice to play hard to get. That had gotten Maynard's attention more than anything she'd ever done on her own.

"Daisy?"

Grace's voice sounded distant as she continued to think about her interactions with Perry. "*We're friends, ya?*" He said that to her, and she'd said it to him. It was true. She would live the rest of her life believing that, for the past two weeks they had become, without a doubt, the best of friends. Then the final barrier crumbled as she realized the truth that she hadn't seen until now.

All this time she'd been fretting about deceiving others. She had deceived herself most of all.

All the wonderful feelings she'd experienced and tried to deny when she was around Perry came to the fore. How she felt sitting on his lap, and when she was in his arms the other night. How she couldn't resist kissing his palm or wanting him to kiss her. The words he'd just said when he sent her away—the ones that had been a blur because she was so determined to set things straight with him about Maynard.

"I fell in love with you . . ."

Daisy felt hot. Then cold. Then hot again, and she stayed that way. She might not be a *dummkopf,* but she was clearly clueless and oblivious. Perry loved her. She did suspect that his declaration might have slipped out in anger, but that didn't mean it wasn't true. He loved her, and she definitely loved him.

She resisted the urge to give in to her emotions, though. Just because she wanted something to be true, didn't mean it was. Or should be. She smiled and turned to Grace. "Can you help me unpack?"

"But . . ."

She went to her suitcase and yanked out the three dresses she'd neatly placed inside earlier. She wasn't going back to Dover, not until she and Perry had a conversation. It might be for the last time, and if it was, she would deal with it. "I'm staying in Marigold."

Chapter 22

Knock. Knock.

Perry waited for Ferman to answer the door. The old man might be moving better and faster, but his house was larger than Perry's and he didn't want Ferman to rush, even though he was the one who had asked him to come over. Perry figured he was probably wanting to talk about going back to work—something he needed to do himself. After Daisy left with Maynard two days ago, he had rescheduled his jobs. He told himself it was because he needed a vacation, but he knew the reason, and it was one he didn't want to think about.

He'd spent his time off doing next to nothing, other than eating PB&Js and moping around. He couldn't bring himself to go into the butterfly room. It had been a refuge after his breakup with Ruby. Now all it did was remind him of Daisy.

After a minute or two, Ferman opened the door. "Howdy, stranger," he said in English and grinned. "Come on in."

Perry followed him to a large living room. Last time he was inside this house, it was before sunrise, and he didn't get a good look at it. Now he could see Ferman had a very nice place. Much cozier and more welcoming than Perry's sparse house, with two comfortable-looking recliners, several muted yet colorful quilts on the couch and backs of the chairs, and some flower pictures hanging on the walls. Definitely a woman's influence that was due to Lovina, he guessed, and probably Polly Ann when she lived here.

"Have a seat." Ferman gestured to the full-size couch across from him.

Perry handed him two puzzle books first. "You left these behind."

"They belong to Rosella Hershberger." He took them from him. "I doubt she'll want them back. There's only one crossword and two sudokus left." He set them on the small table between the recliners. "Thanks for coming over."

"Are you ready to come back to work?" Perry sat down, astounded by how unenthusiastic he sounded. He loved his job, and now that Ferman was feeling better, he would make a great assistant.

"*Ya*, whenever you're ready. "

"What's that supposed to mean?"

Ferman tapped his two forefingers together. "Oh, I'm sure you're missing Daisy."

He scowled, unsurprised that Ferman already knew that Daisy had gone back to Dover. There wasn't any need to feign ignorance with him. Ferman was the only one who knew how he felt, and he regretted ever letting him know.

"Have you thought about going after her?"

Only a hundred times or so. He wasn't proud of how he'd acted when she came over. After she left, he had time to calm down and realize he'd been a heel. She had every right to kiss the man she loved. He'd acted like a baby about it, so much so that, other than telling her to leave, he couldn't remember anything else he'd said, he'd been that furious and hurt. But she hadn't betrayed him, and she didn't know how he felt about her. Thank goodness he never told her, like Ferman wanted him to. That would have been disastrous.

Still, it didn't make him feel any better. And going to Dover wouldn't make any difference. She was with Maynard now. *In his arms.* He gripped the edge of the sofa.

"You okay?"

"Sure," he said, releasing his hands and putting them in his lap. He mustered a smile. "Why wouldn't I be?"

"It's not every day a man loses his *maedel.*"

Perry jumped up from the couch. He wasn't going to listen to Ferman's nonsense anymore. "I'll pick you up on Monday," he said, walking to the door. "We've got a job in Ash Valley, although I'm not sure with who. The client is supposed to call back and give me his name and address."

"I know."

He spun around. "How?"

"We're going to Junior's place." Ferman rose from the recliner, a little slowly, and grabbed his cane. "I called him after I moved back home. You were right, Perry. I should have told him about my hip. Then I could have moved in with him and Polly Ann and not troubled you."

"You were *nee* trouble, Ferman." He clasped the man's shoulder. "I mean that. I even miss the company, believe it or not."

"Living alone can be a lonely business," he said. "I haven't always gotten along with my *sohn* and daughter-in-law, and I'm mostly responsible for that. When I lost Lovina, I kind of lost my mind. And my humanity. Polly Ann is pregnant, by the way." A proud look appeared on his grizzled face. "I'm going to be a *grossdaadi.*"

"Congratulations." He shook Ferman's hand. "Does this mean you're moving in with them?"

"Just when I have my hip replacement and during the recovery. Then I'll come back to Marigold. I plan to stay here as long as I can. It's home and always will be. But if the time comes that I have to *geh*, I'll leave." His mouth quivered a little. "*Danki* for taking care of me. I'm so stubborn, and if it weren't for you and Daisy, I would still be in this house, crawling on the floor."

"That's a little dramatic," Perry said, half smiling.

"You know what I mean." Ferman grinned. "Hey, before you *geh*, I need to get something. Won't take me but a minute. Well, maybe a little more than that. I'll be right back."

Perry nodded while Ferman disappeared to the back of the house. He moved away from the door and looked around the living room again. Seeing all the feminine touches reminded him of Daisy. He glanced away, telling himself again that time heals all wounds, but the clichéd words weren't encouraging. Daisy was gone, and although she didn't know it, she took a piece of his heart with her. That wasn't going to be easy, or quick, to get over.

He meandered around the living room for a few more minutes, then frowned. He'd expected Ferman to be back by now. He headed in the direction Ferman had left. "Ferman?" he called out when he arrived in the kitchen. This room had even more feminine flair. He had his back toward the hall as he looked out the window. Ferman Eash had a nice spread back here. Perry was starting to understand why he didn't want to leave.

"Perry?"

He stilled, knowing that sweet voice anywhere. He spun around to see her standing behind him, her hands tightly clasped in front of her, wearing that butter-yellow dress that she looked so adorable in. *Daisy*.

Daisy clutched her hands, trying to keep her shaking at bay. She'd been the one to set this plan in motion, with the support of *Aenti* Rosella, Grace, *Mamm* from a distance, and of course, Ferman. It wasn't exactly a complicated strategy, and Ferman was the only one directly involved. The rest of her family was just moral support. After she explained everything—and by everything, she meant everything—to Grace, her cousin agreed that she should talk to Perry and tell him how she felt. *Aenti* Rosella and *Mamm* concurred, her phone conversation with her mother surprising her.

"You're what?" *Mamm* said when Daisy called her right after Maynard left.

"I'm in love with Perry Bontrager."

"Oh, Daisy." *Mamm*'s voice was filled with weariness. "Not again."

But when she explained her feelings for Perry and how she'd been mistaken about Maynard—including letting *Mamm* know that she had been right all along—her mother was a little relieved. "Are you sure he said he loved you?"

"*Ya*. I'm just not sure he realized he said it."

Mamm sighed. "Daisy, don't you think you should . . ."

When *Mamm* didn't continue, Daisy asked, "I should what?"

"*Nee*. It's not what you should do. It's what I need to do and should have done in the first place. You're a grown woman and you know your heart."

Considering Daisy's track record, her mother was giving her too much credit and not taking enough of her own. If it weren't for her parents sending her to Marigold, she and Maynard would have had "the talk," they would have kissed, and while it may have been over anyway, she could see herself still trying to force the relationship and Maynard going with the flow. All he needed was a little peach pie to motivate him.

Instead, she'd met the most wonderful man in the world and had experienced what it was like to have someone listen to her, help her, encourage her, and if she was remembering his words right, *love* her. Even if she was wrong about Perry and they parted ways, she was a better person for having known him.

But the only way she would find out for sure was if they talked. Which they were going to do right now, here in Ferman's kitchen, where a rooster pitcher sat in the center of the table. Hmm, she wouldn't have guessed that was his style. Now Perry was looking at her like she was *seltsam*, and she didn't blame him, considering she hadn't said anything except his name. Oh boy, her nerves were going haywire.

He broke the silence. "You came back?"

She nodded. "I never left."

His eyes widened. "Huh? I thought you went back to Dover with Maynard."

"*Nee.*"

"So you've been in Grace's house for the past two days?"

Except when she had snuck out yesterday and visited Ferman and asked for his help. That hadn't been easy, since she noticed Perry's buggy was in the driveway during that time. She guessed he'd had a couple of days off, and she called a taxi to take her back and forth to Ferman's. The man had been glad to help her out, telling her he was always happy to see love conquer all.

"I've had a lot of thinking to do," she said to Perry, "and even more praying. Then there was the listening, the confessing, the journaling, and oh, I finished another cross-stitch. Now I have to start on Grace's for her wedding."

Perry gaped at her. "Why aren't you with Maynard?"

Daisy pulled out a chair. It would be easier to talk if they were sitting down, face-to-face.

Without a word they both sat. She smoothed her dress, ready to tell him he was right to be mad at her for coming over to his house after she kissed Maynard. That had been not only uncouth, but also inconsiderate to both him and Maynard. Yes, she owed him an apology, and then an explanation about her and Maynard, and after that they could talk about their feelings. She had the conversation all mapped out.

Taking a deep breath, she looked into his gorgeous blue eyes and said, "I love you."

Perry blinked. Then blinked two more times. Did he hear her right? He wasn't sure, since he was still reeling from finding out that she wasn't in Dover, wasn't with Maynard, and had been only several yards away from him all this time. Part of him was irritated by that last fact, as if she were playing some kind of game with him. But he pulled back on his thoughts. Daisy didn't play games. She didn't have it in her. And when she explained how she had spent that time in prayer and cross-stitching, he couldn't be upset with her. But that didn't mean he wasn't mistaken about what she'd just said.

Daisy's head fell into her hands. "Oh boy," she murmured.

As was always the case when he was with Daisy, his common sense took a hike. He reached over and gently moved her hands, then tilted up her chin. "Hey," he said, smiling at her sheepish expression. "Did you just say—"

"I love you?" She sat up and met his gaze. "I had this whole conversation planned where I was going to apologize and explain everything."

"Never mind about that." He scooted his chair closer. "You love me?"

Daisy nodded, her smile sweet beguiling and a little sultry, although he doubted she realized it.

"And you don't love Maynard."

"I never did. I'm pretty clueless, I'm discovering. I thought I loved Maynard, but I didn't know what real love was." She took his hand. "Not until I met you."

His heart filled. *This woman* . . .

"And when you told me first—"

"Whoa." He straightened. "When was that?"

"After I came to your house, when you were so angry at me."

"I said I loved you?" He thought back, but that entire episode was just a haze of hot fury.

"Is it true?"

The wistful tenderness in her eyes was his undoing. Without letting go of her hand, he stood and brought her to her feet, then put her arms around his waist. Her eyes widened in delight as he drew her close. "*Ya.* It's true. I love you, Daisy from Dover."

Her eyes grew shiny. "Then I was right."

"About what?"

She touched his cheek, her thumb gliding across his chin. "That God brought us together."

"For Pete's sake, would you two kiss already? I've got a cheese sandwich to make." They both turned to see Ferman grinning in the hallway, only to walk away. "Five minutes of privacy," he hollered. "Then I want my kitchen back."

Perry and Daisy laughed. Five minutes was enough . . . for now. He kissed her, refusing to ever let her go.

Chapter 23

MARIGOLD

NOVEMBER

Perry stood several yards away as the wedding guests mingled around the Hershbergers' backyard. Yesterday he'd volunteered to help Howard, Kyle, and their friends set up the tables and chairs for today's wedding feast. Fortunately, for the next few days, the weather was supposed to be mild and sunny, so they decided to hold everything outside. This afternoon there wasn't a cloud in sight and there was plenty of sunshine. A perfect fall day. So far everything had gone smoothly, thanks in no small part to Daisy's exceptional organizational skills.

The bridal party was already seated at their table. As Grace's maid of honor, Daisy was sitting near her, talking animatedly to other guests since the bride and groom only had eyes for each other. No surprise there.

As for him, he was finding it difficult to look away from his Daisy. She'd arrived with her parents a week ago, staying at the Hershbergers' and helping with the final wedding tasks before the big day. She wasn't the only one who'd been busy. Ferman was still recovering from his hip surgery he'd had in July, and Perry's schedule was full. Until Ferman had taken time off, he hadn't realized how much help he'd been, even in a limited capacity.

Like Daisy, the old man was busy chatting and making the rounds. Currently he was leaning on his custom-made cane, having returned the other one back to Howard, and talking to Micah Wagler and his wife, Priscilla. Perry had given him the rest of the year off, but he was eager for Ferman to rejoin him in January.

He shoved his hands in his pockets and shifted his gaze to the other guests, which included Jesse, Nelson, and their families. He would join them shortly. Right now, he needed some separation from the large group of wedding guests. Thanks to Daisy and Ferman's encouragement for him to get out more often, it was a little easier to be in a crowd than it had been a few months ago. Still, he had to have his alone time too, even if that was detaching himself for a little while before rejoining everyone.

When he looked at Daisy again, she was listening to Kyle's older sister, Rachel, who was talking and sitting next to her. She glanced in Perry's direction, as if she sensed his gaze was on her. She smiled.

His knees nearly buckled. While they couldn't be together this past week, the last few months they had been in contact almost every day. After their extraordinary kiss at Ferman's, Perry took her back to the Hershbergers' and they talked for hours. Not just about their relationship, which had skyrocketed out of the friendship zone, but about everything. When he went back home, he'd never been happier.

She ended up staying in Marigold for another week, then went back home to Dover after they decided to slow things down. *"I moved too fast with Maynard,"* she'd said. He'd done the same with Ruby. Neither one of them wanted to repeat their prior mistakes. During

May and June, they had mostly written letters to each other, but every evening they alternated phone calls to tell each other good night. She returned in July to help plan the wedding, and he visited her in September and met her parents.

But he was getting tired of the long-distance relationship. He returned her smile, ready for the wedding celebration to end so they could finally be alone.

"She's quite *schee*, isn't she?"

Ferman's words jerked him out of his thoughts, and he turned to see the old man behind him. "*Ya*," Perry said, glancing at Daisy again, who had gone back to conversing with Rachel. "Very *schee*," he murmured.

"Ah, young love." His limp barely noticeable, he moved to stand by Perry. "Grace and Kyle, you and Daisy—"

"You and Wanda Yoder." Perry winked at him.

"Pshaw. Where did you get that idea?" But Ferman's wizened cheeks were turning rosy red. "She's just—"

"A *friend*?" Everyone in Marigold was aware that Ferman and Wanda, a widow who had moved to their district back in June, were smitten with each other.

"Never you mind," Ferman groused.

Perry chuckled. After Ferman's hip surgery, he moved in with Junior and Polly Ann, who had their baby in August. When Ferman was able to move back to his home in Marigold, he'd been on the receiving end of more than a few casseroles and *friendly* visits from Wanda. Both Perry and Daisy were happy that he wasn't spending so much time alone. "How's little Ferman doing?"

Ferman's eyes grew shiny. "Growing. Can't believe he's almost four months old. Junior and Polly Ann brought him over the other day. That *boppli* sure can babble."

"Takes after his namesake, *ya*?"

"Humph." But Ferman was grinning. "Looks like everyone's settling in for the meal. I'm going to get my seat." He glanced at Perry. "You coming?"

He was about to say yes when he saw Daisy heading toward him. "In a minute."

"Take your time." With a knowing twinkle in his eye, he went to sit down with the rest of the men.

"Hi," Daisy said when she reached Perry. She looked up at him, her gaze soft.

"Hey." He wished he could take her in his arms right here, in front of everyone, and whisk her away. But she still had her maid of honor duties to perform, and he didn't want to draw attention away from the bride and groom. Still, he was oh so tempted . . .

"You seem a little uncomfortable," she said.

"I'm not." At her dubious look he relented. "Okay. Somewhat. Nelson and Jesse are here. I was going to sit with them."

"Or you could *geh* back home and relax."

That sounded wonderful. "Would Grace and Kyle mind?"

"Not at all. I'll meet you there later, after we're finished up here."

He briefly squeezed her hand. "*Danki*, Daisy."

Her gorgeous hazel eyes sparkled as she smiled. She let go of his hand and went back to the bridal table.

Perry shoved his hands in his dress pants pockets and walked home, grateful for the social reprieve. He would spend time in the butterfly room until she arrived after the wedding was over. Then he would tell her the idea that had been brewing in his mind and heart for the past several months.

Things were about to change for him and Daisy. It was about time they did.

Daisy's pulse thrummed as she knocked on Perry's door. Since she knew he was home, she could have walked on in. But she had invaded his privacy once too often, and after spending so much time apart over the past several months, particularly this week, the last thing she needed was to see him in a state of undress. She missed him enough as it was.

Seeing him at the wedding, dressed in his church clothes and looking not only incredibly handsome but also pitching in to help her family, had filled her heart to bursting. She loved Perry Bontrager, deeply and fully. She was sure of it, and she was positive he felt the same way. He'd told her so many times in their letters and during their phone calls and visits. He'd even said it on their very first actual date when he surprised her by borrowing one of his brother's open carriages and took her for a ride. He was a very, very romantic man, and she wanted more than anything to be his wife.

There was just one problem. He hadn't asked her to be. And she wasn't going to push a proposal or try to force one. She'd prayed for patience, and God gave it to her, not just where she and Perry were concerned. She was becoming less impulsive and more prudent, asking for advice when needed and taking it under consideration, even if she didn't initially agree with it. That also included spending more time in prayer.

She'd even cross-stitched a scripture for herself—Ephesians 4:2: *"With all humility and gentleness, with patience, bearing with one another in love."* She was acquiring patience and humility, something she should have done a long time ago. Dating Perry had helped too. He was more deliberate in his thinking and actions, something she appreciated.

Still, she was getting antsy for her and Perry's relationship to move forward. Seeing Grace get married was lovely, but it didn't help.

When he didn't answer the door, she assumed he was in his butterfly room. Sometimes when he was involved in his hobby, he wasn't aware of his surroundings, just the butterflies. After a pause, she decided to turn the doorknob. It was unlocked, the knob firmly in place.

Here goes nothing.

Daisy walked inside and sure enough, he wasn't there. "Perry?" she called out.

"In here."

She headed to the back of the house and saw the door open to his butterfly room. Smiling, she walked inside. Before she went back to Dover near the end of April and during her visit in July, she'd spent a lot of time here with Perry when he wasn't working and she wasn't helping with the wedding. She knew every square inch of his private sanctuary, and she loved being in here almost as much as he did.

He was sitting at a small desk in the back corner of the room, a sketch pad in his hands. He put it face down on the desk and went to her.

At last, she would be in his arms.

Instead, he guided her out of the room and shut the door behind them, then took her hand and led her back to the living room.

While she wasn't mad that they were holding hands, she was a little perplexed. And exceptionally disappointed. She'd been waiting weeks to hold him again, and now he was going to the couch, the same one he'd slept on when Ferman stayed here. "What's going on?" Daisy said, sitting next to him.

He let go of her hand. He was still dressed in his black pants and white shirt, but he'd taken off his black church vest and hat and had rolled up his sleeves. "I've been thinking," he said, leaning back on the couch and crossing his ankle over his knee.

She didn't know if that was good or bad. And she didn't like that there was so much space between them. Now he was stretching out his arms on the back of the couch, as casual as can be, as if he were ready to talk to her about the weather, the wedding, the butterflies . . . She almost frowned. Didn't he know how much she wanted to kiss him? Wasn't he dying to kiss her?

"We need a new pact," he said, his expression matter-of-fact.

Uh-oh. The last time they talked about pacts, they both had problems to solve. Daisy only had one problem right now—stopping herself from launching at him. Her cheeks heated. She needed some self-control too. "Is there something wrong?"

"*Ya.*" He changed positions so he was facing her, looking serious now. "I have a big problem. And you're the only one who can help me."

Alarm shot through her. "Just tell me what you want me to do, and I'll do it."

"But you don't know what it is yet."

"It doesn't matter." They weren't married or even engaged, but she was committed to him. "I love you. It's that simple."

His gaze filled with tenderness. "What I propose is this." He took her hand, then slid off the couch onto one knee.

She gasped. Finally, finally, *finally*, he was asking her to marry him. "Yes!" She dropped his hand and hurled herself against him. They toppled over, his back hitting the floor as she landed on top of him. "I'll marry you!"

His eyes grew wide. He winced. Then frowned.

She regained her senses. Oh no. All her thoughts about patience and self-control had gone out the window. And he hadn't actually proposed either. For all she knew he could have wanted her to organize his butterfly room. It did need a little tidying up. But why would he ask her that on one knee?

It didn't matter. She'd been impulsive again. "I'm sorry," she said, scrambling off him.

He drew her back, looking less stunned. "For what?"

"Assuming you were proposing."

Perry chuckled, his arms tightening around her. "I was. At least I was going to until—"

"I tackled you." She brushed a wavy lock of hair from his forehead. "Are you okay?"

"*Ya*. Just got a little wind knocked out of me."

She reluctantly moved off him. They sat up, still on the floor, and leaned against the couch. "I'm sorry I messed up your proposal."

"We could try it again. Hopefully your answer is the same."

Daisy turned to him and smiled. "Of course it is. I can't wait to be your wife."

He held out his hand. "Then we have a deal? A new pact?"

She shook it, loving the teasing glint in his blue eyes. "*Ya*," she said. "A marriage pact."

Perry pulled her onto his lap, and she leaned her head against his shoulder as his strong arms went around her.

"By the way," he said, "you can tackle me anytime, Daisy from Dover."

"Deal." She lifted her head and kissed him. *Sigh.*

Epilogue

Perry walked outside onto the patio. The sun was high in the sky, spreading its midday warmth. He spied his wife crouched down in the butterfly garden, weeding the young plantings they'd put in two weeks earlier. So that's where she was. He headed toward her, his hands in his pockets and a grin on his face. Daisy from Marigold. It didn't have the same ring as Daisy from Dover, but it was music to his ears. It also hadn't been a difficult decision for her to move here. *"I already feel like it's home,"* she'd said when they discussed it after their proposal—or rather, pact, as she liked to call it.

When he reached the garden, she stood up and arched her back. *"Ach,"* she said, staring down at her protruding belly. "Look at this. I'm more positive than ever that I'm having twins."

"Chances are *gut* that you are." He went to her, unable to resist placing his hand on her stomach. He felt a kick, and then another one, making him smile. She was due at the beginning of autumn, but she looked like she might go earlier. *"Mamm* would love another set of twin grandbabies." He kissed her cheek and took the short-handled tool from her, threading his fingers through hers. "I've got a surprise for you inside."

She smiled, her plump cheeks turning rosy. "I love surprises."

"I know." While he wasn't a fan of them, he enjoyed surprising Daisy. She was always so excited and appreciative. She had brought him out of his shell, and he wasn't even dreading yet another family gathering they were expected to attend tomorrow. Since their wedding last December, four more babies had been added to the Bontrager clan, and they were getting together to celebrate *Mamm*'s birthday. Having her by his side made everything easier.

"I was thinking," she said as they walked hand in hand toward the house. "If we are having twins, we need to think of backup names."

"I guess we do." They had chosen Perry Jr. if the baby was a boy, and Grace for a girl. "Did you have any in mind?"

"Faith for a girl."

He nodded. "I like that."

"And . . . Ferman for a—"

"*Nee*. No way."

She halted. "Why not? Ferman is a fine name."

"It is. But do you know how big Ferman's head will get when he finds out we're naming our *sohn* after him? He's already got a *sohn* and *grandsohn* named after him."

Daisy smiled and moved closer to him until her stomach met his beltline.

Perry shook his head and laughed. "Fine. Ferman it is."

"*Danki.*" She tried to lean forward to kiss him and almost tipped over.

His arm went around her waist to steady her. "Allow me." He

nuzzled her neck for a second, and once again they headed for the house.

"Oh, I almost forgot to tell you. *Mamm* gave me some news last week."

He opened the back door for her and they walked inside. When they were in the kitchen, she stopped and faced him. "You'll never guess who's getting married."

"You're right because, besides your family, I know exactly no one in Dover."

"You know one other person."

Perry frowned, searching his mind. Then it hit him. "Maynard?" He hadn't heard that name in a while. *Thank God.*

"*Ya.*" She grinned. "*Mamm* said she's nice. I'm happy for him."

He took her hand. He was done talking about Maynard. While he was secure in the fact that Daisy didn't have any residual feelings for the man, Perry didn't want to hear about him again. "Can I show you the surprise now?"

Daisy squeezed his hand. "Yes, please."

He took her to the butterfly room. The door was shut. He put his arm around her and said, "Close your eyes."

She giggled and obeyed. "Okay. I'm ready."

He opened the door and guided her in. "You can open them now."

Her mouth dropped open, and her hand went to her heart. "A nursery?" She looked around the room in amazement, then back at him. "Oh, Perry, it's beautiful. But where are all the butterflies?"

"Some of them are still here." He watched as she walked around the room, looking at several of his butterfly drawings adorning the walls.

"These are all my favorites," she said, then stopped in front of the largest one. "You finished her." She turned to him, her eyes damp.

He moved to stand beside her and looked at his drawing of Lady. He'd worked on it for almost a year, discarding many attempts. He wanted her to be just right, and he thought he'd finally done her justice.

"It's perfect." Daisy clasped her hands together and looked around the room, her gaze landing on the opposite wall where he hung her cross-stitch scriptures. "It's all so perfect." Then she went to the crib he'd placed in the room yesterday while she was visiting Rosella. "What did you do with everything else?"

"It's in storage." At her protest, he added, "For the time being. I know you said the *boppli* or *bopplis* could stay in our bedroom so I could keep this room for myself."

"We could have made it work," she insisted.

He ran the back of his hand over her warm cheek. "You know how much I like our privacy."

She blushed and rested her hand on her stomach. "Then we'll have to add another room for your butterflies," she said.

"I fully plan on adding to the *haus*. But I have a different idea for my collection. I want to share them with my nieces and nephews. And then our *kinner*, when they're old enough. There's plenty to *geh* around."

Her eyes widened. "Are you sure?"

Perry nodded. "It's time. I've kept it to myself for too long. Maybe one or more of the children will take an interest. If not, I can donate some of the materials to Marigold School."

"What a wonderful idea. And so generous." She put her arms around his neck. "Just one more reason why I love you, Perry Bontrager."

He snuggled her against him, his heart overflowing. "I'm ready to have another *boppli*," he said.

She laughed. "We haven't had this one yet."

"If it's God's will, I want more. A lot more."

"It will be awfully crowded around here." She gave him the sweetest smile.

He kissed her and said, "I'm counting on it."

Acknowledgments

It's hard to believe all the Bontrager brothers are finally married! When I first wrote *Written in Love* eight years ago and created the Bontrager family, I had no idea that one of the brothers would be a butterfly collector. ☺ It was such a delight to research the butterflies, and while I was finishing *The Marriage Pact*, a painted lady landed on one of the flowers in my patio garden. Such a precious little gift.

Completing the Bontragers' journey has been one of my greatest joys. Thank you, Becky Monds and Karli Jackson, for your always amazing editing insights and skills. You never fail to bring out the best in my stories. Natasha Kern, words aren't enough to express how much I've appreciated your encouragement and wise advice over the years. I will miss working with you, but our friendship will endure! And a big hug to Amy Clipston, my sweet friend and critique partner. I'm so thankful for your feedback and enthusiasm!

Most of all, thank you, dear reader, from the bottom of my heart. I'm grateful you decided to join me for another reading adventure. My hope is that you enjoyed Daisy and Perry's story as much as I did.

Discussion Questions

1. Perry is passionate about collecting butterflies. Do you have a hobby or activity you're passionate about? Why do you enjoy it?

2. Were you surprised by Perry's hobby? Do you find it strange, unusual, or completely normal? Why?

3. Ferman's hip caused him a lot of pain, and that affected his attitude and mood in a negative way. Discuss some ways we can lean on God and each other to help us get through painful times in our lives.

4. Daisy's parents were concerned, and rightly so, about her unrequited feelings for Maynard, and they impulsively sent her away to protect her from herself. How could they have handled the situation in a better way?

5. For most of the story, Daisy, Perry, and Ferman were deceiving themselves about their true feelings and in Ferman's case, about his role in the strife between him and his children. What do you think are the turning points in the book for each of them to become honestly self-aware?

6. Ferman and Grace both think and talk about how God's ways are different from ours. What does that statement mean to you?

7. Ferman admits that his grief over Lovina's death caused him not to think straight. What advice do you have for someone struggling with intense grief?

8. Perry and Daisy both changed during the story. In your opinion, which character experienced the most change, and why?

About the Author

With over two million copies sold, Kathleen Fuller is the *USA TODAY* bestselling author of several bestselling novels, including the Hearts of Middlefield novels, the Middlefield Family novels, the Amish of Birch Creek series, and the Amish Letters series, as well as a middle-grade Amish series, the Mysteries of Middlefield.

———

Visit her online at KathleenFuller.com
Facebook: @WriterKathleenFuller
Instagram: @kf_booksandhooks

LOOKING FOR MORE GREAT READS? LOOK NO FURTHER!

THOMAS NELSON

Since 1798

Visit us online to learn more:
tnzfiction.com

Or scan the below code and sign up to receive email updates
on new releases, giveaways, book deals, and more:

@tnzfiction

The Amish of Marigold Novels